Don't Be Afraid of Heaven

Don't Be Afraid of Heaven

Clint Adams

With unending love and gratitude,
I dedicate this book to Samantha

ACKNOWLEDGMENTS

Thank you, Samantha, for being the most perfect, most treasured gift I will ever receive. This book is written for you with the same unconditional love you gave me. The meaning of your life is enormous, and it's a privilege to be able to share what I learned from you with the rest of the world.

Thank you, Diane Christiansen, for our eternal friendship; describing what you mean to me is next to impossible. No one I meet will ever be as kind, loving, and selfless as you. You have *always* been there, but the help you gave me getting this book off the ground was extraordinary.

Thank you, Eva Liljendahl, for sharing your outstanding creative abilities and for exercising infinite patience with me. As both a writing coach and editor, the insights, suggestions and support you offered were completely perfect. You were indeed my inspiration for excellence.

Thank you, Dominique Christiansen, future "super-editor," for your brilliant and most accurate criticism. You will forever amaze me; at 14 you comprehend more than most adults will ever know in their lifetimes.

Thank you, Sue Adams, for having provided me with a purposeful life; the colossal contributions you've made are immeasurable. God bless you.

Thank you, Larry Adams, for reminding me that I deserve goodness. This means so much to me. I'm proud to be your son.

Thank you, Johan Borg, for being a close buddy when I needed one. You're exceptional; the fun and serious times we shared will be remembered forever, along with your heavenly cooking. Buon appetito, sempre!

Thank you, God, for having offered so many vital, critical lessons. They were all tough, but I chose to learn rather than ignore them. I will always be grateful for this unbelievable and unique life You have given me.

Thank you, Gloria Wilcox, for not only "getting" what I do, but for making me feel that what I do matters.

Thank you, Mads Christensen for your generosity and support; your desire to help me remains unmatched. Viareggio misses your enthusiasm.

Thank you, Carla & Virg Perez, for always thinking to include me. Your postcards of San Francisco make me feel as if I never left.

Thank you, Frank Di Lorenzo, Davide Forassiepi, Massimiliano Mattei, and all my new friends who continue to provide comfort and guidance.

Don't Be Afraid of Heaven

CHAPTER ONE

Death still scares me. Especially since it almost happened to me again last week. If you count up all the times I was supposed to have died, maybe it's sort of normal to feel this way. Even right before I fall asleep at bedtime, I keep telling myself a hundred times inside my head, "just get over it." But it's so hard.

The exact minute you change from being an alive person to a dead one is something I think about all the time. And wondering what happens next, after that minute is over, is the thing I think about even more times than that. For sure I'm not alone though. There's tons of people all over the world who're afraid of dying, and they don't even have E.B. like I do.

That's what my disease is, a skin-blistering one called recessive dystrophic Epidermolysis Bullosa. If my skin's not wrapped up tight, it blisters and comes apart. My body doesn't make the glue that keeps all the layers stuck together, so I've got to wear bandages like a mummy most of the time. I was born with it. And, most everybody including my mom, told me I'd probably never make it all the way to thirteen. But they were wrong.

In their lifetimes, most normal kids never have to worry that the hug their mom or dad just gave them may end up causing the infection that kills them. They're not forced to take Clorox baths. Their skin doesn't come apart like mine. They get to wear clothes with no bandages underneath. Their fingers don't permanently stick together all the time and have to be separated by surgeries over and over and over again. Whenever they get a blister, it eventually gets better. My blisters are all over my body, they never go away. And their teeth aren't twisted and discolored like Indian corn you only see at Thanksgiving.

My brown skin, brown eyes, and short black hair make me look identical to tons of other kids in California. That's why people usually think I'm Mexican. I'm really half Salvadorian and half white-American though. My favorite clothes are my baggy, comfortable orange jeans and long-sleeve, pullover 49er's shirt that has two easy-to-open front pockets built in.

1

I'm glad I'm more different than the same as most kids though. This is my life. Maybe I'm supposed to hurt for some reason. But what if the pain I feel every day doesn't end even after my life's finished?

Aunt Shirley always says, "E.B. ain't the issue at all, it's fear." Then she usually calls me goomer or a pain in the ass just to make me laugh. Aunt Shirley's funny lots of times. She's kind of like a white-lady version of Wanda Sykes. When she turns serious, Aunt Shirley says fear never should have existed in the first place, it's a man-made thing and people aren't born with it. Since she's pretty much right about most stuff, I guess that's the truth. I think Aunt Shirley's the smartest person around, even though she dyes her hair shiny blue whenever she goes out 80's dancing at the I-Beam on Haight Street.

I'm glad Aunt Shirley didn't die after staying inside her coma. Now, all my guilt can disappear. I don't need to worry anymore if I was part responsible for what had happened. Plus, it was her idea to come over and rescue me from...my fears, anyway. I'm so relieved Aunt Shirley was able to start making herself well so fast. Her doctors never did explain how she woke up from it so quick either. Maybe that part's supposed to stay a mystery.

Sometimes Aunt Shirley just calls mysteries miracles 'cause that way they don't need to be explained. Get it?

"Oh, I certainly hope she forgives me. Those were dreadful things I'd said to her. And that was the very last—"

"Aunt Shirley's not the type to hold a grunge, Mom."

"*Grudge*, not grunge, dear."

Mom did that a lot, corrected my vocabulary words while she was driving. And it's not like she's an English teacher or something, she just wants things to come out right...all the time. We were on our way to see Aunt Shirley for the very first time since she woke up. She's at Kaiser Permanente on Broadway in Oakland, and Aunt Shirley said on the phone that she was so eager to see me.

It usually bites big time whenever I had to go to *any* hospital, mostly 'cause of all my surgeries, but this time was so different. Aunt Shirley was getting back to normal, and her hair even started growing back in. That meant that it gave everybody a chance to see what the real color underneath was. I couldn't wait to see Aunt Shirley and her new real hair.

"Did your aunt happen to say she was looking forward to *us* coming to see her?"

2

"Well, yeah, Mom. Us."

"Did she use that word exactly?"

"I'm not really sure. Us. Me. You. Whatever. *We're* going to see her."

"I only hope she's not still angry with me."

"Hey look, Mom. That car's from Nova Scotia," I said while pointing over to a dirty, mud-covered Canadian BMW.

"And going much too fast, I might add."

Above us was the upper deck of the Bay Bridge, the very same place where Aunt Shirley's windshield got hit by a spinning car tire that came flying off a limousine. Right in front of her. That's what made her car smash into the off-ramp that goes to Treasure Island when she was on her way to get me. It was very serious. Sometimes I couldn't even breathe whenever my mind thought I'd never be able to talk to her again. I'm so happy all those thoughts got extinguished.

Looking out from the lower deck, with the lanes that go to the East Bay, made me wonder about how many car accidents happen on bridges. The news says that the Bay Bridge is the fifth most used traffic artery in the country. From Science class I learned all about arteries, but I never realized they had to do with traffic. I think it just means tons of people go across the bridge to get to work in San Francisco, not that they have heart attacks while they're on it just 'cause it's mostly always clogged.

"You look so very good, Miguel," Mom said as she put her right hand on top of my left hand lightly. Even though I could tell she was a little cautious about touching me too hard because of my fragile skin, I knew Mom loved me.

"You too, Mom. But your hair's different."

"What? You don't like it?"

"No, it looks way cool. Why did you—"

"Hunt wanted... Well, if your aunt can change hairstyles often, perhaps I should try on a new one myself. Let's talk about you. We have so much to catch up on."

It was good to see that Mom was making some changes in her life. Maybe a new haircut's the best way to start. I still worried about her a lot. Hunt's Mom's new husband. He's the kind of guy that calls all the shots. And after the court hearing, Mom moved to be with him full-time at his house down in Malibu. She ended up selling our old apartment at the top of Nob Hill with its killer views. By the way, it was the judge who decided I should stay with Dad instead.

Moving in with Dad, and getting to be away from this guy Hunt, put such a permanent good feeling inside me. It's kind of a bummer though that Mom still had to live with him. Maybe that's the sort of guy she really likes, movie producer-types, or just guys that are really used to people doing whatever they tell them. Or maybe that's just the way it is on the surface. Aunt Shirley said he was "completely bad news." That pretty much summed it up.

Right when Mom had picked me up to drive over to see Aunt Shirley in Oakland, was only the second time I'd seen her since the court hearing from the month before. "Your new place here is charming, Miguel. It's very...artsy," she'd said.

"Yeah, Dad and I both picked it. And, check it out, there's lots of weird stuff that goes on across the street. All over the place there's tons of signs that say Drug Free Zone on the fences that go around the park."

"My goodness. Well, are you about ready, hon? What can I carry?"

"Nothing, Mom. I can do it. I'm just bringing personal things that'll make Aunt Shirley feel like she wasn't ever in a coma in the first place."

I could tell from the way she'd grinned at me that Mom was impressed.

Next, we gathered up my stuff, and headed down the hill to Mom's rental car.

"The Mission district certainly is diverse. Isn't it, hon? Are you and your father going to stay here?"

"Yeah. We *live* here, Mom."

"I mean, he's not looking for a different place? In some other neighborhood?"

"No. This is our home. And, we even have DISH Network with upgrades. Isn't that awesome?"

Mom didn't look too thrilled. But to me, getting to have satellite TV was like a major bonus. Dad and I spent every late night together watching all our regular old shows on either Nick-at-Nite or TV Land. *Roseanne* started up a while ago on Nick, and we're both really excited 'cause of it. Roseanne definitely has it going on. For real it seems like she never has any fears inside her. That's so obvious, especially when she sang that song way bad at that baseball game. Roseanne's hell'a cool.

Mom never cared too much about all the awesome shows on TV. Isn't it strange how some people really love certain things, while other people are into other stuff? Mom mainly likes the de Young Museum, PBS, the San Francisco Ballet, operas, fundraisers, and other junk to do that gives a positive impression to other people. Aunt Shirley never cared about making impressions on any kind of people, good ones or bad. I think just impressing herself is what's most important to her.

On VH1 Cher said, "If you're all the time trying to impress someone, or trying to get someone else to believe in what you're doing, you might as well forget it." I think she really used the *f*-word in between *well* and *forget*. But they had to cut that part out since VH1's basic cable, not premium. 'Cause Cher's famous she can use the *f*-word anytime she wants, and not get into trouble like most other people.

Over halfway across the Bay Bridge, Mom said, "I thought this retrofitting would be finished by now."

"What's *retrofitting* again?"

"Repair work. Before the next big quake."

"Um. Do you want to hear about my new school, Mom?"

"Of course I do, hon. Tell me all about it."

"Well, it's really old. They've got awesome after-school programs…and right next to it is a huge park to play in. I can even hang out at the library that's built right into the park there, the Marina Library."

"Your new school is the Marina Middle School? In the Marina? Will Khadijah will be driving you?"

"No. Dad said I could take the school bus there."

"A bus? Oh, Miguel. I don't now. I think it's best if you're driven there, dear."

"No way, Mom. Dad said it would be perfect. Dad says there's lots of things I can do now. Dad believes in me completely. He believes in all the stuff I want to make happen for myself."

Mom turned silent and didn't have an answer to what I'd just said. She knew that's exactly why I got picked to live with Dad in the first place. She knew that that's the main reason the judge decided Dad should get the custody. So I could be around someone like Aunt Shirley who always believed I'd have a future and end up staying alive. Someone who wasn't going to make me even more afraid than I already was.

"Are you staying well these days, hon?"

"Yeah, oh definitely. Having Khadijah back is so cool. She's the best nurse ever."

"As long as your father's able to afford her, that's terrific."

"And, you know what? She's going to be in a professional dance play at Davies Sympathy Hall—"

"Symphony."

"Sym*phony* Hall in a few weeks. Do you want to come with me to see

5

her do that? Dad can't take me since he has to work every night."

"So, Khadijah did become a dancer after all."

"She's totally psyched. And, she said I've really got to come. Khadijah even told me once that she'd like you to see her dance. Especially since you'd said that that was probably never going to happen for her."

When Mom reached up real quick to adjust the rear-view mirror just after I said that, it made me think she didn't like being reminded of how things ended with Khadijah right before Hunt fired her.

"It's a possibility, hon. Of course I'll need to see what Hunt has planned."

Instead of changing the subject, I decided to do a checklist inside my head of all the stuff I was bringing to show Aunt Shirley. My crammed-full *To Do* list, my report card, what I printed out from the Internet about my new school, the watch she'd given me that doesn't tell time, the picture some tourist took of us when we were at that restaurant in Big Sur together, my favorite drawing of a chewed-up purple Frisbee my brother Jorge made the day before he died, and an extra-big sized Hallmark Thank You card, the over-five dollar kind, for staying alive.

Finding the hospital was simple, and Mom found a parking space right away on the fifth floor of the high-rise garage. "I hope your aunt's happy she moved to Oakland after all, instead of living in the city with us," Mom said.

"Berkeley."

"Same difference," Mom said while turning off her classical station. I felt that being in downtown Oakland for Mom was like a break-in waiting to happen.

"Hey, Mom. Only positive thoughts, remember?"

"Oops. You're right."

Staring at Aunt Shirley with a shaved head in her undecorated, yellow hospital room didn't seem so unusual to me. After all, that's one of the things she's known for, weird hair. The rest of her still looked the same. Being able to actually see her awake again made it seem as if she wasn't even gone for those two months, she was just catching up on some sleep. Having her back made my insides so relaxed too. At first Mom, me, and Aunt Shirley could just make small talk. But then, after the huge excitement of seeing her again began calming down, I asked Aunt Shirley, "Does your TV get Lifetime? *The Nanny's* coming on pretty soon."

"I'm not so sure, doll. Give it a shot," Aunt Shirley said while gently tossing me the remote.

"Shirley! Be careful!" my mom yelled out.

Just as Mom shouted that, it was as if I had experienced this part already. Been there, done that. Dad told me it's called *deja view*. It's like when you've seen it all from before. It reminded me of when Aunt Shirley first came over on the plane from Boston to move in with me and Mom. I remember being so happy then, I could hardly wait to spend time with her. In only one year so much had changed. Seeing how different Mom and Aunt Shirley were together, ain't nothing new though.

Before the two of them could even think about getting into an argument, I thought it was the perfect time to handover my Thank You card to Aunt Shirley. In the silence she read what I had written. Halfway through, in my mind, I was reading the card aloud right along with her.

> *... It's way obvious, but that's why I love you so much, Aunt Shirley. You've taught me about a million different ways to keep alive. Like keeping my To Do list full, saying only positive words out loud, to always believe that what I plan is actually going to end up happening, to throw away anything anybody says to me that has the word no in it, by always wearing the watch you gave me that doesn't tell time, and most of all, to always say thank you. I think with all the stuff you've taught me, all added up, I'll be around forever.*
>
> *Thank you, Aunt Shirley*
> *Love, Miguel*

Without saying a word, Aunt Shirley gave me the most serious look I'd ever seen. It was like she gave me an $A+$ without having to write it down on my report card. It seemed like a mixture of how proud she was, and how much she loved me, all coming out of her eyes at the same time. She had worked so hard to teach me to believe I'd have a future, and I learned it. Aunt Shirley taught me how to get rid of all my fears 'cause that's what I needed to do most to survive.

Since this was the first time in a long while all three of us were together, I thought maybe it would be good for Aunt Shirley to tell us some more of her extra smart ideas. Especially in front of Mom. "Yo, Aunt Shirley. I never did ask you this before, did you know what was happening when you were asleep? On the outside? Like all the news, all the terror explosions and stuff?"

"You bet'cha, babe. I sure did. Same old sh—," then while quickly glancing over in Mom's direction Aunt Shirley said "crap" before she was able to finish what she was really going to say.

"Seriously? You really knew about everything that's going on in the world?"

"Yep. Same old, same old. I don't know what it's going to take for these folks to get it. How much more of a wake-up call do they need?"

"Shirley, you're supposed to be resting," Mom said. "We don't need to talk politics."

"Who's talkin' politics? I'm not referring to you-know-who, I'm talking about everyone. They still don't get it. Fear's the only enemy, folks…get over it!"

"Aunt Shirley, guess what? I for sure don't have any anymore. I'm not afraid of anything. My *To Do* list is way long, see?" I said as I showed her the massively-filled-up printout I'd brought with me.

"You're my hero, doll. You really are."

"Crescent fresh?"

"Most assuredly."

"Crescent *what?*" Mom asked. Then, as they rolled around in teeny semi-circles, Aunt Shirley's eyes said *clueless* for both of us to see. So right after that Mom told her, "I'll always be indebted to you, Shirley, for helping Miguel. He's doing so well."

"For sure, A.S. Ditto. But you know what? There's one more thing. You've definitely got to tell us if there's anything really big you learned while you were inside your coma. Something you could say to us right now."

"You got it, doll! I'm tellin' you, I did learn one *enormous* lesson, something I never would have learned completely if I hadn't been in a coma." Then Aunt Shirley waited a few seconds before saying the rest, probably just so she could have the chance to be more dramatic.

"Well, what was it?" Mom asked.

"To *never* be afraid of dying. Heaven's a wonderful place. It's *so* much better than here. No burdens, no lessons to learn. Total, absolute freedom."

As Aunt Shirley said that, Mom and I both looked over at each other and stared. Aunt Shirley had said stuff like this before, but how could she know? And she said it just like it was the truth, like she really knew what she was talking about.

"For real, Aunt Shirley?"

"Oh, positively. I got to be around you guys all the time, whenever I wanted. Not once did I have to wait for an invitation."

"Shirley, you can't be serious."

"I've never been more. It works both ways too. Anytime you needed me, I was right there for you."

"You can do that when you live in heaven?" I asked.

"You better believe it, bub. And I can't wait to go back."

CHAPTER TWO

Dear Samantha,
Did you get your name from *Bewitched*? Just kidding.
I'm Miguel. And Khadijah, I mean, your Aunt Khadijah asked me to e-mail you to say hi. So I did. E-mail me back sometime, OK? You and I are both going to be in the eighth grade in a few weeks. Isn't that cool? No more middle school after this year!!!
Anyway, maybe you're going to go to Marina Middle School like me 'cause you just moved to Pacific Heights, right? It's really close to there.
I don't know what more to say except welcome to San Francisco. I think you'll like it for sure since most everybody else does.
    Happy summer,
    Miguel
    P.S. I won't add you to my Buddy List yet until you say it's OK.

"Whew. Finding a parking space sure was a challenge," Khadijah told me.
    "It's because of the Mime Troupe, isn't it? I think they're going to be in the park again today," I said.
    "No, something else. I didn't want to be late, so after I found a spot I just ran right over here."
    Khadijah seemed as if she always liked coming over to the city to take care of me. She did this every day, coming all the way from Berkeley. She's changed too. Her face stopped looking like it's about to explode. Mainly because her attitude's a lot more relaxed and casual since Mom's not around, or even more than Mom, Mom's new husband. Khadijah never liked Hunt too much at all.
    "Do you have time to go to the park with me? Before you head back to school?"
    "Sure. Why not?"

10

After hanging out for a few minutes more in the living room, Khadijah and I then went into my bathroom where she started getting me ready for my day. Unwrapping the old Surg-O-Flex bandages. Prepping me for my special medicine bath. Examining my old blisters, and looking me over real specifically...everywhere. This was my regular morning routine...for the rest of my life. "You're doing great, Miguel. No new blisters," Khadijah said, as she started putting medicine on all my old ones. Then, the last step, bandaging my whole body up again, and getting me dressed for the long day ahead. "Which shirt do you want to wear?" she asked, while looking through my closet.

"How about my *Stanford* tee-shirt? Don't tell Aunt Shirley. OK?"

"You got it. How's she doing, by the way?"

"Aunt Shirley's awesome. She'll be getting out soon. She's still mostly got a bald head though. You know what she said to me and Mom when we saw her in the hospital?"

"What?"

"Aunt Shirley said that this is when her life *really* starts, now, 'cause now she'll never again be afraid of dying. And, when you're not afraid of dying there's *nothing* left to be scared of. That's 'everyone's ultimate fear,' she said."

"Your aunt sure is something, Miguel. She's a trip, you know."

"You know what else she said? She says that heaven is *way* better than being on earth. She said she can't wait to go back. I don't get that part. I mean, how come she made me keep my *To Do* list so full in order to stay alive, if heaven's a better place to be?"

"Gee. I'd imagine it's got to be because she wants to keep you around, Miguel. She adores you. I'm sure she wants to spend as much time with you as she can."

What Khadijah said was such a nice thing. It still left me kind of confused though. After getting me all set for my day, Khadijah and I started walking across the street to Dolores Park. Like I had noticed from a few times before, I could see that there was a totally different mix of people there. Some people were trying to get tan lying on the grass...or they were just showing off their bodies, while other people were only hanging out in it. It's cool how parks kind of let people do whatever they feel like doing that's outdoors, free, and peaceful. Even for the drug-deal kids.

Somehow the sirens outside seemed so much louder than normal, everything sounded louder on the outdoors. Being on the inside though, in our new apartment, made me feel so quiet and safe...like nothing else mattered out there, probably because I got to be with Dad. He and I picked out a place that's on the second floor, with a row of palm trees smack in front of our pigeon-pooped windows. But we still got to see some good views through it all. Potrero Hill was right across the park, with a blue-painted water tank sitting right on top of it. The bay was behind that, and the East Bay hills were farther in the distance beyond the bay.

"You think you'll ever move over here, K.? After you graduate?"

"Um, I doubt it. I like Berkeley. The Bay Area's certainly better than most places." Then Khadijah's ears made her stop what she was about to finish saying. "What I'd probably miss most is that. Hearing that sound makes me know I'm home," she continued, as we both listened to the foghorn in the distance. It was a sound you could hear throughout the city, almost anywhere you'd go you could hear its sigh or whatever it's called. It was never sure to me why they've got it. I think it's to keep the big cargo ships from crashing into the Golden Gate Bridge. It's not like an alarm clock either, because the times it goes off is definitely not every hour on the hour.

As we moved closer to the part of the park where tons of people had gathered, we stopped for a moment in front of a statue both of us hadn't seen before. Instead of getting a good look at it, Khadijah asked a funky, flowery-dressed girl passing in front of us, "What's going on over there?"

"A rally. Impeach the Prez," the earthy girl said quickly, as she ran over towards the crowd, down the grass-covered hill.

Khadijah made her eyebrows go up. And that told me that she really didn't care too much about going over to join any of the yelling rally people. Instead, we both decided to look back over to the statue again. "Hey, check it out, K! There's my name," I shouted out, as we both began reading this metal-engraved plaque underneath the statue of the man.

On the early morning of Sunday September 16th A.D. 1810, Miguel Hidalgo y Costilla rang the bell of his church in the town of Dolores, in the new state of Guanajuato, calling the people to mass and to bear arms against the Spanish yoke of 300 years.

"*Bear arms* means *fight*, right?" I asked.

"Yes, fight with weaponry, Miguel. Fight for freedom."

"That's kind of what those people over there are doing, kind of."

Khadijah had to think first, then she said, "In a way it's kind of the same. For the most part, the Mexican people were fighting for something greater."

"Aunt Shirley has always told me that being free is the only way to live, not being controlled by anybody else."

"Sure, that's true. Enjoying many freedomz is what this country's all about."

"All those people in the crowd probably just want to have more freedoms."

"Maybe they do. Or maybe they've forgotten about all the many freedoms they already earned. Their choice to have a rally, to voice their feelings about the president, is a freedom. If my ancestors hadn't fought for freedom, I'd probably end up being a slave just like they were."

"Yeah, right. You? A slave? Well, then. I guess freedom *is* a very cool thing," I said. Then I realized something sort of strange. Although I hadn't been in the park too many times, I was beginning to figure out that maybe the weird bell in the park near 19th and Dolores was somehow connected to this statue we were looking at. "Hey, Khadijah, come on. I want to show you something," I told her, as we headed downhill to that old bell I'd seen from before. Walking from the direction we were going made us first see the bell from behind, the side with the most seagull stuff on it. By the time we stepped around it to the front though, I could definitely tell it somehow belonged to that statue of the bell-ringing guy.

The original bell now stands above the central balcony of the national palace in the city of Mexico where the president rings it at exactly 11:00 in the evening of each September 15th in a traditional ceremony called "El Groto"— the cry of Independence.

After reading about this bell, it made me understand how important getting freed was to people throughout history. Khadijah and I walked away and never talked more about it. It made me think hard about the slave story she'd just told me. It made me think of Dad, and how happy he must have been to have been freed from jail in El Salvador. I think *I* was the happiest overall though. Thinking about the bell, about all the people gathered on the hillside in the park, and about the statue of Miguel made me so thankful. Thankful that I became free from the way I had lived before, with all those fears that were inside me. I'm free. Or I thought I was, until I'd heard what Aunt Shirley had told Mom and me, about not ever being afraid of dying. As usual, I still thought about that one sometimes, and it reminded me that I probably wasn't quite finished.

"That is so beautiful," Khadijah said, while glancing over at what looked like an old Spanish cathedral, but it was really Mission High. "Are you going there next year?"

"I guess. If I last 'til then."

Then after she paused for a second, she said, "Excuse me?"

"Well, yeah. I guess so. Yeah, that'll probably be cool."

"That's strange. I *never* hear you say things like that."

"Well then. To make Aunt Shirley happy I'll put that on my *To Do* list."

"Do it for me too. *'If I last 'til then.'* Oh, brother. I'm going to go back to that Mexican Liberty Bell, pull it down, and crack it over your head."

"Alright already, K."

Khadijah thought I was joking, but I was just being honest. I guess God's the only person who knows for sure how long I was going to last on earth anyway. Thinking about Khadijah taking down that bell made me laugh hard on the inside. On the outside, both of us were quiet as we hiked back up the hill, close to the beginning of the park on the Church Street-side. As we covered our ears from the streetcar wheels screeching loudly on its tracks, we found a bench with only one person near us, a man wearing a tiny little lavender Speedo, stretched out over his beach towel turning really tan. "You like that guy?" I asked as I noticed Khadijah checking him out.

"Shhhh. He'll hear you, Miguel."

"Do you?"

"He's cute. Not my type though. Too good looking. Anyone *that* good looking's probably gay."

"Maybe Dad would like him."

"Has your Dad made any new friends since he moved back?"

"To date, you mean? Don't tell him I said so, but I think he's afraid of getting sick. You know."

"He's a smart guy, Miguel. He also doesn't seem like he's afraid of anything. Hey, by the way, how's that friend of yours doing? Staying healthy?"

"Miguelito? I haven't heard from him in a while. The last couple of times I e-mailed him I never got one back. I hope he's keeping his *To Do* list full, just like I taught him. He's so cool. He really likes all the things I learned from Aunt Shirley, that I ended up teaching to him. Miguelito's my bud."

Miguelito's the guy I got to know after he jumped off the Golden Gate Bridge to kill himself. He didn't die though. Maybe he wasn't meant to. Helping him has sort of been my way of thanking God for making everything turn out the great way it did for me. All the good stuff that happened was like a bunch of miracles all rolled into one. As soon as Khadijah and I were done with Dolores Park, I wanted to remember to make sure and write Miguelito a new e-mail. Maybe he just changed his e-mail address again so he'd get spammed a whole lot less.

Sitting on a bench was just like the way Khadijah and I had done so many times before. Spending quiet and relaxing time with her always made me feel better inside. It's as if she always helped me as my nurse *and* as my friend, both. Having Khadijah as my friend was something I always thanked God for. Some people you help in life, and the others you learn lessons from are maybe the ones you wouldn't normally pick to know. And, sometimes you learn lessons from people who are also the ones who help *you*. Maybe *everyone's* here for a reason.

"Are you excited about starting school again?" Khadijah asked.

"Yeah, I guess so. Taking the bus should be good for a change."

"I'll bet you and my niece, Samantha, will have a few classes together if she ends up going to Marina. She and her parents are still unpacking from the move out here. I can't wait for you to meet her. She doesn't have that many friends. I don't think she knows anyone out here at all."

"They're in Pacific Heights? Right? That's what I'd said when I e-mailed her."

"Thanks for doing that by the way. Yes. Jackson Street. My sister told me they're close enough for Samantha to walk to school. We'll see how she really feels about walking once she begins that uphill climb. She may change her mind."

"Going from the Marina all the way up there has got to be a drag. The bus is hell'a better."

"I agree," Khadijah said.

Then, out of nowhere, I thought for sure I'd heard Khadijah laugh out loud. "What's so funny?" I asked.

"Funny? What do you mean?"

"Didn't you just laugh?"

"No."

"It sounded like you just laughed...or somebody right behind you. But nobody's there."

"Must be one of those confused ghosts again!" the tan man in the lavender Speedo yelled out to us.

"Yes, it must be...those ghosts," Khadijah answered. I could tell she didn't know what the guy was talking about though.

Then the bikini man got up from his towel, and walked right over to us. With all his business kind of showing through. I wasn't sure if he was a nut or not. The majority of him seemed pretty sane. "Did you know what this all used to be? Dolores Park?" he asked.

Both of us at the same time shook our heads sideways and said, "No."

"Dolores Park used to be a huge cemetery, before the big one hit. Hundreds of people are buried underneath where we are right now. When the '06 earthquake happened, they used this land as a temporary shelter, building quickie, emergency barracks on top of every single grave."

Hearing the man say that, gave me a totally weird feeling, it made my stomach shiver.

"I had no idea," Khadijah said.

"Mission Cemetery it was called."

I couldn't think what to say to the man, so I looked over to Khadijah and asked, "How about if we go back home now? Is that OK with you, K.?" And then, in the most courteous and polite way, Khadijah and I said goodbye to the tanned Speedo man.

Both Khadijah and I walked all the way home without saying too much to each other. And while she was in the kitchen making my favorite lunch, I wrote and sent a quick e-mail to my friend Miguelito. It was a short one, and in no time at all I got a response back...except it wasn't from Miguelito. It was from someone else, his older sister, Esparansa. I did my best to read it aloud all the way through, but I couldn't finish.

It began:

Dear Miguel,

We tried calling you so many times. You must have moved already because the number we called has been disconnected.

We really wanted to wait and tell you in person, or at least call you, but we still didn't know how to get a hold of you. I'm so truly sorry to have to tell you this now, this way. Miguelito died almost a week ago. My brother's suffering is over, and now he's gone to be with the Lord. The funeral services are going to be held . . .

CHAPTER THREE

"It's the perfect solution, Miguel. It's what you're meant to be doing. Duh," Aunt Shirley told me.

"Do you really think *fat's* the best word to call it?" I asked.

"It's the *perfect* word, doll. That word says it all. Fear-Ain't-All-That, F.A.A.T," Aunt Shirley said so surely. She was positive that the after-school club I was going to start up had to have *fear* in its title. "It's your turn to help others with their fears. Instead of it being your Mission Impossible, it's your Mission *Mandatory*. Got it?"

"OK. I'll go for that."

"Get it. Got it. Sounds more than perfect to me." School hadn't even started up yet, but Aunt Shirley still knew that's one of the things Marina Middle School's known for, their after-school programs. So then, Aunt Shirley and I spent lots of time thinking up what we'd like to have in the club. "Having everyone make up a *To Do* list is a biggie," Aunt Shirley said.

"The same as mine?"

"A little different. It's going to be an '*Overcoming Fear' To Do* list. Everyone can write down all the things they're afraid of...then they do 'em. They'll confront their fears, then they'll get rid of them. Poof, vanished, gone in a cloud of dust. And when they're done, they'll cross each one off their list once that particular fear is conquered. They'll be history."

"Everyone's going to think that those lists are fly, way fly."

"Oh, absolutely. Fly." I could tell Aunt Shirley didn't know what *fly* meant. But I'm sure she probably guessed its right meaning.

Aunt Shirley and I were at the perfect place to figure out what to do after school. We were right at the school itself. Aunt Shirley ended up getting out of the hospital permanently. And since she knew my school was going to start up soon, she wanted to make sure she met my principal face-to-face, so she could tell all the good things she felt about me. My new principal with long hair, Mr. Lau, looked like a man-Margaret Cho. He

17

seemed like a nice guy. Right off the bat though he started calling me Mikey, but I never let anybody call me that anymore. I just used to let people call me that sometimes when I was younger. No more though. "My name's Miguel, Mr. Lau," I told him, and that's that. Period.

Mr. Lau also said Aunt Shirley had to participate in this club herself, or else it couldn't happen. Aunt Shirley said she wanted me to be the leader though. I hoped I'd do a good job. Except I'd never done anything like this before. "What if no one decides to join our group, A.S.?" I asked.

"Uh, oh. You're cruisin' for one, brother. How many times have I told you that saying *what if* is—"

"I forgot."

"We may have to create something new for you, mister. A *To Don't* list! A list where your first entry is to never ask *what if* again."

"Got it, Shirl. I won't say it anymore."

In a kind of obvious way, Ault Shirley changed the subject by asking, "You want to walk around? Let's scope this place out."

That was actually the right thing to do. I had only seen this new school maybe three times before, so it gave us both a chance to see what I was getting myself into. "When do you think they made this school, A.S.?"

"Well, M. My guess is that it was built during the art deco period. Probably the 20's or 30's."

The front of Marina Middle School had the same look as lots of apartments in San Francisco, with pictures of old-fashioned people and animals carved right into the outside stone-part of the building. On the Fillmore Street-side of the main entrance of the school were two lion's heads chiseled into the walls, two men lions because they both had heck'a big manes. Looking at those lions made me think how special the school must have seemed a long time ago when it first started up.

These days the school didn't seem to be so special. The front lawn had turned all brown, with a few brown weeds leftover from when they were alive. Mixed in with all the dead stuff was a few live bushes that looked sort of pretty, with white flowers growing off them. "White oleander," Aunt Shirley said. She seemed to like those a lot.

From the ground, Aunt Shirley and I peeked in on a classroom, and the ceilings were completely high up, like you could fit three or four regular modern floors into just one of theirs. Maybe that's how all schools were during the old times. It reminded me of the school where that red-headed spinster teacher worked at in *The Prime of Miss Jean Brodie*, one of Dad's favorite movies. "Hey, Aunt Shirley. Did kids have to get real dressed up to go to school in the old days?" I asked.

"I think so. They probably had to wear some sort of uniform or costume. You're probably glad that doesn't happen today. Am I right?"

"For sure. Who'd want to wear stuff that looks like *everyone* else's? Way too boring. When Dad was telling me about going to Catholic school, he said they made him wear gray and white clothes every day. Yech."

"I hear ya."

Aunt Shirley and I started walking around the building towards Bay Street and when we got a little bit away from it I could see words, I mean, names carved into the outside of the top floor of the school. Conte, Raphael, Plato, Galileo, Edison, Homer, Wagner, Euclid, Watt, Emerson, Moses, Milton, Darwin, Newton, Pasteur, and Dante. I'd definitely heard of some of these people. What I couldn't figure out though was why they all just had one name. They're kind of like Pink, Madonna, Cher, or Brandy. You know, people today that don't have two whole parts to their name.

As we kept walking around the school, Aunt Shirley and I found that the Bay Street-side didn't look that much different. Dead and dried plants and bushes seemed to be lined up around the school everywhere. And, just before we continued to walk around some more, Aunt Shirley wanted to peek into one of the windows where the auditorium was. By looking in we could see that it's called the Angelo D'Ambrosio Memorial Auditorium. "Somewhere in here. In back of this auditorium, or someplace around here, is where we'll have the meetings. Our F.A.A.T. meetings."

"Oh, in this one. Cool," I responded without paying much attention to what my aunt was saying, 'cause my mind was thinking about something else. "Does *memorial* always mean *dead*?" I asked her.

Aunt Shirley looked at me kind of shocked and shook her head to say yes. She didn't say anything out loud though. I don't know why, but it seemed for sure like she didn't want to talk about it. "Let's keep at it, shall we?" she said.

We walked back to Bay Street, where the street was lined with lots of two- and three-story apartment buildings on the other side of the school. And, way more than when I had heard them at Dolores Park, the foghorns seemed extra loud since we were that much closer to where the sound starts from. The Marina district is so much nearer the ocean, and Dolores Park is actually a lot closer to the bay. Sometimes though there's gloom all the way around, when it gets stuck in all the nooks and valleys.

As the sky started disappearing above, I told Aunt Shirley, "The fog's coming in. It's going to get a lot colder soon."

"Well then, we've gotta haul."

Behind the school was a blank playground that's paved all black with a few white lines painted in. When we walked towards Chestnut Street in what was kind of a little alley, the school was on our right and a nice, big park was on the left, the Moscone Recreation Center. People were playing tennis on every court there, looking like they were having tons of fun. The two softball fields were full of people watching the players. It all seemed like a real nice place to hang. "Moscone's the one who got murdered. Isn't he?" I asked.

Aunt Shirley paused a second before answering, then she said, "Yes. He was assassin—"

"Yeah, that's what I meant to say...*assassinated*."

"By Dan White."

"Because he ate Twinkies."

"No. That was his defense. Dan White's the perfect example of anger getting the best of you. Blaming two murders on Twinkie-eating is a little too loony-toony for me."

"So, it *wasn't* because he ate Twinkies?"

"No, of course not. His attorney said that eating all that sugar made him act...irrationally, or something like that."

"So, because Moscone's dead now, this is his memorial park."

"I guess you could say that. It's dedicated to him, to his memory. When people appreciate this beautiful park, they're remembering George Moscone. Just like they're remembering Harvey Milk every time they walk through Harvey Milk Plaza."

"That's the other guy who got kil—, assassinated. 'Cause he's gay."

"Dan White was mad for a lot of reasons. Instead of figuring out why, he decided to blame everyone else for all the mistakes *he* made. It's a long story."

I didn't bring it up again, although it still made me think a lot about the whole idea of *memorial*. Was I going to be more important when I turned into a dead person, instead of while I was still alive? Wow, it's starting to seem like people get more attention, for longer, only after they've died. Maybe that *was* the best place to be after all, just like Aunt Shirley'd said. To tell the truth though, getting to be dead seemed like going extremely overboard just so more people will remember me, I thought.

Aunt Shirley did a little bit more walking and talking, and on the flip side of the school I'd noticed the exact same thing that was on the front. Archimedes, Shakespeare, Beethoven, Columbus, Pericles, Washington, Aristotle, and a few others I didn't know too well, were chiseled onto the top floor of the school building. "There's more names on this side too," I told Aunt Shirley. While pointing up to more of these carved-in names, I asked Aunt Shirley, "Are *all* these people famous? I mean, I've heard of Shakespeare and Washington and Columbus. But who's Gutenberg and Aristotle?"

"I'm pretty sure Gutenberg refers to Johannes Gutenberg. He was an inventor in the 15th Century. Gutenberg's primarily known for printing many copies of what's known as the Gutenberg bible. And, Aristotle was a Greek philosopher. He was big into math and logic."

"Math bites. Why would anyone ever want to invent that?"

"It turned out to be pretty important. Trust me. Later on in life you'll be glad you stuck with it."

"All these guys are important?"

"Yep. Important men in history."

"Dead men."

"Dead men, right."

"Does anyone ever name buildings or things after living people?"

"Oh, sure. Lots of observations about death today, Mr. Maudlin."

"It's just that you said being dead is better than being alive. This is evidence of that. 'Cause so many more people get famous after they're dead since that's sort of when things are named after them."

"No, no, no. I wouldn't say *better*. You're remembering what I'd said in the hospital room. The point I was making is that no one should ever be *afraid* of dying. The reason I said that was because it seemed like a great place to go."

"Oh," I said, while agreeing with my head.

"Living life fully is also a great place to be…a lesson in itself, doll."

I had the feeling this conversation was going to repeat itself again a few times until Aunt Shirley got tired of telling it over and over. "Hey, how come there aren't any dead *women's* names carved into the building?" I asked.

"How much time have you got?"

Picking that topic I could tell was going to open up a few cans of worms, so it was just a whole lot easier for me to say, "Never mind."

Behind the school's playground on the Chestnut Street-side was the Marina branch of the San Francisco Public Library, and behind that was some sort of senior lodge building. I figured maybe this was going to be a cool place to go to school after all.

On the first day, everything seemed to be going so well, not too confusing. I seemed to know right where I was supposed to go, and not that many kids stared at me or my bandages. Still, the coolest part of the day was that I was going to get to meet Khadijah's niece, Samantha.

"Did you ever get my e-mail?" I asked as we sat down to eat our lunches together in the cafeteria.

"Yes, I did," Samantha answered.

She didn't explain why she never wrote back, so I asked, "You're glad you picked Marina to go to?"

"Perhaps."

I'd been around shy kids before, and since I'm not, I don't mind that I talk more than most of them. By looking at her closely, I could already tell Samantha was the brainy type. Her hair's pulled back behind her head with a plain brown metal clasp to hold it all together. Her silver-framed glasses were sort of ordinary looking, definitely not designer. And, most of the time when either I talked or she answered, Samantha didn't look at me. She focused on eating her lunch, and that was fine.

"That's a fancy kind of sandwich. What's that on the outside?" I asked.

"Middle Eastern flatbread."

"Oh."

Our conversation at lunch pretty much stayed the same for a while. Then Samantha began to mellow out a little bit. Deep down somewhere, I began feeling she was like me in a bunch of ways. She had mixed parents like me, except hers are still married to each other, and both still live together with Samantha. Even though Samantha's got one black parent and one white parent, it seemed to me that she thought of herself as African-American. That's kind of like the way I always thought of myself, as just Latino.

As it turned out, Samantha and I ended up having three classes together: English, Science, and Social Studies. Knowing that Samantha was related to Khadijah made it a whole lot simpler getting to know her better. I didn't have to think real hard first if she was a good or a rotten person. If she was anything like Khadijah, she's definitely got my vote.

Right after getting out of our Social Studies class, Samantha and I talked more as we walked down one of the north hallways on the second floor. "Are you thirteen or fourteen?" I asked her.

"Thirteen. Quite close to thirteen-and-a-half actually," Samantha answered.

"I'm kind of close to fourteen. My birthday's on October 28th. When's yours?"

"The eighteenth of May."

It didn't take too long to figure out that asking questions was probably going to stay my duty, 'cause Samantha never really asked any. And, all her answers always ended up being a little on the short side. "So, before, you went to seventh grade in New York?" I asked.

"Yes."

"Cool. I used to go to Notre Dame des Victoires over on Pine Street. But I live with my dad now, and he can't afford for me to go there anymore. So this is my first time here, too. You like living in Pacific Heights?"

"Yes."

Then, all of the sudden it came to me...no more yes's or no's. I began thinking that Samantha'd give longer answers if I began asking tougher questions. "What are some of the after-school programs you belonged to in the seventh grade?"

"None."

"You know what? Me and my aunt, Aunt Shirley, are starting up an after-school group called F.A.A.T. We told Khadijah, you know, your aunt, all about it, and she said maybe you'd be the perfect person to join."

"Fat?"

"Yeah, that's right. Except, you don't have to be fat to be in it. It's just a group that's all about fear...getting rid of it. It's about all the good things that can happen to you in your life after you've gotten rid of all your fears."

"Fear, *not* fat."

"Yes. Fear, not fat. That's right. You know Mr. Lau? The school principal? Well, he said it was OK for us to have the group. It's got to have a grown up leader though, or be supervised by some grown up, in order for us to have it. So, that's where my aunt comes in. She told me that that's my mission in life, my purpose. To help people, mostly kids I guess, learn that living without fear is way better, 'cause that's what I showed myself how to do in my own life."

"You don't have any fear?"

"No, not really. Well, just about dying mostly. I still try hard every day not to ever be afraid of anything. Are you like that too? Or are you kind of afraid sometimes?"

"I've been diagnosed as having a total of five extremely different and distinct chronic anxiety disorders."

CHAPTER FOUR

After all my homework was done, one of the favorite things I liked to do was hang out with Dad on one of his nights off. He's hell'a cool. There's probably not anyone else in the world who loves me as much as Dad. Well, maybe Mom too, when she's not around her new husband, Hunt.

Tons of people always used to think that Dad looks like Antonio Banderas. Dad was never in any movies or anything though, and he's got more gray hairs than he had before he left America. One of the reasons we moved to the Mission district was so I could be closer to his "heritage," and learn all about it, he had said. Before, I never used to understand why he and Mom got married if he's gay in the first place. He explained it once, and I guess I understood his reasons enough. Dad said it was mainly so me and Jorge could end up being born.

Everything about living with my dad was so different from when I lived with my mom. Mom could afford more expensive stuff, like Hi-Speed Internet access. Dad's like starting from scratch. It's a brand new life for him since he got out of jail. Dad never did try to figure out if Hunt was the one who set him up either. "The past is the past," he always tells me.

"Dad, sometime I got to show you the *El Groto* bell over there in the park," I told him.

"El Groto?"

"Yeah, the *cry-for-freedom* bell. It's over there in the park. And the guy who started it all's name is Miguel, just like me."

As soon as I said that, I felt just like an alien. Not the illegal kind though. It's like I was speaking a foreign language or something, because Dad just stared at me all confused. I figured I needed to tell more so I said, "You know. So the Spanish would let go of Mexico, so they could be independent. It all happened in the town of Dolores, like Dolores Park, Mission Dolores, Dolores Street. Get it?"

"Well, I'll be damned. Moving here has already taught you something. A lesson for both of us in world history."

That's exactly why Dad wanted us to find a place to live that taught me about different cultures, especially my Latin one. "This area is very much a part of you, Miguel," Dad had told me. I guess when I was living with Mom on Nob Hill I had been learning about the white part of me all along, and I hadn't even known it.

That's what was the coolest part about getting to live in San Francisco, all the different kinds of people and the places they were born in. "Dad, is *gay* a culture? Since there's not some far off country where gay people originally came from?" I asked.

"Well, now. That's an interesting question, Miguel. It probably is. Yes, I guess so."

"So, if we lived in the Castro or Noe Valley I'd be learning more about gay culture?"

Dad rolled his head from side to side a few times to decide on an answer, then he said, "I guess you could."

"My new school is sixty-five percent Asian. So I'm definitely going to get to learn a lot about stuff that's Chinese and Japanese and Filipino."

"That's perfect, Miguel. The best education you'll ever receive."

"Archie Bunker, you know, from *All in the Family*, never would have had a TV show if he had gone to school with other cultures. Right?"

"Oh, boy. I don't know about that one. I'm just glad at least some stereotypes have disappeared on TV."

Dad explained to me a long time ago that stereotypes are things that keep people from realizing the truth about the way people *really* are. Some people actually think that feeling sorry for a person like me is a way to show kindness, except that's a stereotype. I never wanted anyone to feel sorry for me. I just want them to think of me as someone who happens to have E.B., nothing more.

Dear Miguel:
When you have a moment, perhaps you can review some of these entries I've placed on that TO DO list you spoke of:
1. Not to panic if I ever receive a grade less than an 'A'
2. Enter a USTA-sanctioned tennis tournament
3. Ride the ferryboat going to Angel Island
4. Lose my fear of seawater and the creatures living inside the bay
5. Approach foreigners
6. Eliminate my concerns regarding identity theft

Clint Adams

Well, you might say I've already begun working on Number 6, since I'm writing and sending you an e-mail at this very moment.
Onward and upward.
Thanks, Samantha

On some nights, there were weird combinations of noises going on outside. Listening to all the sirens, foghorns, and the metal wheels grinding on the *J*-Church streetcar was especially distracting when the noises all happened at the exact same time. On a night when my dad wanted to have a talk with me, a serious one, I became a little anxious as I expected him to get home. Waiting for him gave me the chance to really look around our new apartment, kind of like studying it. It's on Church Street, in between 19th and 20th Streets. From outside the window in my room what I seemed to notice most were all the wires hanging above the *J*-Church, the ones that give electricity to the MUNI streetcars. I'm still not so sure how that works.

Waiting around made me think back to the old apartment I had just moved out of, my apartment with Mom on the thirtieth floor at the top of Nob Hill. From the window in my room there I could see *everything* almost. What I never could see though was that I'd end up living with my Dad in an apartment in the Mission district. I'd never have been able to predict any of that. Who would have known?

From my new messy room in the Mission I could hear our front door opening.

Dad was home, and soon I was going to find out what he needed to tell me. "So, how was your day?" he asked.

As I walked towards Dad, and as he walked up to me, Dad didn't seem to look too worried. He looked the same as he always did. Then I remembered that Dad's face never showed worry, ever. He understood that *worry* was the exact same as fear, and letting your face look that way never solved anything. "Everything was pretty good, Dad. A pretty good day," I told him.

"Super. What do you feel like having for dinner tonight?"

"How about hot dogs? We haven't had those in a long time." Since I had to be so careful about all the things I ever ate, the hot dog had to be kind of mashed up or else I'd never be able to digest it right. It still tasted good to me, even though it kind of looked like throw up.

"We've got some foot-longs in the refrigerator. I'll get right on it."

Dad's cooking was OK, but I could tell that he's trying even harder 'cause he really wanted to do everything just right. Dad wanted real bad to make me happy no matter what it took.

Not knowing what Dad was going to say next, we both walked into our kitchen and I sat on our stool that looks out the window to where we put the smelly garbage. "So, you wanna tell me now what you wanted to say? Or is after dinner probably better?" I asked.

From in front of the stove Dad glanced over to me. It looked like he couldn't decide what to say next. When he finally could, he said, "Well, yes. As a matter of fact, now would be a good time."

"Good. So…?"

"So, do you remember me telling you about that doctor's office in San Bruno?"

"Yeah, I think so."

"Well, it's a super place and it's so close by, much closer than going all the way to Stanford. It's called the Matthew Morey Care Center, and there's a doctor there who has helped kids with E.B. in the past. His name is Dr. Martin Rosenzweig."

"OK, why are you telling me all this, Dad?"

"Well, Miguel. Dr. de Pascual is leaving Stanford for a while and—"

"Yeah, I know that, Dad."

"This care center is half as far as it would be there, to the Medical Center. And for any kind of surgery, we'd definitely be taking you back to Stanford. For more routine doctor visits though, I'm thinking that it would be best if you started going to the Morey Care Center."

"I don't mind the drive all the way to Stanford. It's cool. And, even though Lefty'll be gone for a while, there's lots of other doctors there who are way cool." As I said that I could tell from the look on Dad's face that there was still something I wasn't getting, not understanding. When I looked at Dad's face even closer, it seemed like the hardest part of our talk was about to come next. How bad was it going to be? Was my dad also sick? Was he going to be going to that new care center place too? For himself?

Dad's chin started to quiver when he began saying, "Miguel, I'm trying so hard. There are so many legal bills, I'm working both jobs. I wish I could give you the best of everything, always. Only…I can't really afford to take you to Stanford for every visit now. My insurance doesn't cover it."

Something I never questioned was that Dad had *always* done his very best, especially when he's doing those things for me. Dad looked so disappointed, like he'd totally let me down. He was so wrong. It made me hurt inside to see him feel like he had failed. "No problem, Dad. I don't mind going to this new place, to have this new doctor."

27

Clint Adams

Dad appeared a little surprised. Then he looked away from me.

"For real, Dad."

"Next year everything will be different. I'll be able to give you all you deserve. Everything."

"Dad, you know what?" I waited 'til he said "what" before I continued. "Getting to be with you is my total grand prize, like my reward, duh. It's way more than I ever could have asked for. Dad, you're the coolest."

We spent the rest of the afternoon and night eating our hot dogs and watching TV.

Our favorite show's *The Munsters,* but we still watched *Cheers* a lot too. Dad used to say all the time that Diane Chambers reminded him of Mom. That always used to make me wonder if Dad actually still thought about her much. I missed my mom. And I thought that maybe it would be good to write her a letter. Maybe that would make us both real happy.

The next morning I turned on Dragon, my voice-activated word processor, and began dictating:

Dear Mom,

You know what? Sometimes we don't talk about it too much, but I wanted to write this letter to you now to make sure you know that I miss you lots, and I love you a lot too.

Are you happy down there in L.A. full-time? Are you meeting lots of cool movie stars? I hope so. Is Hunt being nice to you?

Dad is taking real good care of me, and he's really concerned about the way I feel inside. Maybe you could come up again, and we all could do something together, like take a ferry ride over to Angel Island, Sausalito, Tiburon, or even to Marine World in Vallejo. Maybe we could even take my new friend Samantha with us. I can tell she's got a lot of courage deep down. She even started up a *To Do* list just like mine. Isn't that awesome? Don't forget, it's not too late for you to start one either.

Anyway, thanks for coming up to see Aunt Shirley with me. That was way cool that all three of us were together again.

Aunt Shirley's helping me out a lot with my after-school group, and that's going really well. She said that helping people overcome fear is *the* greatest thing I could do. And, sometimes, you know what? Having my group, and knowing that maybe it's going to help someone, makes me feel kind of important, like I'm doing something worthwhile. 'Cause you know what? I don't know for sure if what I'm learning in school is going to pay off after all. Right now, I think it's just killing time. Aunt Shirley even said once that the lessons you learn outside of school are the most meaningful, since you're the one who DECIDES to learn them. I like that part.

Every day I hope that you'll decide to be unafraid...of everything. That will be a great day.

Love,
Miguel

Writing Mom's letter felt good, like it was a way to make sure she knew I was always thinking about her, and that I haven't forgotten all about her just because she moved away.

Next, all of the sudden something inside me made me feel like I wanted to immediately tell Aunt Shirley about the letter I'd just wrote to Mom. So, I called her. On the third ring she answered by saying, "Yo, what's up?"

"I just thought I'd call and tell you I wrote Mom a letter, and I think I'm going to do that more often...just to let her know I haven't forgotten about her."

"Good for you, doll."

"In my letter I told Mom that I hope she gets rid of her fears."

"No kidding, Miguel. Wow, that's fantastic. What a beautiful wish for her."

"Oh, then it was good I did that?"

"Of course. You're meant to help *a lot* of people, doll. They're going to learn so much from you. That's where F.A.A.T. comes in. That's where it all begins."

Whenever Aunt Shirley said stuff, it's like she always knew something that few other people did. She always made it sound like there were way more reasons why things happen than you first think of. She always said that even the tiniest piece is an important part of God's plan for us all. They're all parts of what it takes for us to get to where we need to go next in life. So, I guess F.A.A.T., and the letter I wrote to Mom, just like everything else I ever did in my life were all connected to each other, and they had to do with the way I'd turn out.

"You're sure a positive-thinker, A.S."

"Keep remembering what I told you, it's not just positive thinking, it's *believing*! *You* make it all happen by believing it will."

"That's true."

"The more you live this, the more people who'll be influenced by you.

Just like I taught *you, you'll* teach them."

"Maybe that'll be my job in life, to become a teacher."

"And, you'll be great at it, doll. But, keep learning. Maybe you've got a whopper of a lesson headed your way now, maybe your hardest one yet. So, stay alert and watch what comes your way. You'll be happy you did."

When she said that, the strongest feeling came over me that the lesson coming up next was huge. Rather than thinking about it though, I tried my best to put the whole idea out of my head. I told myself to just live life, and have plenty of faith that what I did was the best I could do, and...the rest is out of my hands once I throw it all back into God's.

CHAPTER FIVE

"Miguel, you don't sound quite the same today," Samantha said to me over the phone.

"It's just that time again, I can tell."

"What do you mean?"

"I have this feeling like I'm going to get sick again, real soon. I hate it. I'm so sick of being sick all the time."

"Maybe you've just got the blahs. Perhaps you have some minor depression that runs in your family."

"I'm just in an *I-don't-care* mood. Sometimes I don't care if I live anymore, it's such a pain."

"Miguel, I don't know what to say. I don't know if I'm the person you should be talking to right now."

"Don't worry about it. I'm not looking for support. I just don't care."

"Well, please remind me. On what day are we going to the zoo again? Although those monkeys and alligators terrify me, I'm eager to cross that one off my list."

"So, you're still up for that?"

"Oh, of course. We've got to. I've been afraid of going to the zoo forever."

"Tuesday."

On a day when one of the blisters on my right shoulder needed extra medical treatment, Khadijah took me to see my new doctor in San Bruno. The care center place where he's at is right on the way to the airport, and going anywhere near it always gave me an excited feeling. So, before I even met this new guy, I was already in an OK mood.

As Khadijah and I were driving south on 280, we noticed a huge cemetery that seemed to go on forever. When we passed by it, we could see a big green sign hanging above the street that read, *Golden Gate National Cemetery*, so I asked Khadijah about it. "That's a military cemetery. I've driven past it many times," Khadijah told me.

From the freeway we could see mini red, white, and blue American flags waving right next to the headstones, like in a kind of patriotic way, I thought. "Does that mean just army people are buried there?"

"I think veterans and their families. Pretty impressive, isn't it?"

"Maybe not *impressive*. It's definitely huge though. Can we drive into it, K.? Or are we going to be late for the doctor?"

"Go *into* the cemetery?"

"It looks like there's another entrance to it right over there," I said as I pointed to an open, fenced gate, right off Sneath Lane.

"Well, we can spend a few minutes there if you *really* want to. We do have to be at the doctor's office by 2:30."

"That's good enough. I just want to see the inside of it."

After Khadijah agreed, she drove us into the cemetery when a feeling like awe came over me. There's no way I could believe all of what we were seeing. There were graves everywhere, all over the hills, beside the trees, on flat ground, some closer to the freeway, others far away from it. And, the thing that made it all so eerie to me was that all the headstones looked absolutely identical, they were all the same, like Stepford Stones. Since they were completely alike I asked Khadijah, "Did all these people die at the exact same time? From some war?"

"No, I don't think so. I mean, I really doubt it. Why?"

"Because all the headstones are the same, the same shape, the same look."

"Oh, I get it now. That's how all military headstones are. I'm pretty sure they all look similar in any veteran's cemetery."

"I want to make sure mine looks like nobody else's."

"Yours?"

"Yeah, you know, when it's my time to go. Sometimes I worry that the people who bury me aren't going to know how to do it just the way I want."

"Miguel, I don't think you need to be worrying about any of this right now. We'd better get going. We don't want to be late."

"Can we stop to see just who one person is? Was? Just one? Please. That won't take up too much time."

"You mean, to read one of the *headstones*?"

"No, I don't think of it that way. I want to see a person's name so I'll know somebody on the other side before I get there. I'm afraid that when I go nobody else will be there. Or they'll all be strangers to me. I don't want that to happen."

Khadijah looked at me like I was a weirdo. She seemed like I'd just said a bunch of swear words straight in a row 'cause of her so shocked look.

"OK," she told me, as we continued to drive through what seemed like millions of gravesites. It was all so big. It's as if we really could have used a AAA road map to find our way around the place. Within the cemetery there were actual street signs, Hopkins, Strauss, Crocker, and a few others. It's like this cemetery was an actual city, a city where everyone in it just happened to be dead.

Khadijah kept driving until she asked me where I'd like to stop. "Let's stop right over there," I said while pointing to a tree that looked real shady. Under it seemed like the perfect spot to be buried in, like some sort of extra fancy suite instead of just an average room. Khadijah pulled over to the tree and parked. I could tell that she hadn't yet figured out my reasons for wanting to stop. Maybe she would when we both got out of her car.

The moment I opened my door all by myself, the air felt so much colder than it had been in the Mission district. "Which site do you want to visit?" Khadijah asked.

My eyes wandered over the many headstones in front of us. Then my feet stopped walking as soon as I saw something that both shocked me and scared me at the same time. On a headstone with the name Pvt. M. Jesus Martinez on it was carved my birthday, October 28. The year on it was different from the year I was born. So much of everything else was exactly the same. My first name begins with *M* and my middle name's Jesus. "Oh, my God. Come here and look at this," I shouted over to Khadijah.

Khadijah walked right to me, but then she looked at the wrong headstone before she also shouted, "Oh, my goodness. Look at that. It's your birthday? Isn't it?"

"Keep looking."

"The first initial *M*. He even has the same middle name as you."

"I know. I can't believe it."

"What a coincidence. It's amazing to think that you picked out this particular one. Is that why you walked up to it?"

"I hadn't even seen it first, I just stopped walking...right here."

To myself I began thinking about my aunt, and in the most natural way I asked out loud, "I totally wonder what Aunt Shirley would think. She's the one who keeps saying that there are no coincidences, nothing's an accident, and absolutely everything's meant to happen."

"Give her a call when we get back."

"I don't know if I can."

"Why?"

"I'd be sort of afraid to find out what it all means." After telling Khadijah that, we walked back to her car, got in, and again headed to the new doctor. The ride the rest of the way was pretty quiet. I could tell that Khadijah was thinking. I could tell she was thinking about something she was waiting to say to me.

"You've never even talked to this doctor, right?"

"No, never."

"I bet it's a good idea to let him know about all you do to keep yourself well. Your *To Do* list. The way you say 'I will' rather than 'I want.' Speaking only positive words out loud. The fact that you always *believe* you'll have a full and fulfilling life. Tell him about F.A.A.T."

My mood started to get a little better after Khadijah began reminding me of those things. "OK. He'll like that stuff. And, Aunt Shirley'd be glad I mentioned it all."

After taking two wrong turns in a row on El Camino Real, Khadijah and I ended up finding the building we were looking for, the Matthew Morey Care Center. And it sure seemed to pretty plain, nothing so special about it at all. The outside was painted dull grey and it totally matched all the other businesses around it. The whole thing altogether looked just like it was once part of Tanforan Mall, just without McDonald's, KFC, and Burger King all lined up on the inside.

Khadijah and I walked in the main entrance door, and a pretty red-headed girl receptionist asked who we were there to see. She was super-friendly and said, "My name's Becky. It's good to meet you both. Have a seat and the doctor will be with you shortly. The paperwork is already done."

When we both sat down, Khadijah said it before I did, "I like it here."

"Totally." Inside me I felt like this was all going to work out fine. I mean, a person doesn't get to be a doctor if they don't know what they're doing. From what I've heard they've all practiced a really long time before they do it for real.

Khadijah and I waited in our chairs for a while, then I got up to get a magazine. I picked up *People* 'cause Ashton Kutcher's on the front of it. He's way whacky sometimes. He seems like the kind of person who does stuff before he thinks about it. When I sat back down, some new nurse opened the door to the waiting area, and as she smiled she said, "Veronica. Veronica Kepler."

Then a girl sitting to the left of me got up and walked over to her.

"May I come too?" a woman who was probably the girl's mom asked, then got up, and walked through the door.

About five minutes later the same lady opened the same door, smiled just like last time, and said my name. Khadijah and I both stood up and headed inside, except the woman stuck her hand out, stopping Khadijah from going in. "I'm sorry. Just Miguel. The doctor would like to speak with him alone."

"I'll be your nurse this afternoon. I'm Lucinda, and I'll be prepping you for your visit with Dr. Rosenzweig," the new nurse said.

Lucinda seemed like another friendly person in this brand new place. I couldn't wait to tell Dad that this all worked out so well, and he shouldn't feel bad that I had to come to this care center place instead of Stanford. The insides still looked like a place for doctors-only though, kind of like a real mini-medical center. "They don't do surgeries here, right?" I asked.

"Well, we actually do. Simple surgeries."

"Not big ones?"

"No. We're not equipped to handle major surgeries. Those take place in some of the nearby hospitals." Asking that question wasn't really necessary, because that's what I already guessed in the first place. "Today the doctor wants to get to know you, and re-dress and re-medicate some of your lesions," Lucinda said as we were still walking down the very long hallway.

Finally we got to the very last examining room. It seemed so far away from everything. For a second I wished Khadijah was with me after all. Instead of climbing up onto the table with the white roller paper on it, I sat on an uncomfortable, metal chair. Since I knew the table wouldn't be too cozy either, having to sit on that chair didn't matter so much to me.

"Well, Miguel. I'm going to step out now, and in a few minutes the doctor will meet you. I'll be coming back if the doctor needs me."

Many different and weird-shaped instruments were all lined up on the counter close by. Some of them I had seen many times before and others were brand new to me. A few of the tools were there for the doctor to cut off old bandages, like fancy kinds of scissors with ends that were soft, not pointy.

Over and over again my eyes scoped up and down and side to side like a periscope to find something that I'd find more interesting. That never happened though. The room I was in was on the ground level, so in between the window blinds I was able to see a few of the mall people walking back and forth in the parking lot. The feeling I had inside was way different from the times I went to Stanford. Stanford Medical Center was always extra fancy and real classy. And this new place was more generic looking, like a place where you'd find everyday low-prices, Wal-Mart.

Through the door to my room I could hear a man's voice real nearby on the other side. My guess was that it was Dr. Rosenzweig. Finally I was going to get to meet this new guy who was about to become one of my main doctors. The door opened quickly, then the man who opened it looked right over to me and said, "You're not on the table. What are you doing sitting there?"

"They said we were going to talk first," I told him.

"Oh, I see. Always on the table. I always speak with my new patients on the table. Saves time that way."

"OK, sorry about that, sir."

"Doctor. Dr. Rosenzweig. You may call me Dr. Rosenzweig, young man."

"Yes, sir, Dr. Rosenzweig."

Just as this new doctor helped me get up onto the table, part of me began to get scared all of the sudden. Was I just being a big wimp? Or was I feeling something that was very for real? "Up, up, up," Dr. Rosenzweig said, as he motioned for me to move more to the middle of the table.

"Do you—" I started to say.

"How have you been digesting lately?" the doctor asked.

"Food?"

Then, instead of answering, the doctor just glared at me. Both of his eyes said, "Of course, food."

"Um, pretty good. My Dad cooks different from what I used to eat when I was with Mom, but I'm doing OK."

"Fine. Any dairy?"

"Sometimes I eat—"

"No dairy. None at all. Never."

"You know what? Maybe Khadijah should be in here too. She's my nurse, and she'll definitely remember in her head all this stuff you're going to tell me."

"No. Not necessary. We'll be finished before you know it. Time is money."

I wasn't sure what that meant. I figured it was best to give him a benefit of a doubt though. Maybe he was really an alright guy if he just relaxed a little.

"Another person you should meet sometime is my Aunt Shirley. She's way cool, and she's thought of a million ways for me to stay well."

"A doctor?"

"Aunt Shirley? No, she's not a doctor. She—"

"Which ways would those be?"

"A whole bunch. She believes that as long as I keep my *To Do* list full, the longer I'll have to stick around to do everything, because I have to. She also taught me that whatever you say out loud is what's going to end up happening to you in life. If you say bad, negative things, then that's what's going to happen. The biggest is that I always say 'I will' instead of 'I want.' Get it? See, that way I end up making what I want to happen happen, because I've already said 'I will' do something instead of just wanting it to happen, which isn't ever enough…to actually *make* something happen. Isn't that cool?"

The doctor looked at me after what I'd just told him and said nothing, he just stayed silent for a while. It was like he was watching one of those foreign movies, except he didn't seem to understand the language it was in. After about a whole minute he told me, "In my presence, I'd appreciate it if you mention none of this again. I don't believe in God, I'm not religious. I'm a doctor, a professional. On your next visit, please keep these notions to yourself. Also, it would be more cost-effective if, from now on, I do all the talking and you listen."

At home, looking into the kitchen cabinet with all my medicines inside, I was able to convince myself that this new doctor of mine was just having a really bad day. He's the one who's responsible for giving me the medicines I need, so I'll close my eyes and keep my mouth shut. Everybody has rotten moods every now and then. Maybe he'd be completely different with me next time, I thought.

CHAPTER SIX

During an August morning when everything seemed pretty normal, I got a phone call from Khadijah. She told me Samantha wasn't going to school because the government just announced it was an orange-terror alert day. I asked Khadijah a few times more about why Samantha wouldn't go. Khadijah kept saying over and over, "she's terrified, she's terrified."

Something inside me made me call Aunt Shirley, 'cause I knew she'd be just the right person to realize the answer for what was happening. On the speaker phone in my room I called her, and she answered right on the first ring by asking, "What?"

"Aunt Shirley, did I wake you up? I'm sorry," I told her.

"No, doll," she said in a groggy voice. "What's up?" she asked next.

"Well, Khadijah just now called me and said Samantha wasn't going to go to school today, since they just made it an orange-terror alert day. Samantha's totally afraid. She's got tons of anxieties."

"Not to worry, doll. It's a no brainer. If you really want to help Samantha out, give her a call. Then plan on doing something specific that'll make her unafraid. Think of a task that will make her brave."

"Something brave. Like only someone who'd be unafraid would do, something that goes against this alert, against this fear they've made up."

"Exacta-mundo, hon. Not *too* daring…or else your mother's gonna be on my case in a heartbeat."

"Maybe I should call her now."

"Go for it. After all, this *is* your calling. Get it?"

"Oh, brother. Hey, thanks a lot, Aunt Shirl. Except for that stupid joke."

"Oh, get out. Go call. Love you, doll."

"Love you too. Bye."

When I hung up with Aunt Shirley I felt like what I needed to do next was something I *had* to do. Especially since I didn't learn how to get rid of all my fears by accident. That took lots and lots of hard work unlearning all those fears I was around when I lived with Mom. Those lessons were difficult to swallow, especially when I ended up in the hospital nearly every month from the fears that were making my body so sick. I hated being alive then.

The best thing to do next, I figured, was to call up Samantha immediately. Khadijah had given me Samantha's number a while ago, so I dialed it right away.

"Hello," a proper lady's voice answered.

"Hi. This isn't Samantha, right?" I asked to make sure.

"No. This is Samantha's mother. Who's this?"

"My name's Miguel, Miguel Estes. Khadijah asked me to call...Samantha."

"Khadijah?"

"Yeah, she's your sister, right?"

"She certainly is. Only, Mee-gheel, I'm not so sure Samantha can come to the phone at the moment. She's—"

"Yes, I know why she can't, Mrs. Parker."

"No, *Khadijah's* last name is Parker. My last name is Austin."

"Well, whatever. I think it would be good if I could talk to her, Samantha."

Without even knowing too much about the lady, I had the feeling maybe she was a little bit the way my own mom was with me all the time, overprotective. I never heard much about Khadijah's sister before, all I knew was that she was about five years older than her. "Khadijah knows that I like to help people. And since Samantha and I have so many classes together, she felt that maybe I could help her get unafraid of going to school on a day like this."

Then there was a silence on the phone, and I realized that no one was there on the other end anymore. Samantha's mom had gone to get her. I wasn't expecting to be able to speak with her. Then she asked in a really scared voice, "Miguel, you aren't going to school today? Are you?"

"Well, yeah. That's the whole reason they make up these terror alerts...to scare people even more."

"No it doesn't. It means we should stay inside and protect ourselves."

"Protect ourselves from *what*?"

"Miguel," she said, while making it sound like it should be so obvious to me by continuing to say, "from bombs, from toxic water, bio-terrorism, from everything."

39

"What's to be scared of about going to our school? Who'd want to bomb Marina Middle School anyway?"

"Miguel, Homeland Security says we shouldn't travel today. It could be too dangerous."

"Samantha, you only live twelve blocks away from school."

"I know. I—"

"Hey, how about if your Aunt Khadijah drives us to school together? How's that? She's coming over here to get me ready anyway. I'm sure it would be cool with her to pick you up too, so we could all go together."

"But we all might—"

"I want to help you, Samantha. I used to be exactly like you. Except, I learned that life's a whole lot better when you don't freak out. 'We all might' a lot of things...it shouldn't keep us from living our lives."

"My therapist says that during times like this I shouldn't become over-stimulated."

"Over-stimulated? What the...? Anyway, I did my part. I want to help you with this, but you have to want to change. It's a lesson for *you*. Only *you* can make changes happen for yourself. Your therapist can't, and neither can I."

After a short pause, Samantha said, "I suppose you're right, Miguel."

"You know what? I've actually got to get my own bad self going now. I've got a Spanish test today, and I still have to study un poquito."

"OK, I'll go. I'll go to school."

"Awesome. That's sooooo cool. When Khadijah comes over I'll ask her to go to your house. We'll pick you up, and we'll go from there. How's that?"

As soon as Khadijah came to my apartment she didn't have whole lots to say. She sure did thank me over and over again though. Part of me thought that since she remembered what my life was like before, when I lived with...all that fear, she knew that maybe it was possible for Samantha to get rid of hers, too.

For about an hour Khadijah got me all bathed, bandaged, and dressed for my day ahead. Then we got into her car and headed for the tip top of Pacific Heights where Samantha lived. I noticed that the city seemed so busy, so extra busy. From outside the car window Khadijah and I both could hear lots of people yelling, I guess at each other. Hearing homeless people do that all day was a totally normal thing, except this time it looked like it was way more than just homeless people. "Hey, watch it, you asshole!" a business-type, financial district pedestrian yelled out to a convertible Audi coming too close to her in the middle of the street.

"*Everyone* must be on edge today," Khadijah said to me as we continued driving north on Van Ness.

"The orange-terror alert. That's what it is."

"No," Khadijah said, while scrunching up her face in disbelief.

"Seriously. I'm not kidding."

"Oh, I don't think so, Miguel. Nobody really pays attention to those warnings."

"What about Samantha? She's totally freaked by it. Even though people may not pay extra attention, it still makes them maybe a little more scared than when the warning was whatever color it used to be before orange."

"You could be right."

"Oh, definitely. For sure. Aunt Shirley says that those Al-Qaida terrorists got exactly what they wanted and much more. Exactly."

"They got…?"

"That was their Number 1 main goal. To make America, I mean, Americans afraid."

"That's awful."

"Aunt Shirley said that forcing people to be afraid of living is way more dangerous than any bomb could ever be. She said that Osama bin Laden must be dancing a jig every day because the U.S. reacted just the way he wanted them to. They reacted with fear."

Because it was during commute hours, no cars were allowed to make left turns onto Broadway from Van Ness, so Khadijah decided to turn right onto Green Street. Then right onto Polk Street, and then we finally made it onto Broadway, heading up the hill to Pacific Heights. Being on Polk Street, even for a little bit, reminded me of my friend, Miguelito. Every time I thought about him I always felt like I deserved an *F*, like I didn't do enough to help him to stay alive.

Being on Polk Street made me think seriously about Miguelito, and about how young he was to die as a teenager. It made me wonder about his life, and what came before that made him decide to become a hustler, a prostitute who walked up and down Polk Street just to make money. Maybe that was Miguelito's destiny. Then I thought, 'did he learn all the lessons he was supposed to while he was alive?' But out of nowhere, a flashed picture of Aunt Shirley came into my head. She had once told me, "the lessons we've been given are not lessons we're *supposed* to learn, they're lessons we *choose* to, or don't choose to learn from. They're opportunities for us…for us to become wiser."

"K., do you think prostitutes like being prostitutes?"

With a puzzled look on her face, Khadijah asked, "What on earth made you ask that?"

"Being on Polk Street. All those boys there who look twice their age."

"Oh. The male prostitutes there. Were you thinking about Miguelito?"

"Yeah, being there made me remember him. I miss him. He was way cool."

"I never met him. I'm certain he was grateful to you for having helped him before he...left."

"Do you think he liked what he did?"

"Miguel, wow. I don't know. I have no idea. Who knows what motivates anybody to do anything."

"That's true, I guess. I just hope I learn all the lessons I choose to before I die. And, I hope I won't ever feel guilty for anything I've ever done," I said.

Khadijah never responded to that comment. Every time I talked about dying, or talked about being kind of afraid of dying, Khadijah usually either didn't answer, or she'd end up changing the subject. "So, you're taking the bus back home, right?" she asked.

"I guess so."

"Because I'll have to be back in Berkeley later today. I have two classes this afternoon."

"What about Samantha? Will she be OK to walk back to her house all by herself?"

"Oh, by the end of school. I'd hope so."

After Khadijah said that, I got to thinking about something, something that may be able to help Samantha out, by tackling another one of her fears big time. Telling Khadijah about what I had inside my head wasn't going to happen though, because I wanted my plan to stay a total surprise. Waiting to spring it on Samantha during one of our breaks at school, I figured, was going to be the best way to do it.

At about a block away Khadijah and I eventually made it over to Samantha's house. I was absolutely sure of what I wanted to do to help Samantha next. But when we drove up to their house, Samantha wasn't waiting outside like she was supposed to. I wasn't quite sure why. Maybe she'd changed her mind, maybe she just wasn't ready yet. Khadijah and I waited outside a few minutes. Then she asked me to get out of the car and knock on the front door.

Don't Be Afraid of Heaven

Samantha's house was totally fancy. The closer I got, the bigger it seemed. It had three or maybe more floors. And the gardens in front looked like they were from *Sunset* magazine. Their doorbell was some sort of combination ringer and alarm system that lit up as soon as I pressed it. I buzzed it three times in a row just to make sure it worked. A woman answered the door with black hair pulled back tight just like Samantha's, and a look on her face that I should definitely have rung the bell only once. She just stared at me after she opened the door and didn't say a word. Because she didn't say anything first, I said with a smile on my face, "Hi. Are you Mrs. Austin? Samantha's mom?"

She looked absolutely shocked, and eventually she was able to say, "And you must be Mee-kwehl."

"Yes, Ma'am. Is Samantha ready?"

"I'm afraid she's had a change of heart, dear."

"Change of heart?" I repeated, like I knew what that expression meant. Assuming it meant that Samantha changed her mind, I went on to say, "Oh, but I have something real special planned, something we *have* to do today."

"Well, you're welcome to talk to her if you want. Please come in."

"Khadijah's waiting in her car though. We can't be late for school."

"No, you don't understand. Samantha *won't* be going to school today."

"Yes I am, Mommy," Samantha said while walking towards us both. "If Miguel and Auntie Khadijah were kind enough to come all the way here to pick me up, the least I can do is go with them."

"But, darling, you're—," Samantha's mom tried saying.

"We'd better go, Miguel."

As fast as she could, Samantha practically sprinted out her front door just like Jackie Joyner-Kersee. And, before you could cross the finish line, Khadijah had dropped us both off at the entrance of Marina Middle School. All it took for Samantha was a little head start.

In between Science and Social Studies, the last classes of the day we had together, I began to tell Samantha that I thought of a great plan. Before you knew it, it was time for our next classes, my Spanish and her Russian. But, right before I left her, Samantha finally insisted that I tell her when she asked, "What's the big deal you're planning? I'm dying to know."

"Are you sure you won't get too anxious or whatever if I tell you?"

"Oh, I can handle it. Come on. Tell me now."

"OK. After our last classes we're going to get on a Golden Gate Transit bus, the Number 10 that goes to Mill Valley, except we're getting off at

Fort Point. Then we're going to walk all the way across the Golden Gate Bridge."

With a shocked look on her face Samantha shouted out, "No way. Absolutely not. There's no way, Miguel. On an orange-terror alert day? Are you crazy? Don't they close the walkways on days like this?"

"No, they just have more National Guards on duty there. They patrol both ends of it. I think they walk up and down it, too."

"But, why *that*?"

"Because, walking over the bridge is something you're afraid of. Duh"

Just like lightning striking, that moment was another reminder that maybe I was meant to be doing all this. Somehow, as if God had whispered it into my ear, I knew for sure Samantha and I were supposed to know each other for a very definite reason. I could tell that somehow I was helping her be able to erase all her fears, one by one.

After school, Samantha very reluctantly agreed to go and we got on the bus. Passing by all the tourists who were mostly spitting over the railing, Samantha and I began walking on the bay-side of the Golden Gate Bridge, with the wind blowing at us softly from the ocean-side of it. Without saying too much, and after about a hundred yards or so, I could see Samantha become a little more relaxed, comfortable, and proud. After a while she even looked like she was beginning to enjoy herself. We walked and walked and walked. We laughed, we pointed to the big ships in the distance, and we occasionally stopped to take a look at the magnificence of it all. By the time we had gotten all the way to the bridge's north tower, we stopped again. Actually it was my feet that stopped moving forward.

"What's wrong, Miguel?" Samantha asked.

I looked over at her, and it took me a while to say, "This is where my friend jumped off. His name was Miguelito."

"Oh, my God. Did he die?"

"No. I got to know him after he jumped. I helped him the best I could. He died a few weeks ago." Thinking about Miguelito just then made me wonder if I was going to end up living as long as he did. Or would my life end before I turned seventeen?

CHAPTER SEVEN

Sitting in front of Aunt Shirley's living room window on a quiet Friday evening was as comfortable as it had always been. Like so many times before, this window with the awesome view of the bay, was where I made up my dreams. Sometimes though I couldn't decide what I really liked more, looking out at the panoramic view of the world or getting to spend some extra special time with my aunt.

As she came from behind to catch me by surprise, Aunt Shirley said, "What's up with you right now, Mr. Man?"

"I was thinking about something cool. That time you took me to the waterfall in Big Sur. Remember? We sat on that bench at the top of where the ocean was, so we could thank God. Wasn't that awesome?"

"Yes, sir. I'll remember that moment always."

"I wish we could do something special like that again. How about if you and me go to Hawaii sometime?"

"There's only one problem with that. I'm broke. Something closer."

"Um, Bodega Bay. How's that?"

"Weren't you there with your dad recently?"

"OK. Someplace closer *and* new, huh?"

"I'm thinking Lake Tahoe. Isn't riding on that glass-bottom boat still on your *To Do* list?"

"Oh, definitely."

"Well, then. Let's hit the road, Jack."

"What? Now? We can't just leave now. I didn't plan on it though."

"Who says you have to plan *anything* in life? I've got a friend who has a cabin up there. He never uses it. I'm going to call him right now. Start packing your bags, doll."

"I just *un*-packed."

"Perfect. Then you should be quite the expert at it by now."

Inside my luggage I threw in everything I could think of. The cabin was all ready for us, Dad didn't mind, Aunt Shirley had no other plans for the weekend, and I didn't need Khadijah to help me with all my medical stuff. It's like it was all meant to be, in a real spontaneous kind of way.

"It'll take us about four hours to get there, plus or minus a few minutes to stop and pee."

"Aunt Shirley, you're crazy."

"Oh, good. For a moment there I thought you might have thought I wasn't. What a waste that would be."

"How did you ever get to be this way anyway? You're *so* different from Mom."

"I don't know. Probably from living too close to oak trees all my life. Some people say they make you nuts."

Within a matter of minutes Aunt Shirley and I were on the road. From Berkeley we hit the Warren Freeway to 24, to 680, and then we took Highway 80 all the way to the Sierra Mountains to a town called Truckee. All the in between parts, like Sacramento and stuff, weren't really worth remembering though. Maybe it's better just to skip over all that.

"Quickest? Or most scenic?" Aunt Shirley asked.

"Um, most scenic." I liked it when Aunt Shirley gave me choices. Dad hardly ever did that too much whenever we drove together, and Mom never.

"OK. Highway 89 it is. It'll take us to Tahoe City on the north shore."

"Hey look. They have a McDonald's here," I yelled out while Aunt Shirley sneered at me in a disgusted and funny way at the same time. I always joked with her about that 'cause she always liked Wendy's way better.

Cruising through the mountains was so cool. Along the highway we were driving down, there were a few cozy-looking cabins and country-type wood houses scattered around. It made me think about what kind of people lived in places like that, and how lucky they were to be near something so beautiful *all* the time. While looking through my passenger window, I noticed that not all the pine trees were the same. I mean, they were all green, duh. Some had long needles, and others looked more like the Christmas tree kind from Walgreen's parking lot.

"It's gorgeous. Isn't it, doll?" Aunt Shirley asked me.

"Totally. This is kind of like the way it is on the way to Big Sur. That shorter part that goes through the woods. Except you told me those were redwood trees, right?"

"Yep, redwoods. You got it. And, you know what, in about ten or fifteen minutes we're going to pass by something real special. So keep those eyes open."

My eyes were already open. I wondered what it could be. On Aunt Shirley's side of the road she pointed out the Truckee River. It looked bigger than average to me, and it was real pretty and clear. "It runs from Lake Tahoe all the way up to Reno, then through it. It empties into Pyramid Lake on the Paiute Reservation about 35 miles north of Reno. One of the few rivers in the U.S. that doesn't empty into an ocean."

"Wow. No kidding."

"Pyramid Lake still looks like it did during prehistoric times. Someone even caught some prehistoric fish there as recently as the 40's...and it was *alive*."

"No way. Like a dinosaur?"

"Yep. Some places on earth never feel like changing."

That's what it seemed like to me, like going into the country was somehow like going to a place where changes didn't happen too fast. It's like the opposite of San Francisco where changes happen all the time, right in front of your eyes. Sometimes it's hard to catch up. Which is better? Aunt Shirley, over and over again, kept telling me that that's one of the main reasons why we're all alive. To change, to grow, to learn. "Do lessons come to *all* kinds of people? Or just the ones who *want* things to change?"

"Lessons come to everyone, whether they're ready for change or not."

"Everywhere?"

"*Everywhere*. Lake Tahoe. El Salvador. Oakland. New York. Nowheres-ville. Everywhere and anywhere."

"When people live in a place like up here, is it easier for people to die 'cause maybe it's already like heaven anyway?"

Instead of answering my question, and without any warning, Aunt Shirley quickly pulled over to the side of the highway. I'd been looking toward the opposite, driver's side of the road the whole time but forgot about my own. Aunt Shirley swiftly parked her car right under some kind of big metal bowl with a huge burning flame coming out of it, like a barbecue that got too much lighter fluid sprayed on it. And there was another burning-flame bowl on the other side of this road. Before I could ask what's up, Aunt Shirley told me, "It's the Olympic flame." She said that just at the same time as I read what was right above the blazing fire bowl, "*Squaw Valley: Home of the 1960 Winter Olympics*."

"The *Olympics*? 1960 was a real long time ago. They keep that fire burning all the time? Doesn't that sort of waste energy?" I asked out loud.

"It's a reminder, doll. Keeps the memories alive. It's a reminder that something very extraordinary took place here."

"I think the Olympics are cool."

"Me too. What else can you think of that makes the Olympics extraordinary, hon?"

"Somebody gets to win a Gold Medal."

"You're right, athletes win medals. Some see the Olympics as a major competition, I see it as a gargantuan opportunity. A chance to learn from others, from different types of people united."

"All those countries. They said that at the last Olympics there were something like over a hundred countries all mixed in together."

"Bingo. That's it. I think there should be an Olympics of some sort every week. It shows the world that getting along with people that are different from us ain't such an impossible task after all."

"Good one, Aunt Shirl."

"More to see, doll. More to do," Aunt Shirley said. That was her way of telling me that it's time to move on.

When I glanced over to her when neither of us had anything to say, I felt deep down that Aunt Shirley'd end up being my best and smartest teacher for life. No one ever made me feel the way she did. Almost the total opposite of the way other people did. She seemed to get *everything*. Everything to her was either a lesson, an opportunity, a gift, a blessing, or a new way to learn something in a different way. Wishing that everyone could think like her though was like a total joke, I mean, get real. I knew for sure that I'd never meet anyone like Aunt Shirley again for the rest of my life.

Closer and closer we got to the lake. As I began to see it from the distance up above on Highway 89, I couldn't get over how huge it was. "How come they don't call this an ocean, A.S.? It's so big," I said before realizing how dumb my question was.

Next, we came to the little city on the lake Aunt Shirley mentioned before called Tahoe City. It's built smack on the lake. What a cool place, I thought. Sort of like the feeling I remembered having with Aunt Shirley in Big Sur, I was starting to have again at Lake Tahoe. I felt as if I was about to not only discover some new and special place, soon I was going to learn something important about myself. It made me want to store up this memory inside my head forever.

Aunt Shirley turned onto Highway 28, the one that twists and turns around the north and east parts of the lake where there were lots of teeny towns. What a different feeling the people must have had from living in cities, I thought. Were they more relaxed people? Did they come from somewhere else before moving to this place?

After we passed through the town of Kings Beach, we headed up a hill in some other town called Brockway, and then we crossed across the Nevada border. There were a few casinos and hotels there, and the whole atmosphere was way different from on the California-side, like a lot more mysterious and magical. "Here we are," Aunt Shirley said.

"Check it out, Nevada's a Spanish word. I learned it from Dad."

"This is where we're staying, hon. Be on the lookout for Tuscarora Road. It's coming up soon."

"In this town? Is this where the cabin is?"

"Yes, sir. Right here in Crystal Bay. I remember it's up on one of these side roads somewhere, right off the highway."

"You've been here before?"

"With a friend of mine, yes."

"Which friend, Aunt Shirley?"

Without answering my question Aunt Shirley said, "This cabin was built in the early-20's. My friend mentioned to me that when he bought it, the owner told him that Marilyn Monroe had actually slept there."

"Wow. Are you serious? Marilyn Monroe? She's way famous. She's like the original Madonna, right?"

"I guess you could say that."

"She's called a legend, too. Is *legend* the right word?"

"Yes, Miguel. That's what she is."

"Can some people be legends if they're still alive? Or is being dead the part that makes them the legend?"

"No, there are many legends that are living."

"I think I'd like to turn into a legend *before* I die, so that way I can have fun being one while I'm still alive."

As it turned out, Aunt Shirley found Tuscarora Road before I did, and started to drive up it. After that, she knew exactly how to get to the cabin. When we got right up to it, although it didn't look too fancy at all, it was still heck'a cool. It was real woodsy, with tons of trees around, and about a billion flat-stone steps to walk down from the road. "This is kind of a far place to park."

"No garage, no carport."

"So, Marilyn Monroe stayed here," I said, while imagining that such a famous person would have slept at someplace way more fancy. Without a response, Aunt Shirley began walking down the steps to the cabin, and I followed her. She said she'd come back up to get our stuff out of the trunk later. Walking down the steps was like a fairytale, with squirrels and chipmunks running up and around the trees, lots of different birds chirping, and then the silence came. This was definitely a different world for me.

I felt like I knew what Marilyn, Monroe not Manson, must have liked about it. This was a place where she could forget about all the things she had to do to be such a famous, movie star, sex symbol legend. I thought maybe when she was inside this cabin she didn't even have to paint her mole on, she could just forget all about it and chill. What a cool thing. I hope she had this same good feeling when it came her time to die.

Seeing Lake Tahoe from inside this tiny cabin was like looking into a painting. It seemed like it was all made up, but it was real. "Thanks, Aunt Shirley. This place is totally perfect, like a dream."

"Hey, I'm glad you like it, doll."

"Definitely. Are there cool close by places we can go exploring up here?"

"Absolutely. Tomorrow. I've already picked out the perfect spot. It's in a town that hasn't changed in over a hundred years, Virginia City. I'm taking you to the cemetery there."

To make the whole experience pretend to be more permanent I started unpacking all my stuff I'd thrown into my suitcase. Aunt Shirley showed me my own special bedroom that totally smelled like Airwick solid, the pine flavor. Neatly as I could, I put my socks and shirts in a drawer, my pants on the hanger, and my shoes on the floor. As soon as I finished, Aunt Shirley yelled out from the other room, "Before we explore Nev*ada*, your homework's got to be termin*ada*, señor."

Oh, brother. I just knew she was going to tell me that. Doing my Social Studies would be the most fun I figured, so I took out that book first. When I opened it to the section about the Masai people of Kenya in Chapter Three, a folded up piece of white binder paper was stuck inside it. As I unfolded the typewritten note, I began reading.

Dear Miguel,

I must apologize in advance for not having the courage to tell you this in person. Unfortunately this letter is the only way I am able. I certainly do appreciate your efforts; I'm even flattered you chose to help me. But, Dr. Herman, my psychiatrist, said it would be in my best interest to abandon your group, F.A.A.T. He even suggested that I work on my anxieties solely with him, using only the methods he employs.

Dr. Herman says that fears and phobias are highly complex. He believes it's not possible to eliminate them; it's better to in fact, coexist with them. I don't mean to offend you; he says the ways in which you deal with fear is perhaps best for you, but too dangerous for me. So, for my own well-being, I'll no longer be spending my free time with you. But, I do look forward to the classes we share.

I'd appreciate it you'd convey these thoughts to your aunt as well. Thanks.

> My best regards,
> Samantha

CHAPTER EIGHT

Stop and read as you pass by,
As you are now, once was I,
As I am now, You will be,
Prepare for death and follow me.

Reading that sign made me feel real creepy inside. Above the poem were lots of rules and regulations that all the visitors who went inside the cemetery had to obey. After parking on some dirt road, Aunt Shirley and I found a few signs with directions on them. Then we watched a family of tourists head towards what seemed to be the popular path up the hill where most of the other tourists were. Aunt Shirley decided to take me on the lower road though, where no other people seemed to be walking. "Where does this one go?" I asked her.

"You'll see," she said. As we walked more into the cemetery I could tell why it was called the Silver Terrace Cemeteries, all the graves were spread apart on different flat, leveled hills, with a few dead trees and sagebrush mixed in between. The paths were made of cat litter box gravel, clean of course. And they went in all different directions to a variety of burial places. The desert breeze blowing by us felt so velvety on my skin.

No one else was around us. No one living, I mean. All the graves had their own, little individual fences around them with entry gates attached, like little built-in backyards right on top of the graves, something I'd never seen before. Some were metal and some were made of wood. Even some of the tombstones were wooden, with what's written on them faded away long ago from the blistering sun.

Aunt Shirley and I followed the road to the end and walked underneath an old, fallen-apart metal gate that said, "Blessed are the dead who die in the Lord." Then, more up the hill we walked until I stopped first to look close up at one of the tombstones. It belonged to a child. The name on it was John Henry Higgins, who died on September 23, 1869. Age: 10 years, six months. On his tombstone was another poem that read:

> *Sleep on Sweet Child,*
> *And Take, thy Rest,*
> *God, called thee Home,*
> *He thought It Best.*

How come God did that? Thinking about John Henry Higgins made me remember back to a question I'd asked Aunt Shirley over and over, "How are kids supposed to learn all their lessons in life if God makes them die that young?" Why did this boy only live to be ten years old? Was he already finished with the lessons God had given him? I totally didn't get it. Was I going to get to finish all I needed to do? Or was God going to call me home 'cause He thought it best? How come Aunt Shirley took me to this place? What did she want me to learn from it all?

Way by surprise Aunt Shirley said, "What a lucky boy. To have lived during those times. I wonder where he is now. I wonder *who* he is now."

"His soul, you mean?"

"Yeah. He's probably come back a few times since then. Maybe we've even run into him somewhere already, and we just never knew that he used to be John Henry Higgins from Virginia City."

"Sometimes I forget about that, people who used to be somebody else before they're here this time."

"Oops, I shouldn't have brought it up. Forget about it. Don't bother focusing on any of that. Who someone was before, who they're going to be the next time around. Who knows. Who cares."

Why did Aunt Shirley bring it up if she wanted me to drop it in the first place? I always thought that guessing who or what people used to be was kind of interesting. Somewhere, somehow though in an obvious way, Aunt Shirley was trying to make some sort of point. She always made *me* be the one to figure it out though…then that way, it became a lesson for me 'cause I sought out the answer. Something told me all this didn't have to do with how long we're on earth but how short. I felt pretty sure that that's what she was trying to get across to me.

We left the spot where John Henry Higgins was buried. Then we walked around some more. Up and down hills, through the weeds, and taking a few time-outs for it all to sink in. In between the sound of our footsteps crunching the gravel below us, I just listened to the constant electric buzz-noise made by some insect that's not a cricket. The bug must have not gotten too tired of doing it either, 'cause the sound went on forever.

Over half of the headstones we spotted belonged to kids, kids buried in this desert, kids who never got the chance to have a future. "When a kid dies, and just like the tombstone said that it's *'cause God thought it best*, is that a good enough answer? Especially for the moms and dads?"

"They must have believed so, or else they wouldn't have had that inscribed on the tombstone."

"That sure seems like it's sort of lame to me, to have that much faith in what God decides."

"What do you think God is teaching *you* right now?"

"God? I have no idea. You're the one who brought me here."

"Well, if you see our trip here as a lesson perhaps, what do you think He's teaching you?"

An idea had been rolling around inside my head for a while, except I never did tell Aunt Shirley what it was. Maybe I was learning my lesson right as we were speaking, maybe when I was looking at John Henry Higgins, or maybe it was when I started asking about God. Instead of letting it just roll around upstairs in my head, I decided it was time to spill the beans. I told Aunt Shirley, "Even though our soul comes back a few times, the time we're actually here ain't so long. I mean, each time we're here…on earth. You know what I mean? So we better do the most we can."

"Yippee! Doll, that's exactly how I see it."

"Just like you in your car accident. You didn't know that was going to happen, and it almost killed you. You almost went to heaven without even knowing anything about it beforehand."

"You said it, sweetie. Everything I do now, everything that happens to me, I appreciate. And, the more unusual, the better."

"That's like thanking God all over again, every single moment."

"Oh, absolutely. I don't know how long I'm going to be here. I don't know how long *you're* going to be here. But I'll be damned if I'll let a second go by without appreciating it all, without appreciating my life, without appreciating you."

My head just shook back and forth after Aunt Shirley and I left the cemetery in Virginia City. Everything I experienced was like it was from some meant to be kind of story. It's true, I had no idea how long I'd be around. And, I guess all along I should have stopped worrying about how and when I was going to die. Anytime. Anywhere. It's anybody's guess.

On the front porch deck at the cabin in Crystal Bay, Aunt Shirley and I watched the sun set over Lake Tahoe's west shore. It was like a massive rainbow in the sky. Like the clouds were painting the most colorful pictures right in front of our eyes. Purple. Red. Orange…and the clear blue water beneath it all.

It was the end of the day, and after what Aunt Shirley and I experienced in Virginia City, I saw it all as not just the end of a day but the day's departure for heaven. The day was something we both appreciated so much. Then it was time for the day to go away, to go to heaven, and never come back again the same. Nighttime was coming soon, and I looked forward to the new day that was coming up next. And before it had even gotten there, I appreciated it.

My sleep that night was so peaceful, a lot of my worries were gone. What I appreciated even more than ever before was my Aunt Shirley. That night made me appreciate her so much more. It made me remember my time talking with God, asking Him to make her wake up from her coma. And, more than anything else, it made me remember what Jorge had told me once in a dream. I don't know what made him think of it, but I'll never forget him saying, "Listen and learn from Aunt Shirley…it's the last time she'll be here." What made Jorge tell me that?

When I got out of my bed in the morning, I stepped into the living room. Aunt Shirley was already there. She was sitting on the end of the cozy brown couch in the dead silence. I didn't want to disturb her, so instead I just looked at the expression she had on. Whenever Aunt Shirley was alone and I happened to see her, she always had a mixed look on her face. Part of it looked peaceful and the rest of it looked real sad. I thought that if I went up to her and said, "Good morning" it might cheer her up. Only, I remembered having done that a few times before, and it only seemed to work halfway.

Before I had a chance to walk back into my bedroom unnoticed, Aunt Shirley said, "Are you practicing to be the next *007*?"

"The next double-oh-seven? What's that?"

"Oh, that's right. You're *way* too young. James Bond, 007. A secret agent, or spy, or one of those."

"It seemed like you were thinking hard about something, and I didn't want to disturb you."

"You could never disturb me, doll. I was thinking about my life. What I've done with it thus far. What I still need to do."

"Trust."

Like I had just unleashed a weapon of mass destruction, Aunt Shirley became totally shocked, and could only respond with one word by asking, "What?"

"Trust. That's your last lesson. I spoke to God about that. I asked Him to take you out of your coma so you could learn your last lesson, to be able to trust someone and have a relationship with them."

Then a totally rare event happened when Aunt Shirley said, "I'm speechless, Miguel."

"Your baby that got killed, and that guy you were with that did it. Dad told me about it. I hope you don't mind."

In a startled way, Aunt Shirley asked, "He told you?"

"Yeah, when he called me right before he flew back to America."

"I can't believe this," Aunt Shirley said in a much quieter voice.

"It's because of something Mom said right when we found out you were in a coma, when she found me sitting in the lobby of the Fairmont all by myself waiting for you to pick me up. Dad said that's what made Mom…" Then, all of the sudden I realized how much of a big deal all this was, and that it was maybe more Mom's business than my own about the real truth of what had happened to Aunt Shirley's baby when she was a teenager. I finished by telling Aunt Shirley, "Probably the best way is for Mom to tell you sometime."

"Tell me what?"

"No, it's really none of my business. Maybe we should talk about something else now."

Being a tattletale was never my thing, but this time it happened like a total accident. Blabbing stuff out without thinking beforehand was something I did sometimes, and this one was huge. Aunt Shirley still appeared speechless. The face she showed me was confused and stunned all at the same time. "Miguel, I just don't know what to say."

"You know what? You should definitely have a talk with Mom sometime. It's not right for me to say anymore."

"How long have you known about this, Miguel?"

"Not too long."

"Wow," she said like a whisper, and said no more.

"Samantha, your mom and dad should take you to Lake Tahoe sometime," I said.

"We never have the chance. Vacations get in the way of Mommy and Daddy's lives. Their work keeps them very busy," Samantha responded.

"Oh, I used to take vacations with my mom all the time. And the only thing that *ever* kept us from going on them was whenever I got too sick. Later on though, with planes and terror and stuff like that, Mom became too afraid of going to most places. Right about then is when a lot of changes started happening."

"I know about all that. Auntie Khadijah told me everything that went on." In a way, when I heard Samantha say that, I got kind of embarrassed.

"What else did she tell you?"

"All about your mother's new husband. He sounds dastardly."

"Ooh, that's a good one. That's a word straight out of one of those old, classic cartoons on Boomerang. Did she also tell you about my Aunt Shirley?"

"Oh, yes. Are all those stories true? All she's done?"

"I won't even ask you which stories. I'll just assume whatever you heard is true."

"Auntie Khadijah filled me in on your father, too. He's from South America, isn't he?"

"No, *Central* America. El Salvador."

"Oh, *that* was the place. And, he was just released from…?"

"Prison there. I don't mind talking about it. I'm not humiliated or ashamed at all. He was set up by somebody."

"I don't watch many police dramas. What does *set up* mean again?"

Asking about my dad was one thing. Asking about the way he got put in jail was something that began making me a little uncomfortable. I figured maybe that's what made Samantha so smart though. Like I remembered hearing a million times, 'it's only the smartest people who ask the most questions.' "*Set up* means that Dad never did anything wrong, someone else got him into trouble. *That's* what it means," I told her, in a very definite-sounding way.

"Tell me, what was he arrested for again?"

Once more with the very personal questions. Maybe Samantha didn't know me that well after all. She never knew when to shut up. I never thought of myself as a totally private person, but there were definitely certain things I liked to take my time telling. "Do you really need to know that part?" I asked.

"No. Not really. I'm sorry. No, not if it makes you uncomfortable."

"OK."

"I don't need to know, I *want* to know, Miguel. That's how I can learn to trust you. As you know, I don't have very many friends. And, it's only after someone's confided in me, divulged something rather intimate, that I begin to trust anyone. That's why I decided to call you again after I'd written you that letter."

"I'm totally glad you did by the way. I felt like such a loser when I got it. Then—"

"I'm so sorry, Miguel."

"That's OK. I just figured, you can do what you want with your doctors. I still wanted to stay friends at least. You should always do what *you* think is best, *you* decide. Trust your instinct."

"Instinct? I'm not so sure I'm all that perceptive."

"Don't you ever have a first impression of something?"

"Well, yes. I guess so."

"Going with your first impression is usually always the right way to go. Trusting your first impression will definitely help you with all your fears, I mean, anxieties."

"How will first impressions help relieve those?"

"'Cause fear is a man-made feeling. When you go to do something and just do it, you won't have time to think about it, being afraid. You don't have time to think about how whatever it is may or may not turn out. You just go. You just do it."

"No one's ever told me that fear isn't natural, that it was created by man."

"Man, society, the news, AOL. We've all *learned* to become afraid. God never created fear. We did."

CHAPTER NINE

"Aunt Shirley, you're acting kind of nervous. What's up with that?" I asked.

"I want *everything* to be so special this evening, like a dream come to life."

"You still haven't told me who's coming over. Are you ever gonna?"

"No way, José. What kind of surprise would it be if I told you?"

Usually Aunt Shirley wasn't big on secrets or surprises. This time was way different. Something extra huge was brewing, and I didn't have a clue about what exactly. Aunt Shirley had spent all day long cleaning up her whole house and spraying it with Lemon Lysol after. And I had just spent what seemed like all day waiting. I'd gotten myself ready a long time before, and Aunt Shirley was acting like Tom Cruise or Ben Affleck was popping over for a date.

"I bet it's Dad. You haven't seen him in a while. Am I right?"

"Nope," Aunt Shirley answered while running away from me. "Shit, I forgot my earrings," she continued. Wearing earrings was so *not* Aunt Shirley. Actually, wearing *any* kind of jewelry was so very definitely not her.

The only clues I was ever given was that the person who was coming over was someone I liked, someone who was probably a man, and someone who'd always wanted to eat at Chez Panisse but could never get in. Well then, it couldn't have been a movie star, because their way-famous name could have probably gotten them into anyplace anytime.

Catching me by surprise was a really loud knock on the front door. "Aunt Shirley, whoever it's supposed to be is here," I yelled out all the way to her bedroom upstairs. I was so positively sure that she heard both the loud knock and me yelling upstairs, except Aunt Shirley didn't respond to either. "Do you want me to get it? Or not?" I shouted out again.

Aunt Shirley started running downstairs, but then ran right back up again. From up at the top of the stairs she shouted over to me, "Answer it…pleeease. I'm too much of a wreck."

Opening Aunt Shirley's front door was easier than most because it has those European-type handles on it, so I never was forced to grip onto a knob or anything, I just had to push down and voila! Looking through the peephole first was something Aunt Shirley never did, so I didn't either. I just pressed the door handle down and then I became totally shocked to see someone completely weird-looking on the other side.

It was a woman whose ears must have been pierced in about a million different places. Her shiny purple hair was cut in a bowl shape, and was even dyed up like a rainbow on one side. Her clothes were a purple flannel shirt and ripped jeans, not designer. Who was this? Aunt Shirley had told me the person we were having dinner with was someone I liked and probably a man. I was completely baffled. Maybe I was wrong. Then I began thinking, *what a strange-looking* man. After a moment though I remembered that I was in Berkeley, a place where *any*thing goes even more than in San Francisco.

Greeting me like she or he had met me before, a female-sounding voice boldly said, "You must be Miguel."

"Yes, that's right. I'm Miguel. And you're…the surprise?" I asked.

From the top of the stairs I heard Aunt Shirley yell, "No she's not."

What a relief that was, finding out that this woman was not the surprise Aunt Shirley and I were both waiting for. No offense. She's just not anyone I was expecting. Seeing her made me more curious than before though. With the front door still open I could see the raindrops falling onto Aunt Shirley's perfect garden of pretty multi-colored mixtures of roses and snapdragons. The sky was turning into something dark and stormy, like a big, old drama was about to begin.

"Hi there, Miguel. I'm Mary Agnes. It's a pleasure to meet you," she said, while reaching her hand out to shake mine. Seeing that I had no fingers, she stopped for just one second, then grabbed my hand softly and shook it in a real friendly way. I liked that.

At first, I felt like I had to explain how E.B. made my fingers go away. Then I just told the new lady, "Hi, Mary Agnes. Aunt Shirley's up—, oh, well, here she is," while Aunt Shirley joined us at the front door.

"Come on in, Mare. What's happening?" Aunt Shirley said.

"Nothing much. I'm door-to-dooring it this evening. And wouldn't you know, it just began raining."

"What's on the agenda tonight?"

"Legalizing euthanasia. We need scads of signatures in order to push this through," she said.

"What's that?" I asked.

"What's *euthanasia*? It comes from the Greek word, *euthanatos*, meaning *a good death*." Then, like she turned into another person, Mary Agnes got completely scared when she looked over to Aunt Shirley. Watching her was like when a person shoves their foot into their mouth but not for real.

Very straightforwardly Aunt Shirley said, "It's OK to talk about it. Miguel's cool with that. Tell him."

"Yeah, tell me. What's youth in Asia? And, why do they need to have a good death?" I asked.

"Oh, no, Miguel. It's a word. Euthanasia. It's defined as the practice or act of ending the life of a person who suffers from…"

"From what?" I asked, while I waited for her to finish her sentence.

"From a terminal illness or incurable condition," Mary Agnes answered. Then she looked away from me.

"I've heard of that. That's what that one guy does a lot, and he always ends up in jail 'cause of it."

"Yes, Dr. Kevorkian. Dr. Jack Kevorkian." Then Mary Agnes began to motion *bye* like she was going to leave, except talking about all this made so many questions mold inside my head. So, I had to ask her, "Is it more like killing? Or suicide?"

"Well, we call it *assisted* suicide."

"So, then it's *not* killing?"

"Absolutely not. Because these people who are so ill have *chosen* to die. They're never going to get any better. Assisted suicides help them finish their lives in peace. Their agony comes to an end, their suffering is over…all because they've *chosen* to end their lives."

"There's still lots of people who think this is wrong, right?"

"Correct." Then Mary Agnes, still standing on the inside of the doorway began to open it. At that very same second the doorbell rang. It was the real person Aunt Shirley and I had been waiting for all along. Mary Agnes glanced over to Aunt Shirley for a moment, and then the three of us, all at once, saw who the mystery person was as the door opened completely.

"Oh, my God. Lefty. What are you doing here? I don't get it." I couldn't believe my eyes, and inside my brain I was saying, "What's wrong with this picture?" It was more than way-weird to see my old doctor from Stanford standing right out front of Aunt Shirley's house.

"Miguelito, you sure are a sight for sore eyes. How are you?" Lefty

Clint Adams

said.

"I totally don't get it. What are you doing here?" I asked.

"I'm going to have dinner with you," he said. Then he noticed Mary Agnes there right in front of him, and he introduced himself by saying, "Hello. I'm Dr. de Pascual."

"Hi there. I'm a friend of Shirley's, Mary Agnes," she said.

"Hey there, doc," Aunt Shirley said.

It's like I had just come in from some foreign place, like maybe even from outer space, where *I* was the only person I knew. It just didn't make any sense to me. Aunt Shirley had been acting so unnatural, this new, weirdly-dressed up lady was getting signatures to help people die, and then Lefty shows up when he's supposed to be in the hospital at Stanford. What was going to happen next?

"You were the person we were waiting for? How come it's you?"

"What? You're disappointed?"

"Oh, no. Totally not. It's definitely good to see you. It's just, you're not at Stanford. It's like it's not right to see you here. That's all," I said.

"Well, hey y'all. Let's sit down and have some coffee. Come on," Aunt Shirley said. She seemed so much more calm than before. I guess with the woman being there, it kind of took all that nervousness away. "You three go have a seat. I'll go make us something. Miguel, what would you like, hon?"

"Grape juice is good." As I said that, all three of us that were left sat down with the view of the bay in front of Aunt Shirley's dream window. And before anyone else had the chance to say anything, I had to tell Lefty something real quick. "By the way, I don't call myself Miguelito anymore. Just so you know...I'm older now."

"Oh, I'm so sorry. I forgot."

"That's OK, Left."

"So *you're* Lefty? You've got to tell me how you got that nickname," Mary Agnes said.

"My first name is Elefterios. Miguel's the only one who calls me Lefty," he answered. Then, it probably hit him that he had no idea who this rainbow-headed woman was. So, he politely asked her, "Will you be joining us for dinner tonight?"

"No, I just happened to be in the neighborhood."

"She was collecting signatures to make legal youth in Asia," I said, assuming I got it right.

"Euthanasia. Legal? I see."

"To drum up support. It's not headed for the ballots anytime soon. We're trying to raise awareness. That's our primary goal, you could say."

"*Assisted* suicide is what it's also called," I told him.

"*Some* consider it that, Miguel. Others don't necessarily," he said.

Somehow I felt like I'd missed something, because there was a brand new tense feeling in the relaxing living room that wasn't there before. To make things easier I thought I'd tell Mary Agnes, "Lefty does surgery a lot. Isn't that cool?"

"It sure is. Very admirable. I have so much respect for doctors, I do."

"Thank you, Mary Agnes. I'm glad you see merit in medicine, in what it can accomplish."

"I see merit, of course. I don't, however, believe in prolonging misery. There's already too much suffering in the world."

"Aunt Shirley told me that suicide's just another way to die. It's not a sin at all like the way those religious people tell it. That's a made-up invention."

"To clarify though, there's a very strong distinction between suicide and *assisted* suicide."

"Oh," I said, and didn't know what to say after that.

"How do you feel about doctors who perform abortions, Dr. de Pascual?"

"Call me Elefterios, please. I truly see abortions as being an entirely different matter. Ending lives of the unborn is a decision that ultimately rests with the parents. And, that's another issue in itself. Is a fetus an actual life or not?"

Before Mary Agnes could answer that question, from the kitchen we heard Aunt Shirley accidentally knock over a pot or pan, and then try to cover it up by shouting, "What's going on out there?"

"You should get in here, it's getting real juicy," I shouted back.

"Oh, no. What are you all talking about?"

"Just about abortions and people dying, A.S.," I replied.

Aunt Shirley came sprinting into the living room with a fresh stain on her brand new dress and said, "OK. Enough. Although I despise trivia, how'd those 'Niners do today?"

No one ever really answered that question, and Mary Agnes and Lefty continued with the conversation they were having from before. The two of them never did get mean or anything, except their opinions about what was right and what was wrong were definitely on opposite ends of the speculum, like the North Pole and the South. Aunt Shirley and I joined in a couple of times, but our voices didn't seem to count nearly as much as the others. Because I didn't get the chance to talk too much, euthanasia gave me a whole lot to think about on the inside.

Who *wouldn't* want to have a *good* death, as opposed to a bad one? Duh.

More and more time had gone by, and from what I could tell, Mary Agnes and Lefty just sounded like they were mouthing off to each other. Arguing just ain't my thing. I don't know why, but all this talk about different ways to die made my death fears flare up all over again. It also kept making me think of Jorge. Missing him was something I never stopped doing. Then, I began wondering how come I stopped dreaming about him? Remembering those dreams, even though they were kind of whacky, made me believe that he still knew what was up with me and my life.

Jorge's the one who'd always told me, in my dream, that Aunt Shirley only had one lesson left. As I thought about exactly what he'd said, I turned to see Aunt Shirley sitting on her chair. With her hair still growing in from being shaved off, I began wondering just how long she was going to be around. I wondered if the times when I talked to God, asking Him to make her wake up from her coma, made any difference at all. Did He remember when I told Him that Aunt Shirley still had one more lesson left, a huge one? Maybe that's what did it, and made the tide turn around.

Although I had never asked before, I realized I must have been more than just a little clueless to not get that Lefty may have been over to Aunt Shirley's house for more than dinner at Chez Panisse. And out of nowhere, Lefty somehow must have known I was just thinking about him, because all of the sudden he stopped talking about dying and abortions and asked me, "So, you and your aunt had a good time at my place by the lake?"

"That was *yours*? The place where Marilyn Monroe slept?"

"Well, that's what the previous owner had said. I really can't verify that for certain though."

With an honestly shocked look on top of my face, I began to understand that *some*thing was going on that I never would have expected in a million years. "We had an awesome time. My favorite part was when Aunt Shirley secretly let me put a quarter into the slut machine, and I won twenty dollars," I answered.

"*Slot.* Gambling. Shirley, you're too much," Lefty told her.

"Hey, maybe it's none of my business, but how come you guys know each other now? I mean, you know, since I'm not in the hospital anymore?"

"Yeah, I'd like to know the answer to that myself," Mary Agnes said.

"You never knew this, Miguel. When you were at Stanford I'd come over here to the East Bay a few times to check on Shirley's condition."

"So, you're like a couple now?"

Lefty looked over at Aunt Shirley and at the same time, they said, "I guess so."

Before I had the chance to become happy or not for them, I still stayed shocked. All I was able to think about was the fact that maybe Aunt Shirley had finally come upon her very last lesson. If she trusted someone enough to have a relationship with them, that meant there'd be nothing left. She'd already learned everything else. And after that she might be gone.

Dear Miguel:

Here's the updated document you requested. This attachment's already been scanned for viruses, so there's no need to worry over that. I'm assuming you have the newest version of Microsoft Word for PC. Should any compatibility issues arise, please inform me.

Thanks once again for keeping me motivated; as always, I admire your persistence where I'm concerned.

    Best, Samantha

When I opened the file, I couldn't believe how much she'd already accomplished. I glanced through several pages of Samantha's *Overcoming Fear To Do* list, but my curiosity of what's left to be done made me scroll down to the final page.

33. ~~Stop wiping keyboard with disinfectant~~ after every use.
34. ~~Don't change channels whenever a violent scene appears on TV.~~
35. ~~Step~~ outside, even if only once, when thunder and lightning appear.
36. ~~Make an effort to try out new, unfamiliar strategies~~ on the tennis court.
37. Go fishing.
38. Walk across the wooden footbridge in Crissy Field.
39. Believe that ~~food prepared in any~~ restaurant isn't contaminated.
40. Don't be afraid of the unknown.

CHAPTER TEN

"What you expect is what you will not have," Aunt Shirley said.
Although Khadijah mostly did it for fun, Aunt Shirley still felt like she needed to tell her her own opinions about what a psychic lady had just told Khadijah. Aunt Shirley sounded so completely sure about...expectations.

"So, I guess I wasted my time," Khadijah said.

"Hey, these are only *my* thoughts. I don't understand how these people know this stuff. Maybe they truly are gifted. Knowing anything about your future, and telling others about theirs, I feel, is horribly wrong."

"The way she was speaking made it all sound as if she was trying to *help* me."

"Telling you anything about your future ain't at all helpful. You, you, you, you, you, you *make* it all happen. I'm not kidding."

How many times have I heard Aunt Shirley say that out loud. Like thousands. Khadijah still didn't seem to care one way or the other that Aunt Shirley was almost scolding her for what she had just done. I guess friends can do that once in a while and still get away with it.

"I believe you, Shirley. What's the harm in seeing it as entertainment though?"

"No, no. Whatever you hear from these people makes you, at some point in your life, expect. Instead of *making* these things happen, you wait. You'll expect them to happen. Then, of course, they never do because you never *made* them happen."

"So, these psychic people don't really know things that other people don't?" I asked.

"Maybe they do. I guess. Like I said, I guess you can think of them as being gifted. I'd rather put my faith in God rather than in anyone else though. And to top it off, how on earth would we learn any lessons if someone told us what they were going to be ahead of time?"

"What if one of these psychic people had told you in advance that you were going to be in a car accident when you drove over the Bay Bridge? And you were going to end up being in a coma?" I asked.

"I don't know, doll. I'm just glad I had known nothing about what was going to happen. Like I told you before, I learned something from that whole event, something incredibly valuable. I wouldn't have traded that experience for any other."

"You're not serious," Khadijah said to Aunt Shirley.

"I'm completely serious. That's the very first thing I told Miguel, I learned to be unafraid of dying. There's no longer one ounce of me that's afraid of moving on when it's my time. That's what I learned from having that accident. It was all supposed to happen exactly the way it did. Thank God."

"Shirley, you're an absolute trip. That's for sure."

"Yep. One of the kind," I said.

"Good to hear. Having one of me around is more than most people can handle anyway, that's what your mother used to tell me. Hey, what time is she meeting you in the city?" Aunt Shirley asked.

"She told me she's checking-in at around 3. At the St. Francis this time."

"We better get going then," Khadijah said.

Seeing that Khadijah and Aunt Shirley were becoming good friends made me feel a little bit more cozy and comfortable inside. It's funny to see that Aunt Shirley was totally right from a longtime before that they were meant to meet for a reason. Meeting each other a year earlier was so supposed to happen. My whole life was way different back then. I had no idea where I'd end up, and all that was going on with where and who I'd be living with, was what was making me the sickest.

Living with Dad took a lot of the pressure away, and made me a lot more relaxed. And more than anything else, a lot less afraid. Before seeing Mom, I wondered how she ended up liking life since she married this dude, Hunt. Soon, I'd know everything.

Without too much traffic, Khadijah drove me from Aunt Shirley's house in the hills of North Berkeley to my apartment in the Mission. After she double-parked, Khadijah watched as I was able to use my own key to get in and open up the entry door all by myself. As I walked into the building, I could see Khadijah through the glass door giving me a *thumbs up* as she began driving off. Khadijah believed in me lots. She was, waaay more than any of the others, the best nurse I ever could have picked out. I hoped Mom was going to think the same when we all got together later on that same night.

When I got inside my apartment I felt a little worn out. And with Dad at his new Sunday job, I decided to take a serious nap on our new blue Laz-E-Boy from Levitz. As soon as my head hit the pillow I was asleep, and right after that I began dreaming about my brother.

"No way, dude. These have got to be new ones. They can't possibly last that long," I said.

"Sure, keep looking. You'll find some," Jorge told me.

"This one looks like it's really old. Oh, never mind. It says 1874."

"Let's walk up the hill to that other cemetery. Even from here I can tell they're pretty much ancient."

"Are *all* these people pioneers? What does that mean exactly?" I asked Jorge.

"I guess so. That's what the sign said, something like, *what's through these gates is a dedication to these true Nevada pioneers.*"

"But, dude. What's a pioneer?"

"A pioneer is some sort of person who goes into unknown territory and decides to live in it. I think they're called settlers too."

"OK, I've heard of *them.*"

"Yep, lots of them moved on a lonnng time ago."

"To heaven?"

"No, *from* heaven. Most of these people died so long ago that they've come back a few times already."

"Back to *earth*? So, what Aunt Shirley always keeps telling me is *true*?"

"Like you always say, bro. *Duh.*"

"When's it your turn to come back? Are you ever allowed to be you again? Or do you always have to be someone else the next time? Do you know?"

"An even bigger duh. It's impossible to be the same person again. Been there already, dude."

"No new lessons to learn, I guess."

"Hey, let's keep looking. We still haven't found the very oldest one. Up here," Jorge said, while pointing to the top of some new hill we'd discovered. That's what Jorge and I were doing, looking for the absolute oldest headstone. The one that belonged to the first person buried there. Lots and lots were from the 1870's, except we wanted to find some that were even older than that.

When I had been to this same cemetery in Virginia City with

Aunt Shirley, she and I never did any of this. Jorge and I were on some sort of adventure mission though, like right out of *Spider Man*. It was way fun, and hanging with Jorge was always hell'a cool.

"I'm getting kind of burnt out on this. Let's do something different," I said.

"Well, did Aunt Shirley take you up to the Opera House here?"

"No way. Why?"

"Let's go there then."

"Get out. I'm not going into any opera place."

"That's just what it's called, fool. It's ancient. They've had performances there for nearly 150 years. Let's go."

"Are you sure?"

"Yeah. Come on."

"OK," I said, while we began our walk downhill, out of the cemetery. Throughout this Old West town there were so many Western-type tourists. But where Jorge and I were headed no one else was going. Up another new hill onto a narrow street we hiked. What was the weirdest thing to realize was that it's probably some of the same people who used to go to shows there, the actual audience at that Opera House, who were people whose names we'd just seen on the tombstones in the cemetery.

Staring up at the old, white-painted brick building was like standing in front of a place where time became extinct. "Do you think *I* was ever here before, Jorge?"

"Who knows?"

"So, you don't know stuff like that?"

"Nobody needs to know stuff like that. Been there, done that. Get on with it, that's what everybody should be doing. Learn from your past so you'll have somethin' better now. This means you, Miguel."

"*Me?* I'm no dumb ass. I've learned a lot."

"What's up with F.A.A.T. these days?"

"How did you know about that?"

"Everything you've learned you've gotta share. Go for it. You get that fear makes people stuck," Jorge said, as we walked up the creaky, broken down wooden stairs leading to the lobby of the Opera House.

"I know that already. Fear sucks."

"You need to get your club off the ground. You need to teach more people what you've already learned. It'll help them."

Just as we stepped inside the entrance of this way-old theatre, I could see that Jorge and I were in a place that had never ever become modern. It even had the smell of something alive that had turned dead.

"So, this is where the operas were? Wow. It's a little spooky."

"Enrico Caruso sang here. Harry Houdini did magic here. And Mark Twain spoke from this stage. Many famous plays were performed here," Jorge told me.

All this fascinated me completely. Then Jorge took me over to an antique-looking, glass-covered, wooden case. It had a printed program booklet from some performance back in 1878 displayed on its inside. I couldn't believe something like that had survived for so long, just so other people could look at it over a century later. "Is that really from a play or whatever that actually happened here back then?" I asked Jorge.

"It sure is. A comedy. About a very interesting girl who happened to be forever fearful...that was the name of it."

"People thought *that* was funny?"

"All things can be funny, amusing. Think back to at all the stuff we used to make fun of."

"I had to learn that there was nothing funny about being afraid. I had to learn to *not* be afraid in order for me just to survive."

"That's what makes you different, dude. So few folks know how deadly fear can really be. Like I said, you've gotta teach 'em. And you need to be doing it now."

Again Jorge was telling me that I needed to teach people about fear, about getting way over it. How strange, I thought. How come he picked me to be the one? Then something made me look at the faded play program booklet in the case. "I can barely read any of this, Jorge. I can't even make out what it says underneath the title. Can you tell?" I asked, while Jorge pressed his face up against the glass to see closer.

"*Forever Fearful: Samantha's Lament*...a tragic-comedy in three acts," he told me.

That was the last thing Jorge was able to tell me before I woke up. My time with him was over. When I realized Jorge was gone, I looked over at the clock in my room, and saw that it was almost five. Mom was coming over soon to pick me up and take me out to dinner. And, to watch Khadijah's dance concert. I couldn't wait for both.

Right on time Mom came over. And she seemed sort of cheery and in a real peppy mood. "Where would you like to go for dinner, hon?" she asked me.

"Gee, I don't know. Maybe a place we haven't eaten at yet."

"A casual restaurant? A little different? Bull's. How does that sound? It's somewhat close to Davies, where Khadijah will be."

"They have country food, Mom. Old West barbecue kind of stuff. Don't they?"

"Yes. Let's give them a call. Let's see what you might be able to order there."

"OK," I said in a totally surprised way. Mom usually didn't go for any of that kind of food, anything that wasn't fancy.

The whole evening Mom seemed like she was a little less afraid than I'd seen her before. She never picked at her face with her fingers, and we ended up having a great dinner at Bull's. They made something especially for me that I'd be able to digest well and not get sick, chicken gumbo soup. I even got to eat a little cooked, mushy cactus that actually came out of the desert. And the whole time Mom and I were there, I felt like I was in Texas or someplace way-far southern. Yee-hah!!!

Mom could hardly wait to see Khadijah dance. Performing in a professional show had always been Khadijah's big-time dream, and it finally came true. Seeing her name in the playbook program was especially exciting to me. That's what made it all seem for real, like evidence in a courtroom.

The performance Mom and I watched was divided up into three separate sections, and Khadijah got to be in all three. She danced in a totally new way I'd never known about before, that's why it's called modern dance. There were so many boy and girl dancers and all of them were real muscley. Lots of them were doing stuff that's more like those floor-routine gymnastics you see on ESPN. Maybe that's what the modern part of it was.

Hearing Mom say, "Isn't Khadijah impressive? She's really something," at intermission was like I was imagining things. I wondered what Mom was going to end up saying when the show was all over.

In a whisper during the third section, I asked Mom, "Can we go backstage after and tell Khadijah that she did good?"

"*Well*. Not good, dear. Of course we can. I have a gift for her. We'll give it to her then."

"You bought her something?"

When the end of the show came, all the dancers stood in a line on the stage as all the people in the audience clapped for them. They all did so *well*. Just as she said she would, Mom took me to the backstage part of the theatre and I got to see Khadijah. At first, when she saw us together, Khadijah didn't know quite what to tell Mom. So Mom talked first by saying, "Khadijah, we're so proud of you. You said this was what you wanted to be doing most, and you're doing it! Brava! Here's a little something from the both of us," Mom said, while handing Khadijah a small, gift-wrapped package that still had Tiffany & Co. showing through the see-thru paper.

As Khadijah unwrapped her present I couldn't believe my eyes. It was a shiny gold metal statue-pin of a girl dancer leaping up into the air, with her arms reaching straight up. It was real pretty and classy. "I'd gotten it for you when I was in Paris on my honeymoon. I wish I'd given it to you a long time ago. Well, I'm so thrilled to be able to give it to you now. Thank you for all you've done for my son."

Khadijah was more than speechless. And eventually all three of us were just glad to celebrate that things were getting way better for all of us. Mom still stayed stress-free, so she took Khadijah and I both out for dessert at Max's Opera Café down the street from the theatre on Van Ness. As soon as we began entering the restaurant door, I shouted out, "Samantha, what are you doing here?"

"It's on my list. Remember?" she answered.

"Oh, yeah." It was nearly impossible to believe that we just ran into Samantha in a place that's crowded full of people. Especially in a restaurant, where she had had so many food-eating phobias. Khadijah already knew that Samantha wasn't able to go to her dance concert 'cause that's still a little too much for her. The two of them getting to be together right after it though, was like a surprise party for everyone.

Samantha was at Max's with some new governess or nanny or whatever, and everybody introduced themselves to each other. Everyone else sat around and ate real fancy sugary sweets. I had a plain old, bruised banana instead. We all talked about what was going on in life. And I could tell that Mom liked Samantha a lot. "You are absolutely charming, dear. You're wise for your age," Mom told her.

"Thank you for saying that, Sharon. Sometime, I'd like you to meet Shirley too, Samantha. She and Miguel's mom are sisters," Khadijah said.

"Shirley and I already met at a F.A.A.T. meeting."

Then that reminded me about being over at Aunt Shirley's. "Khadijah went to some psychic lady on Shattuck in Berkeley today, Mom."

"Oh, I just did it for fun. Nothing more really," Khadijah said.

"Did you ever ask anything about me, K.? Anything about Samantha?"

"I think those people frighten me. I'm not so sure I feel comfortable discussing this," Samantha said.

"Miguel, I'm so sorry. I didn't get the chance. I did happen to ask about you, Samantha. And, don't worry. I was only curious if you were going to be having a future as a tennis pro."

"And, is she?" I asked.

"That's just it. Samantha, you'll be very relieved to know that the woman didn't seem to have any answer. She kept repeating, 'I don't see it...I'm not seeing anything.' And that's all she was able to tell me."

CHAPTER ELEVEN

"Dr. Beaumont told me that I now have Social Anxiety Disorder," Samantha said, right after we both got out of school. She had been waiting all day to tell me this. Except after I thought about it, I didn't really figure I could be much help to her. What Samantha told me she had, sounded a little too fancy for what I was even able to understand.

"I thought your psychiatrist was Dr. Herman," I said.

"I have a new phobia specialist now."

"What's a *disorder* again?"

"It's just another way of saying *ailment*."

"Samantha, I don't know if I get it very good, all the things your doctors tell you you've got, have something to do with fear, right?"

"Well, yes. They do. They've all been clinically diagnosed. My phobias are different from my anxieties, and my anxieties are separate and distinct from my panic attacks."

Part of me realized that Samantha knew I was actually able to get rid of all, I mean, most of the fears *I* used to have. Maybe that's why she trusted so much. Telling me all about her fears was maybe easier for her to do than telling somebody else who was still afraid all the time. "So, what ways is Dr. Beaumont able to help you with your Sociable Anxiety Disorder? Are your fears disappearing?"

"He helps me *manage* them all. I've tried beta blockers, tricyclics, MAOIs, SSRIs, benzodiazepines, and a wide variety of therapies. I don't know what's left."

"Samantha, I've never heard of any of those."

"I still need to take them. I couldn't survive without my prescriptions."

"I couldn't either. I need my oatmeal and medicine baths, my special wraps, my ointments, my treatments, and I need to be extra careful about my skin every second of the day. What I definitely couldn't survive without even more though is believing."

"Believing that what you want to happen will. That makes fear disappear?"

"Yes, definitely. Absolutely," I told Samantha for about the millionth time, as I could see that a little bit of what I'd been telling her was finally beginning to sink in. Knowing that I had made some progress, I decided to take it a step further by asking, "Hey, you like Justin Timberlake, right?"

"Oh, yes! Are you kidding? He's my man."

"And, I totally like Christina Aguilera. Why don't we go to their concert that's coming up. They're still touring together through the end of November. Let's definitely go," I insisted.

"Oh, no, Miguel. Never. You don't get understand. I could never go to anything like that. If I couldn't attend Auntie Khadijah's dance recital at Davies Hall, I could never go to a concert in a large arena. Never."

"You walked over the Golden Gate Bridge on a day when you said you were never coming out of your house. You've already done tons of stuff on your *To Do* list, most of it on your own. Duh, you need to keep the ball rolling. Facing your fears is what it's all about. Believe that going to a concert, one that you totally want to see, is going to be great. Serena ain't afraid of *any*thing. That's what makes her a champion."

"I *know* that, Miguel. Well, how do you know the concert's not sold out?"

"If my Aunt Shirley were here she'd be saying '*What if? What if? What if?*' She got so pissed at me saying that so much, that I never said it again."

Samantha didn't have anything to say after what I'd just said, but it looked like her brain was still working overtime. Maybe that's what makes a person afraid in the first place, *thinking* too much. Whenever I saw Samantha off guard it seemed like she was constantly thinking hard about something. And, I always wondered if whatever she was thinking about really mattered that much to begin with.

Maybe it's the people who aren't so smart are the ones who have the least fear, I figured. 'Cause they don't think too much. If only Samantha'd been born dumber she'd have a lot fewer fears since her head would have stayed a whole lot more empty.

Before I left for my bus to go home, I told Samantha, "Think about it. Or don't. Or instead, ask yourself one question, '*Yo, Samantha, how much do I really want to see my hottie, Justin?*' If you really do, then it will make you really want to go. If you don't, then we can just forget all about the whole thing."

Mr. Lau told me I needed to create an agenda, and plan our F.A.A.T.

meetings way in advance so he could make sure more students knew about it. Taking nearby field trips on MUNI Metro or BART could be a cool, fear-eliminating thing to do, I thought.

It sure wouldn't take much too much total time to ask all the people what they'd like to do most, because there were still only three of them signed up to be in my group anyway. Well, four, if you include Aunt Shirley. Knowing that she'd for sure have some great ideas, I decided to call her up.

"Hey, A.S. I've got to come up with more ideas for F.A.A.T. My principal told me I should be doing more planning, and I have to turn in some sort of schedule."

"I'm a little bit out of it now, doll. How about your *To Do* list. Give him that."

"Maybe a *To Do* list for everyone. That's what I'll give him. That should be good enough, I guess." Then there was a long pause, but I thought it was just a cell phone thing. "Aunt Shirley, are you there?"

"Yes, hon. Is tomorrow OK? I just got out of the pool...and..." As I was waiting for Aunt Shirley to explain what she was telling me, it sounded like she was beginning to cough real hard in the background.

I couldn't tell if her ear was still pressed to the phone or not, so I yelled out anyway, "Aunt Shirley? Are you there? Are you OK? *What* about tomorrow?"

After a few more seconds Aunt Shirley said, "Doll, I'm sorry. I...haven't been feeling well. I was only able to swim a few laps today. Is there any way we can work on this on Wednesday?"

"Oh. Well, sure. We don't need to talk today. Tomorrow's fine. No problem."

"Great."

As soon as I ended our call, my constant worries started up all over again.

On a rare night when my dad didn't have to go to his nighttime job translating stuff, he decided to take me across the bay to see the Dunsmuir House near San Leandro. He kept telling me what a really cool, historic place it was, and we were both excited to get over there. I loved driving with Dad. He always knew to go see special things that most people didn't seem to remember.

While we were stopped in commute traffic on the lower deck of the Bay Bridge, it made me remember about when I'd been on it with Mom when she was worrying about retrofitting. "Isn't this the part that almost collapsed?" I asked Dad.

"During the earthquake?"

"Yeah, isn't right about here where it happened?"

"Could be, Miguel. It was the upper deck, one entire panel in every one of the six westbound lanes."

"Where were you when all that happened again?"

"Oh my God. I'll never forget that night. It was about a year before you were born. Your mom and I were at the World Series game at Candlestick."

"I never knew Mom liked baseball."

"I had to talk her into going. That's when everyone in the Bay Area became a fan. They called it the Bay Bridge World Series, Oakland against San Francisco. The A's versus the Giants. And your mother thought that that night was the end of the world."

"We're *you* afraid?"

"Oh, definitely. It was a catastrophe. October 17, 1989. I'll never forget that date. It was like being in a war zone. Smoke and flames throughout the city. No electricity. No water to drink. No phones."

It was hard to imagine San Francisco had ever been like that. San Francisco always seemed like a city that could handle all types of situations. Even lots of years later, there's still tons of stuff that still has to be repaired because of the damage. "Did you think you were going to die?"

"Your mother certainly did. She thought everyone would end up a casualty. I just prayed for it all to be over."

"And it finally was. How long did it last? A couple of hours?"

"The earthquake only lasted a minute or so, but it was still so violent. I can remember when we happened to be inside our apartment when the power came back. Your mother noticed that there was one message on our answering machine. When your mom played it, we just howled. It was the funniest thing we'd ever heard."

"Why?"

"It was from Shirley. She's crazy. She'd heard about it on the news, and didn't sound the least bit worried about us. She said, 'I hope you both got a kick out of God's rollercoaster ride. Shit happens.' Then she hung up. Only Shirley could say something like that."

"*Nothing* scares Aunt Shirley. She's not even afraid of dying."

"That's pretty amazing. I admire that."

"What do *you* think's on the other side, Dad?"

"The other side?"

"Yeah, after we all die. What do you think comes right after that?"

"I guess heaven. I'd imagine it's a wonderful place."

"Then, how come mostly everyone's afraid of dying? If heaven's such a wonderful place?"

No answer. Dad just shook his head in a way that said, "I don't know." What was way different this time was that I was asking Dad this question when all along I knew that Aunt Shirley was the only one who really knew about this kind of stuff. Part of me felt like, at that moment, I was supposed to be having this discussion with Dad though.

By the time we drove off the bridge and made it onto 880 South in the East Bay, Dad nervously asked me, "Are *you* afraid of dying, Miguel?"

If Dad had not been the person to have asked me that particular question, I would have made up something different. Dad, more than anyone I've ever known, always spoke only the truth. I never lied anyway, except lying to Dad was something that would like *never* happen, ever. "I am, Dad. I'm scared of dying all the time."

What I said caught Dad completely by surprise, and he had to stop and look over at me right then, rather than watching the traffic...just to see if what was said had actually come out of my mouth. "Miguel, I don't know what to say."

"I'm just being honest, Dad."

"You're so hopeful and optimistic though. Your *To Do* list. Everything you've learned from Shirley."

"Nobody lives forever, Dad. I'm just scared about the way it will happen, and when, and what happens after that. It all scares me. Sometimes it makes me stop breathing. And when it gets real bad, all my muscles start twitching. Don't tell Aunt Shirley though. OK?"

"Miguel, when you're afraid, please tell me, anytime. We need to take care of this."

Dad still had a real concerned look on his face. It's like he had discovered something about me he never could have predicted. Like when you find out your next-door neighbor's really a mass cereal murderer who just happened to bury the leftover bodies underneath the basement with all their Christmas decorations.

After telling Dad the truth about the way I felt, made me somehow feel sort of relieved inside. And, in a real flattering way, Aunt Shirley was beginning to see me only as the boy who got rid of all his fears, and changed his life forever. That wasn't exactly the truth though. In a way it was kind of extra pressure for me to stay alive, to show people that by getting rid of fear, is what makes anything possible in life, even surviving. Telling Dad also made it easier for the next time I wanted to talk to him about something. So, I'm really glad that I'd gotten that stuff off my chests after all.

Driving across the bay, and seeing San Francisco from the east made me shake my head in amazement. It was hard to imagine that a place so spectacular could have been destroyed and ruined, and that some people even moved away from it just because they had become so scared of California earthquakes. Right then, I thought that no matter when it was my time to go away, I wanted to stay in the Bay Area until up to the very end.

"Only a few more miles to go, Miguel," Dad said to me, as we approached the historical old Dunsmuir House.

"What movies were filmed there again, Dad?"

"Gee, I'm not sure exactly. There have been many. One with Bette Davis, one with Jet Li. A good variety, I suppose."

When we got closer to the fancy front curly metal gate that opened to the Dunsmuir House and all the gardens there, I was able to see why lots of people wanted to make movies around it. Everything was so spectacular, like from the *Beverly Hillbillies* house. Parts of it we were driving through even looked like being in the middle of the Lake Tahoe forest. Dad decided to park right next to one of the tennis courts there, and seeing it up close made me think of Samantha. I even wondered once what it would be like watching her on a tennis court like this sometime, playing against Venus or Serena Williams. That would be her most massive dream come true.

And as we watched a dead bunch of leaves blow from one side of the court to another from the bench we sat down on, I asked, "Hey, Dad. Which one is the biggest tennis tournament again?"

"Oh, boy. I'm not necessarily a tennis buff. I'd have to say Wimbledon. It's definitely one of the oldest."

"Maybe that's what my friend Samantha needs to do most, go to the biggest tennis tournament there is, in person. That would be the coolest thing. To see all those famous tennis players, up close."

"I don't think you ever told me she plays."

"Oh, yeah. She practices a lot. Just with her coach though. Her Sociable Anxiety Disorder makes her too afraid to play against other girl players. How far is Wimbledon again?"

"Wimbledon's in England."

"England? Oh, that's way too far. What about a closer one?"

"I'm not so sure. Who knew you'd be so interested in tennis."

"It's not really for me, Dad. It would be kind of fun. It's a way I could totally help Samantha out, help her to believe."

"So, she wants to be a professional tennis player?"

"Yeah, she said it's on the back of her head. And more than that, maybe it's something she has to see to believe. You get it? If she sees that all that's for real, it'll probably make her want it even more."

"That could be."

"And even huger, she'd have to face her fears and get rid of them for good, if she really wants her dream to come true. It'll be the ultimate big-time lesson of her lifetime."

CHAPTER TWELVE

As soon as I got home, without any kind of warning at all, Dad told me Aunt Shirley had gone back into the hospital. She had some kind of serious pneumonia thing going on, and she needed to be around doctors again. Although I didn't want to have to admit it to Dad, I was getting way scared ten times more than I ever had before. I celebrated forever that Aunt Shirley had recovered from her coma. But just like last time, I had to worry all over again about what's going to happen to her next.

All I could think to do was what I'd done so many times before, talk to God. Immediately I walked into my dark bedroom with the curtains still closed. It had been a while, but I hoped real bad He'd still listen as I began to say out loud,

"Dear God,

How's it going? Well, it's me again. Miguel Estes. I know I haven't talked to You in a pretty long time, but what I have to say now is way important. You know why? Because Aunt Shirley started doing really good, I mean so well that she's even dating someone...my old doctor from Stanford, Lefty. Can You believe it? Neither can I. Check it out though, the biggest thing is, after all these years, she started trusting someone. By the way, I'm being serious with You right now, I'm not just mouthing off.

Except, the thing is, right now Aunt Shirley's in the hospital again. All because of the way she got aspiration pneumonia from when she was in her coma. They said her lungs were damaged, and now there's some sort of infection inside them.

God, please don't think I'm a whiner, 'cause I'm not. I just needed to tell You, if no one else hasn't done it already, that Aunt Shirley learned a huge lesson from being inside her coma. Aunt Shirley learned not to be afraid of whenever she's going to die. She said that going to heaven is absolutely the coolest place to go ever.

Is that true by the way? I figured You'd know for sure.

Well, I think her lesson that's left has more to do with trust than anything else. So, to learn that one real good, she has to be real healthy. Am I right? Another lesson Aunt Shirley learned was that long illnesses mostly happen for the people around the person who's really sick. It's like the person who knows they're going to die gets to a point when it becomes way obvious that they're really ready to go, like they *want* to. But the people who love them still don't want them to. Is that why so many people have to suffer? Just for the people around them who love them so much? To get *them* all prepared before the sick person goes away?

Anyway, in order for me to learn more from Aunt Shirley, You have to make her well again. OK? Please make this happen. Plus, Aunt Shirley's the adult supervisor of my new after-school group, F.A.A.T. Without her, the group will have to get defunct. You wouldn't want to see that happen now, would You? After all, Aunt Shirley said that's my mission, to help people get rid of their fears once and for all.

So, God, if You can, please do Your best. And I will look forward to the day when Aunt Shirley will be healthy, wealthy, and wise once more. Well, I guess she was never wealthy. But, whatever.

Love You lots, God,
Miguel"

Talking to God about Aunt Shirley got me thinking about all the things she'd tell me if she weren't in the hospital. Since she's the one who always nagged me, I mean, reminded me of what I needed to do for F.A.A.T. I decided to take another look at my own *To Do* list. Ever since I moved in with Dad I'd just thought that since so much of my life improved, that I forgot to be doing everything that it took to make me stay well in the first place, like especially making sure that my list was full all the time.

Seeing my list for the first time in nearly a few months was both good and bad altogether. It still looked pretty full to me, although many of the ideas I'd written down I hadn't crossed off yet. That meant I hadn't done them. And, there's no point in keeping my *To Do* list full if I never get around to doing most of the things on it.

Aunt Shirley said that whenever I was healthy, there's no excuse not to be accomplishing as much as possible that I want to do in life. I guess what she was maybe trying to tell me was, "Do as much as you can now 'cause you never know when your number's up." Anyway, that's kind of the way they describe it in the old movies on TCM.

As I was remembering some of those oldies from the seventies I'd seen over and over like *Grease* and *Carwash*, I got a call from Marshall, Marshall Glickman. He's the other kid that joined my group, even though when I very first heard from him, he thought he'd joined a group just for fat kids. When Samantha and I told him it was really a group that had to do with fear, he decided to stay anyway.

"Hi, Marshall. I was just thinking about you and our club."

"No kidding, Mee-kvgwel. Hey, what are we supposed to be doing again?"

"Well, make up a list of all the stuff you're afraid of. Then we do 'em. We do 'em as a group. You, Samantha, and I."

"Are we ever going to do anything fun?"

"Sure, like Samantha really wants to go see Justin Timberlake. But being in a place full of people like in the Oakland Arena is way too scary for her."

"Yo, I'm into Justin. I'll go. That would totally be da bomb."

"Christina Aguilera'll be there too."

"She used to be *such* a babe. Now she's lookin' a little too hoochie for me. When is it? I'll ask my mom to drive us."

"No, what we're going to do is take BART over, 'cause that's kind of the whole point...to do stuff we're afraid of."

"I'm not afraid of BART. What's up with that?"

"Samantha is. It would help her. It would be good for us to show her that there's nothing to be afraid of. Going under the bay should be no big deal."

"Oh, I get it. Whenever I've seen her around school it seems like she's scared 24-7."

"Marshall, some people are like that."

"Hey, what made you want to help scared people anyway? I mean, because of the way you are and stuff?"

I could tell Marshall was talking about my E.B. Marshall wasn't the most intelligent guy I'd ever come across. And I don't mind answering questions like that though, mainly because I've already answered them about a thousand times before. So, it was like no biggie.

"The story's way too long to tell, Marshall. But, yeah. I just learned the hard way that living life without fear is definitely the way it's meant to be done. It's the way God created us to be, to do whatever we wanted."

"God? You're into that shit?"

"Um, yeah. I guess I am."

"So, you're telling me you're not afraid of *anything*? That means you'd go out there and dance naked in the school auditorium if I asked you to?"

"No way, dude. Dancing naked doesn't mean I'd be unafraid. It means I'd be a total dumb ass if I did something like that."

"You've *got* to be afraid of something...or else you wouldn't be human."

"You see, I do lots of different kinds of stuff in order for me to stay alive. I'm real hopeful and I only say positive words out loud. Except, sometimes...well, a lot of the time, I think about dying and what it's going to be like when I go."

"Whoa. Are you gonna die soon, dude?"

"I don't know. Who knows? I have the kind of E.B. that's the most dangerous, recessive dystrophic."

Marshall looked like he definitely didn't understand too much of what I was saying. I've seen that stupid look so many times before though that it didn't really matter to me. Whatever. Then out of nowhere he said something smart that made me think real hard. "So, that's what you need to work on most. Not being afraid of dying. Isn't that a fear like all the rest?"

Realizing that Marshall was absolutely right, I said, "Yes, it sure is. I don't really know what to do about it though. Some days I think about dying all the time. I actually spend more time wondering where exactly it is I'm going after here. The whole thing scares me real bad. Once I didn't even go to school 'cause of it."

"What a waste. I'm not being mean, dude, but you should watch *Ricki Lake* or *Jerry Springer* once in a while. They've even had people on who've gone to the other side and come back. Most of them seem pretty skanky though. They're forced to put on those shows to make them seem more interesting, because mostly they've just got hos."

"That's why I usually don't watch those kind of shows. Just a bunch of hos."

"Your aunt should be on one of those shows."

"She's ain't no ho," I yelled out to Marshall.

"No, dude. I mean, that's what she's all about. She's been there. Didn't you tell me that? When she was in a coma you said she knew what heaven was like."

"That's not exactly what she said. She just said she realized that *going* to heaven was a good place to go. She never described what it was like."

"Yo entiendo, bro."

Even telling someone as goofy as Marshall about my one last fear felt kind of good, almost like a total relief. Maybe by telling people, friends, is what was going to end up being the most helpful thing for me after all. Although Marshall seemed like a simple guy, the way he said things always seemed to come out the most honest way. I liked that a lot.

Marshall and I talked for about another five minutes or so. Then I got another call from my call waiting. At first I thought it was a telemarketer telling me about the cheapest long distance or AOL for Broadband. But, it ended up being my new doctor, Dr. Rosenzweig. After saying, "Hello," he asked me, "Have you been your taking your minerals?"

"Minerals?"

"Yes. Don't you recall that long list of supplements I gave you the last time you were here?"

"Um, you know what, I'm on another line right now, Dr. Rosenzweig. Can you hang on? I'll get rid of my other call."

"No, I can't. I've got to earn a living here."

"Yeah, Dr. Rosenzweig. My dad got all—"

"You couldn't possibly have. We never received an insurance inquiry."

"But, Doctor. I really *have* been taking them. *All* those pills."

"Is your father home?"

"He's at work. And, Khadijah's at school."

"I'll need to see you again in my office. I have an opening in my schedule tomorrow afternoon at four-fifteen. I'm assuming that works for you."

"I'll need to get a ride from someone. Yes. I'll be there right at four-fifteen. It's just, like I said, I *have* been taking—"

"Very good then. I'll see you tomorrow," Dr. Rosenzweig told me, right before hanging up.

I couldn't believe what I'd just heard. I clicked back on to speak with Marshall, but he'd already hung up. I felt so completely worthless inside, like a total loser, and I didn't know why. Part of me felt like I'd just been *Punk'd* by Ashton Kutcher and the whole thing I'd just experienced was really a joke. How could Dr. Rosenzweig have accused me of that, when he didn't even know me that well in the first place?

Instead of calling Marshall back, I text-messaged him. There's no way I felt like talking with anyone anymore. I definitely wanted to apologize though for not getting back to him quickly on the phone.

At school the next day, Marshall walked right by me in line at the cafeteria. All he had to say was, "Sup." And then he kept walking right past me, to pick out his sandwich for lunch.

All that day at school I was a little angry and ashamed. Four-fifteen. Four-fifteen. At least I'd have Khadijah on my side, she'd be able to tell the doctor the truth. Khadijah'd stand up for me for sure. Khadijah told me over and over how much justice meant to her, so this was a good chance for her to practice it again for herself, too.

Real close to three o'clock, after I had gotten out of the school library, I could see Khadijah right there on Fillmore Street, waiting to pick me up. And guess who else was in her car? "Samantha's going to come with us. Is that OK?"

"Sure. Hey, Samantha," I said.

"Do you need anything at home, Miguel?" Khadijah asked, after I'd gotten in.

"No, I'm pretty much ready."

"Great. We're all set to go then."

"I hope you don't mind me tagging along. I'd just like to be there for you, Miguel."

Wow. That sure was nice, I thought. Khadijah and Samantha kept telling me not to worry about anything. Slowly but surely I began to feel a lot less stressed about everything. As soon as we got closer to San Bruno though, I got a little nervous all over again. "It's not after four-fifteen, is it? He'd be totally pissed if we were late," I told Khadijah.

Just like the first time the both of us had been there, the office people seemed really friendly. And, surprising me completely was when Dr. Rosenzweig came right up to us immediately in the waiting room. "Thanks so much for bringing Miguel in on such short notice. And how are you doing?" he asked Khadijah.

"I'm fine, thanks," she answered.

"And, who's this?"

"I'm Samantha. I'm here with Miguel. We're friends."

"Oh, that's fine. Kah-seejah, you're the one who supervises Miguel's diet. Is that correct?"

"Yes, I am. And, Dr. Rosenzweig, Miguel *has* been taking all the nutritional supplements you asked him to take."

Dr. Rosenzweig shaked his head up and down to show some sort of recognition for what Khadijah'd just told him. He seemed like a different person. I'd heard of Dr. Jekyll and Mr. Hyde before, so I guessed that's just something that happened to doctors. Go figure. "Miguel, how have you been feeling lately? How much energy have you had?" he asked me.

"Lots, I guess," I answered.

"Super. Well, Kah-seejaln, I'm going to take Miguel into one of the exam rooms for a bit to jot down some numbers. It shouldn't take too long at all."

"May I go with him? I'd like come along, Dr. Rosenzweig."

"Oh, don't bother. It'll just take a few minutes."

After the doctor said that, I gave Khadijah a look that said it's OK, then I looked over to Samantha and made the same look again. I wasn't scared a bit anymore. Everything seemed cool. Dr. Rosenzweig walked me into the room I'd gone into last time. He got out the thing that listens to my heart, and while he was starting to do that he asked me, "Do you tell Kahl-deejan everything you and I discuss?"

"Um, not everything. Don't you want me to?"

"Please don't. And please tell her nothing about this discussion either. Is that clear, Miguel?"

"Yes, sir."

"I'm a professional, I'm your doctor. I know what's best for you."

"Yes, doctor."

"I'd like to speak with your father...about the specifics of your insurance coverage."

"Oh, you don't need to do that. He already feels..."

"He feels *what*?"

"Well, I can't go to Stanford all the time anymore 'cause of the insurance he's got. He can't afford it. It's cool."

"So, I'm a substitute. Is that it?"

"No. Not at all, Sir. Doctor."

"From now on please show me respect. I'm better than any physician who'll treat you at Stanford. And you shall keep all we discuss confidential. Understand?"

All I could think about after the doctor told me that was Aunt Shirley. I knew what *confidential* meant, and Aunt Shirley's the one who'd always told me that secrets were like the same as lies. That's how come she always called herself an opened book. Staying confidential, I had a feeling, was something that was going to end up hurting me more than my E.B. ever could.

CHAPTER THIRTEEN

Just minutes before we were all supposed to head over to the East Bay, I was so positive I'd get a call from Samantha saying that she wouldn't be able to go after all. That never happened though. It ended up being like the total opposite. Right before leaving for the Powell Street BART Station, Samantha called me and was completely excited about going.

Showing that he trusted me to do more and more responsibilities on my own, Dad dropped me off at BART, told me he loved me, and wished me a good time. There I was, the only bandaged-up kid in sight, waiting all alone outside on the plaza level for Samantha and Marshall to show up.

The first to arrive was Marshall, who decided to frighten me to death by walking up from behind in a really crowded tourist spot. "Yo, what up?" he yelled out, just as I caught a glimpse of the glow-in-the-dark Disneyworld t-shirt and Blues Brothers sunglasses he was wearing.

"Hey, Marshall. You excited about going?"

"Hell, yeah. This is what it's all about."

"Samantha should be getting here soon. Look out for a brand-new, pomegranate red Mercedes to pull up on Market Street. We're all supposed to meet right here on the upper level before heading into the station."

Marshall and I hung out right around the intersection of Powell and Market along with all the prostitutes and drug-dealers for at least ten minutes. And before you knew it, there was Samantha's mom's car parked in a red, no-stopping zone on the Market Street-side of the station…just sitting there. As Marshall and I walked over closer to her car, I could see Samantha inside agreeing with her head, like her mom was telling her something real important, something she should be concerned about.

The minute Samantha saw Marshall and I, she immediately flung her door open, yelled "goodbye" to her mom, and then we were all set to go to the show. Samantha was so excited about going until we got closer to the BART entrance when she asked, "Why is there an escalator here?"

"That's how you get into the BART station," I said.

"I can't take escalators."

"Sam, you gotta chill. It's no big deal," Marshall said.

"No, you don't understand. I can't go if I have to ride down that."

All of the sudden, Samantha's enthusiasm turned into total panic as she realized that to get into most BART stations you have to go down or up some sort of escalator. And, the station we picked out, Powell Street, happened to have the longest escalator of them all. Remembering what Aunt Shirley always told me about wanting something badly enough, I tried to explain it all to Samantha the exact same way Aunt Shirley would have if she'd been there. "You really want to see Justin, don't you? You were totally excited about that," I told her.

"Yes, I *know*. I definitely want to go. Escalators scare—"

"Good. So, this is the only way for us to get there. If we were to call and ask somebody for a ride now, we'd be totally late and miss whoever opens."

"Don't they have an elevator here?"

"Yes. For handicapped people," Marshall said.

"Except, you're not handicapped. You can walk just fine. Being afraid doesn't qualify as a physical handicap. It's something you can get over. It wouldn't be fair to those people who don't have the ability to walk," I said.

Nobody said anything for a while. All three of us just stood there staring down the filled-full-of-people escalator. Every single passenger looked like they never gave any thought as they got on or off, it seemed like a complete piece of cake. What Marshall and I had to do though was try real hard to accept that some people, like Samantha, were nearly afraid of almost *everything*. Marshall was more of a pushy kind of guy than I was, so I told him not to put extra pressures on Samantha. He seemed like he did his best to understand, and said, "It's your call, Sam. We all three go, or we all three stay."

In her own style, Samantha began figuring out a way for her to move ahead. "If you stand in front of me," she said to Marshall, "and you stand behind me, Miguel, I think I can do this. As long as there's something for me to hold onto."

"We're set to go whenever you are," Marshall said.

"OK. On the count of three. Well, wait 'til this group gets on. Let them go first."

"One, Two—" I started to say.

"No, I didn't finish explaining. *I* will count to three. And when I say *three*, you get on, Marshall. Then, I'll get on. Then you, Miguel."

After a few more tourists got on the escalator, Samantha began the countdown. Marshall got into position, and when he heard *three* he got onto the escalator. Samantha reluctantly jumped on and uttered a gasp when she felt the jerk of stepping on. I was right behind her, reaching out to offer my right hand to hold onto. She grabbed it, and none of us said a word as we waited for the ride to be over. Samantha's eyes were kept tightly shut the entire time, with her left hand outstretched holding onto the moving railing next to her left side. In a soft, relaxed voice I said, "Samantha, we're almost there. Open your eyes so you can see when to step off."

She must have opened them, because even though it was pretty awkward, Samantha knew just when to stick her foot out to get off the escalator. Stepping off for her was probably a combination of things, relief *and* victory. Samantha had conquered another one of her fears. I figured that maybe having this experience won't be nearly as bad for her the next time. Maybe it was going to be easier for her to do a bunch of new things she hadn't ever attempted before. "Samantha, you're kickin'," Marshall said to her.

"Yeah, Samantha. I'm so proud of you. You did great."

Samantha also looked so proud of herself. It seemed on her face as if all the fears she'd lived with for so long, never should have existed in the first place. Samantha was becoming a hero to me, and it made me feel like a hero for helping someone else to feel like one.

Next, without any effort at all, all three of us entered the underground BART station and we waited in line to buy three round-trip tickets headed for the Coliseum Station in Oakland. After purchasing our tickets, we stuck them into the entrance slot machine, and real quick we found the right place to stand for the train we'd be taking. Seeing the Richmond train approach, a train headed north, was maybe a good experience for Samantha. It gave her an idea of what they looked and sounded like close up as they moved into the station, just before we actually had to get on.

No more than five minutes passed and the train we needed to board was nearing the platform. "You guys ready?" I asked.

"The sign says Fremont. We're going to Oakland," Samantha said.

"The Fremont train is the one that stops at Coliseum BART, *hell-lo!* You've got a lot to learn, Sam," Marshall said.

Although Marshall's not the most tactful person on earth, he used the absolutely perfect word. That's exactly what Samantha was doing...learning. On the BART train all she did was talk about the concert coming up. Her excitement was all over the place again. Every other word was Justin-this and Justin-that. She never seemed to mention Christina Aguilera, so Marshall did instead. All three of us just couldn't wait for the concert we were about to see. Samantha had even forgotten to be afraid about riding the train just as it was about to go underneath the bay. I guess it slipped my mind too, to remind her that we'd have to go under the bay in the first place.

What did come as a total shock to Samantha though was when we got to the other side of the bay and the underground train turned into an above-ground one at West Oakland. "Wow, I wasn't expecting that," Samantha said, and she unfortunately went on to say, "That scared me."

"Not a big deal. I like seeing the sights over here on this side of the world," Marshall said.

In just a short while we we're going to be at the Oakland Arena, right after stopping at the Lake Merritt and Fruitvale stations. All I kept thinking was, that everything that was happening, and the ways it was happening, was like it was all planned out in a real particular way. Maybe it was all part of God's plan. Maybe that's what God had planned for a *whole* bunch of people...to get rid of their fears and really start living.

It made me wonder why trying to get over fear ever had to happen at all. What made people on earth learn to be afraid anyway? Where did the world go so off-course? When did people begin to replace faith and believing with fear? God must think that it's all one huge lesson for people to learn. Aunt Shirley said that God doesn't really get pissed off, but I wondered what He thought of people who chose to stay afraid and stuck, rather than getting on with it all.

When we got off at the Coliseum Station it was like Samantha had never seen that many people, all in one place, ever before in her lifetime. What was she going to be like once we went inside this huge arena? "Now where precisely is my aunt going to meet us?" Samantha asked.

"At the ticket booth for the baseball games, at the outdoor stadium. Where the A's play," I told her.

"Chill. Don't worry about it," Marshall said.

Together, the three of us walked down the very long walkway to the indoor arena, all in a row with what seemed to be like thousands of other people on both sides of us. Most of the girls were dressed up like Christina, with way too much makeup, short skirts, and huge hair. And some of them carried hand-painted signs they probably made at home. A couple even said, "Marry me, Justin." Yeah, right. I'm *so* sure.

"These chicks are totally hoochied out," Marshall said.

"Quiet. They may hear you," Samantha said.

"Have either of you heard of The Black Eyed Peas? They're the opening act," I said.

Neither Samantha nor Marshall had heard of this band, so I wasn't alone. Justin and Christina were all anybody cared about anyway. As we got closer to the arena we could see that the front entrance was completely mobbed with people kind of crushing into each other to get in. "Stay in line, people," some guard kept yelling out on his Mr. Microphone. I could see that Samantha was getting a little bit nervous. "We'll be in in no time. These lines move fast," I said.

Samantha took a deep breath, and all three of us made it through the line and inside we went. Everywhere we turned around there were mostly girls wearing *JT* and *Stripped/Justified* tour t-shirts. "Are you OK?" I asked Samantha.

"I think I just need to sit down."

"You guys go ahead. I'm gonna bail for a while and get some nachos. You want anything?" Marshall asked us.

"I'm not hungry," I said.

"Neither am I," Samantha said.

After a walk that seemed like forever, Samantha and I found our seats. They were completely awesome. Right on the main floor, smack in the middle, and only twelve rows from the front of the stage. Being away from Marshall gave Samantha and I a chance to talk alone. It was my time to tell her how well she was doing with all this stuff coming at her that's new. "I'm totally impressed with you. You're doing great," I told Samantha.

She looked at me and shook her head in a way that made it seem like she was in total disbelief. "I can't get over it, Miguel. Thank you so much for wanting to help me. A few weeks ago I never would have thought I'd actually be doing something like this. Thanks."

"You're welcome. I like helping you, Samantha. It makes me feel good inside. It's also the best way I'm able to thank God for all the miracles He made for me. Don't forget, I used to have just as many fears as you."

"Not as many as me. Seriously?"

"My Aunt Shirley told me I'd never be around too long whenever I had any fear left inside me. She told me it's a killer."

Samantha had a totally surprised look on her face. I guess she never realized exactly how horrible and destructive any kind of fear really is. At the same time, we stopped talking and just looked around at all the people around us. From the distance we could see that Marshall was totally lost and looking for us from a few wrong sections away. Eventually he made his way over to us with only a few minutes to go before the show began. Of the three of us, Samantha was definitely the most ready for it all to begin. The fact that she was surrounded by tens of thousands of cheering fans, the first time ever in her life, didn't seem to affect her too much at all.

"You weren't frightened, Samantha?" Aunt Shirley asked.

"No, everything about it was perfect."

It *was* perfect. Even the opening act was OK. "Christina came out first. And, you know what? Justin even knew to say, *What's up, Oaktown?* when he began singing *Rock your Body*," I said.

The day after the concert Aunt Shirley decided to come to the city and take Samantha and I out for lunch at the Mission Rock Café. It's a funky, seaweed-smelling kind of burger place right on the docks where all the even-numbered piers are in San Francisco, just south of China Basin. Aunt Shirley also invited Marshall, except he had to go to violin practice instead.

"Sam, you certainly deserve what I'm about to give you, doll. A real, honest-to-God, F.A.A.T. gold star. You did it! You faced your fears…and you came out the winner," Aunt Shirley said.

"Yeah. Bravo, Samantha. You're a winner."

"Do you feel any different, hon?"

"No, not really. I'm not sure. It wasn't such a big accomplishment."

"The hell it wasn't. It was a *huge* accomplishment. Most people just *accept*. They don't do a damn thing about their fears. Oops, pardon my French."

"It's OK. My daddy swears all the time."

All three of us being together was like a for real party, an incredibly important celebration. A good old big, F.A.A.T. happening. Samantha brought her *To Do* list, I brought mine, and as she looked them over, with many of the things crossed off, Aunt Shirley began clapping her hands. Our waitress even brought a huge carrot cake over to us with lit candles on it. "Whose birthday is it?" She asked us while setting the cake in the middle of the table.

"It's nobody's birthday. We're—"

"But it *is*. We're all born today. Today's the day we're saying adios to fear. Goodbye and good riddance. Eliminated from our existence," Aunt Shirley told her.

"Even better than a birthday. It's a re-birthday. That's what it is," the waitress told us all.

"You better believe it. Want a slice? Take a load off," Aunt Shirley said.

"I can't. I've got to work. Thank you though. Congratulations. Congratulations to you all."

Just at the same time our waitress walked away after bringing us our re-birthday cake, I saw two people who looked familiar to me heading up towards our picnic table. "How are you, Miguel?" the woman asked.

It only took a second to recognize who the couple with the sad faces was. And remembering who they were, instantly made me so sad inside. "I'm fine, Ma'am," I answered.

In her party-like, way-too-happy way, Aunt Shirley said, "I'm Miguel's aunt. And this is our partner in crime, Samantha."

"It's nice to meet you both. We know Miguel from… Well, we're the parents of his good friend, Miguelito, our boy in heaven."

Aunt Shirley looked so embarrassed. Then she said, "Oh, I'm so sorry. Miguel told me so much about him. They were great pals."

"We came over to thank you, Miguel," the father said.

"Thank me?"

"Yes. Because of you our boy left for heaven in peace," he said.

"You helped him live longer. You helped him leave without worry. You were his guardian angel. God bless you, dear Miguel. We will always be so very grateful to you," the mom said before she began to cry.

CHAPTER FOURTEEN

"So, that's the last thing I can think of. Does anybody have any questions or comments before we end?" I asked the members of our F.A.A.T. meeting.

"How full is our list supposed to be when we bring it in next week?" our newest member Amanda asked.

"Just a page. That's all. It'll take us a while to do them all. And, make sure to put the thing you're most afraid of doing right on top."

"Later," Marshall yelled out, as he got up and started to head out the door.

"Wait, Marshall. Let's say 'good job' to our newest members, Amanda and Wilfred, for joining up today."

At the same time Marshall, Samantha, and I again thanked our brand new F.A.A.T. members. They seemed to fit in just fine. More than anything else, I noticed that they were a little afraid to speak up, afraid of asserting themselves. I totally forgot, but I wished I'd remembered to tell them what Aunt Shirley had always told me that "the best things happen to you in your life only after you believe in yourself completely."

Amanda and Wilfred are brother and sister. They're also in the Cantonese-American program at school. Maybe they were afraid to speak up because learning English was still kind of new for them. It was Mr. Lau's idea for Amanda and Wilfred to join in the first place. He thought it was good for them to get acquainted with other kids, so they could practice telling English conversations.

Even after Marshall walked out of our meeting room behind the school auditorium, the rest of us hung out for another ten minutes or so. At first I thought it would mostly be fun and sort of entertaining to have a group like F.A.A.T. Then some new feeling was beginning to take over after our meeting had ended. I started experiencing what Aunt Shirley told me a long time before when I asked her what my reward in life was going to be...for suffering so long. "Your reward is that you will have an opportunity to help others. It's not what you're going to get, it's what you'll be able to give…that's your reward," she had said to me. For the first time I could tell that she was probably right. My life was beginning to feel kind of more meaningful, like it was all on purpose.

Samantha, Wilfred, and Amanda ended up leaving the room, while I stayed on a bit longer to clean up and put the chairs back to where they had been. While I was organizing my last row of seats, a woman walked into the room, stared at me, and asked, "Are you Mih-kwel Estus?"

"Yes, Ma'am. I'm Miguel."

"Hello, Miguel. I'm Mrs. Sponheim. Renate's mother."

"Oh, yeah. Hi. She was maybe going to join us today."

"She won't ever be joining your organization, Mr. Estus. I don't know exactly what your health issues are, but who are you to impose your values onto these children?"

I didn't have a clue of how to respond. I actually couldn't speak up at all.

"I thought that after-school programs require an adult to be present at all times."

"Well, Ma'am. My Aunt Shirley couldn't make it today. She's—"

"I'm having her investigated as well. Young man, have you read the bible? Any of it? Do you attend church regularly?"

"What? What does that have to do with my group, Ma'am?"

"It has everything to do with it. My Renate told me you've been *preaching*, speaking of faith. You're no minister. And, taught in this school of all places. It's shameful."

"Hey wait, Mrs. Sponheim. It means 'faith in *yourself*,' not a religious kind of faith. I'm not really into any religions. Faith's just the word that's the opposite of fear. Our group helps people to get over fear. That's all it does."

"Well, it sounds blasphemous to me. And I won't stand for it. Mr. Lau's been no help at all. Where can I get in touch with this aunt of yours?"

Knowing that Aunt Shirley could explain what our group was about a whole lot better than me, I gave Mrs. Sponheim Aunt Shirley's number. But I figured that I should be the one to call Aunt Shirley as quick as I could before Mrs. Sponheim got to her. From the payphone near the auditorium, I called Aunt Shirley's cell phone. "Hey, it's me," I said.

"Yo, doll. How was today's meeting?"

"It was way good up until a lady came over to me and said how our meeting was totally blasta-mess."

"What lady?"

"Renate's mom. That girl I told you about who was going to join. Then decided not to. The lady's her mom, and she's going to call you. She's really upset."

"That's OK. No problem. If this should ever happen again, Miguel, please tell any one of these people to call me. I'll take care of it."

"You're not worried?"

"Of course not. She's just scared. That's all. I encounter people like this all the time. I do two things with people like her. I accept them for who they are, and I have as little to do with them as possible from that point forward. After all, *I'm* no saint. That's for damn sure."

"What's she scared of?"

"She's afraid of your power, doll. People like her are extremely limited. You can't expect them to, even for a second, grasp what it would be like to live without fear. Fear of change, fear of moving, fear of leaving a bad marriage. This woman's probably afraid of her own shadow. She probably never learned one thing from her own past. "

"It sounds like you've met people like her before."

"Every day of my life. I used to spend so much time wondering what I'd done wrong to make them so upset with me. Then, I assumed they were jealous of me. That's what it was, I thought. Then it hit me square in the face. They weren't really jealous, they're scared sh—less. They've got to make up something in their minds, something false about me, something they don't like because they're so afraid, afraid of my power, afraid of the way I live my life. This woman's afraid of your power, Miguel. That's all."

"I didn't know I had any. Is that what makes a person powerful? Not having fear?"

"You better believe it, bub. Look into the mirror sometime. Living our lives the way God intended, without fear, is the ultimate power trip. I can't wait to talk to this woman."

"Maybe you can help her."

"Talk about your impossible mission. Forget about that. I just want to clarify a few things with her, about F.A.A.T. That's all I can do. Trying to help people who are so against any kind of change is a colossal waste of time and energy. After our chat I hope to never hear from her again."

Aunt Shirley tried to make me feel better about being bashed by this lady, except I still felt pretty bad. "Since God didn't give you thick skin, you've got to make it yourself," Aunt Shirley had told me. She was making a pun because of my E.B. and how my skin is so fragile. But, Aunt Shirley was really talking about when I had to deal with people like this mean lady.

When I got off the phone with Aunt Shirley I decided to take a drink from the water fountain in the auditorium's lobby. As I was drinking from it, three other kids I had run into from a few times before came up and stood in back of me, waiting for me to finish. "You should bring your own," a boy I didn't know said to me.

"Now it's not safe for anybody else," another boy I didn't know said.

"I didn't do anything wrong though," I told him back.

"No one else can drink out of this now. You've contaminated it."

"I'm not contagious. I haven't contaminated anything."

"How come you look like that? Like a mummy? Why do you wear all those bandages? You look like a freak."

Just because I was over my limit for all I could handle that day, I apologized for drinking out of the water fountain to the three kids. And, as I left them I walked behind the school so I could be all by myself, so no one else could be mean to me. I found a place under a tree at Moscone Park, right behind the softball field. Under the nearby tree all by itself was a homeless guy asleep who I had seen a few times before. I walked over to where he was. Somehow I felt a whole lot safer being near him than near anyone who could have come from my school. I always felt that homeless people were a lot less cruel than regular people could ever be.

Sitting down under the tree was a real safe place for me. And looking out to what was going on in front of me started making me realize once again just how different I was from everyone else. Playing softball, playing tennis, or even playing on the swings in the children's playground were all things I was never able to do. As a little kid Mom never took me to any playgrounds because the sand could have gotten in between my bandages and skin. I thought I was over all that. The part of me that knew I was sick, and always would be, was beginning to make me forget about what the rest of my life was like, the life I'd made up for myself in my dreams.

Was I going to have a future? What was the point of trying to help other people when there was really no one out there who could ever help me? How come there had to be so many mean people in the world?

That's all I did under my tree, looked out and wondered.

"What are you doing here? I thought you'd gone home already," a voice said from behind, a voice that didn't belong to the asleep homeless man.

As I turned around I saw Samantha walking up to me. "I came here...to kind of be by myself for a while," I told her.

"Do you still? Want to be by yourself? Or can I hang out with you, too?"

"Oh, definitely. Have a seat."

"This is the same tree *I* sit under. I've never seen you here though."

"*You* come out here? When? What do you do, sneak out in between classes? After school?"

"All the time. That's Alfred. He's out here a lot too, always relaxing under this very tree."

"You know him?"

"Sure. He's a nice man. We've talked about everything. He always asks me how I'm doing."

"I think I've seen him around sometimes."

"I'm not so sure he has a place to live though."

Realizing that Samantha knew this guy made me think differently about her. It made me think back to Charlie, the homeless guy from Huntington Park I used to talk to all the time when I lived on Nob Hill. Talking to homeless people was something probably no one else from our school ever did, I imagined. Homeless people always made me forget about thinking about myself. They made me think about how difficult it must be to still have to be struggling after getting all the way to be a grownup.

"I wanted to come here before I had to go back home. Renate's mother yelled at me after our meeting. She told me that what I was doing was wrong. She thinks F.A.A.T.'s about religion, and it's something we shouldn't be doing in school."

"You're not serious. Wow, that's hard to believe. You know what though? You should do what I do when I'm here, under this tree, not think. This is the place where I don't have to think. This is where I don't have to worry about anything. This is the one place where I'm not afraid."

"That sounds totally cool to me. Perfect. You, me, and Alfred. And we don't have to think about anything."

"It's like heaven," Samantha said.

"Samantha, that's what I think about too. Places that remind me of what heaven must be like. Someplace where you don't need to think, where you can take a huge break from having to learn lessons."

"So, you believe there is a heaven, Miguel?"

"Oh, for sure. Aunt Shirley talks about it all the time."

"Every time I see the sign for this park I wonder if George Moscone knew he was headed for heaven when he was elected mayor. That's what Harvey Milk always thought about when he was supervisor. He knew he could be assassinated at any time just for being gay, and that's exactly what happened."

"Maybe that's what was more important to him. He must have believed so much in what he was doing, being different and honest at the same time, that being killed wasn't anything he was scared of."

"Maybe they're in heaven right now, glad we're remembering them, remembering that they were not at all afraid of dying."

"It's cool this park's named after Mayor Moscone. That way more people will always know him for a very long time, forever."

"Will you always remember me, Miguel?"

"Duh. What do you mean? Where are you going? Nowhere."

"You'll remember me, won't you?"

"Of course I will. Are you going to remember me?"

"There's no way I'll ever forget you. You teach me courage. Because of you I've already been able to face challenges I never thought I'd ever be able to go anywhere near. Thank you, Miguel, for having taught me so much."

"It's nothing, Samantha."

More and more I was realizing that my life has been something worthwhile after all. Helping someone else seemed to be turning into exactly what Aunt Shirley told me it was going to be, my ultimate reward. Helping Samantha take control of her fears, was more than a pleasure, in so many ways helping her was also helping myself.

Knowing that my life could end at any time didn't terrify me as much as it used to. I thought that maybe reaching my fourteenth birthday was going to turn into a victory for me. Spending any time thinking about what would come after fourteen was no longer my goal. All those hours writing up my *To Do* list got me to where I wanted to be, and if I ended up already accomplishing my last thing to do, that's cool with me.

Samantha ended up walking home to Pacific Heights, and at the corner of Chestnut and Fillmore, I waited for the MUNI bus to take me back to the Mission. When the cars on the street passed by me I wondered if any of the people driving ever thought as much about all the things I'd always thought about, like dying and going to heaven. Did everyone ultimately want to go there? Or were most people afraid of it? Or were most people just real busy thinking about totally different stuff other than that?

When the bus pulled up in front of me, somehow my eyes made me focus close up on the people riding inside it. I got to examine their different faces and the expressions on top of them. This time I seemed to see even more, I could see what's underneath them all. What I saw was the exact same thing under every face. It wasn't misery. It wasn't stress. It wasn't exhaustion. It wasn't hunger. And it wasn't ambition. Some of the people had some of these things, but what I could see was that all of these people weren't totally happy. Not all of them at least, not feeling this way all at the same time.

What my life had been like was not much different from mostly all the people around me. Whoever made up that happiness was our true reward for living a good life was a total liar. That person should have been told that giving us all such a completely unrealistic expectation did way more harm than good. How come we weren't all told from the very beginning of our lives that the real purpose of life is to learn the lessons God gave us?

Some were easier than others, but overall, life's really hard. And, for the people who think it's too easy, they're not making as much of an effort to learn lessons as the other people who choose to. In my opinion, the people who've decided to learn from it all, from life, are the ones who end up being the real heroes of the world.

CHAPTER FIFTEEN

Expecting that I'd end up in a hospital room that smelled like a freshly-opened box of Band-Aids again was something I should have been planning for all along. Stanford, just a year earlier, had been the place I'd spent so much time at, so I just got way over being there. Still, I hated it, and I hated my life even more. Seeing Lefty again was a plus, but the surgery I needed to have was kind of more complicated than average. As usual, it was because of an infection that happened to one of my blisters. This time on the skin right below my stomach.

Having Lefty do it was a lucky break for me. He still wasn't back at Stanford full-time, so catching him while he happened to be there was like a totally early Christmas present for me. Two nights before I was going to have my surgery, Lefty came into my room and said, "I just consulted with your regular doctor in San Bruno. He said the treatments you've been having with him there are going fine."

"Yeah, I guess so," I told Lefty.

"You like him? He treats you well?"

For more than a few seconds I had to think hard about the way I was going to decide to answer those two questions. Then I made my body language say "yeah" by putting both hands up in the air. This way I never had to lie, since I never spoke a single word.

"I'm glad everything's been going well while you're there, seeing him."

Massive relief was what I felt after our conversation ended that way. If I'd told Lefty the truth about what the other doctor was really like, meant that Dr. Rosenzweig would end up telling Dad. I figured it's better to just bite the bullet than do or say anything that would make Dad feel any worse than he already did.

"When's Aunt Shirley coming to see me again?"

"Tomorrow, in the afternoon. I'm not certain. Your mother is going to be here first thing in the morning though."

"I know. I can't wait to see her. She called me about an hour ago. She told me she's planning a big birthday bash for me. She said I'd better get well quick in order for me to be at my own party."

"Is her husband coming up with her?"

"No, I don't think so. He's in Europe somewhere, doing some new movie about the Holocaust. You know what the Holocaust is, right?"

"Yes. Unfortunately, I do."

"Do you think all those people who died in it went to heaven?"

"Heaven? I assume so, Miguel."

"Aunt Shirley said that *everybody* goes to heaven, no matter what they did on earth. 'God doesn't judge people,' she always says to me. And she tells me that since God never judges people, neither should I."

Talking to Lefty this time was so like I was talking with a stranger I had never met before. Before, he used to question almost anything about what I believed, except that's changed. It's like he and Aunt Shirley, people that were so much like Poland opposites before, had learned a little something from each other. Instead of thinking Aunt Shirley was probably some sort of nutcase, I had the feeling that Lefty truly appreciated what she stood for.

As usual Lefty had positive words to tell me the next night too, the night before I was going to have surgery. He had told me this conversation lots, but I always tried to pretend it was my first time hearing it all. What it told me about him was that he would do his absolute best. Hearing positive words seemed to always make my mind feel better, no matter how things actually went during or after any kind of surgery. Positive, hopeful words were so good to listen to, they kind of canceled out anything negative that the other pessimist people always told me, like, "we'll just hope for the best," or "at least you're in excellent hands." What a bunch of B.S.

When my nurses gave me the drugs to get me ready to go to sleep for the night, I thought about what it would be like to not see them again, ever. What a relief it would be to not have to go through all this one more time, I thought. Maybe this would be my final surgery. Maybe something would go horribly wrong, or someone may make some awful mistake that can't be taken back, and it'll all be over, my very last time. What a total, worth-waiting-for relief. Looking forward to seeing Mom was what came into my head next though.

By the time I got to sleep I began remembering what it was like when Mom and Hunt came to visit me the last time I was in the hospital, the time when I had gotten real, real sick. That visit was a turning point for me. In my dreams, Jorge had told me to be very, very cautious of Hunt, Mom's husband. I remember that part of me didn't really care if anything bad ended up happening to me or not. Although I always seemed to be scared of dying even back then, it would have been totally OK for me whatever way things worked out. That was then, and although nearly everything I had wanted to come true did after that time, I still felt that I'd learned plenty, more than enough lessons in my life.

That night's sleep didn't come too easy for me. Inside, my brain was overflowing with a tension-filled headache like you see on commercials, and all I could do was wait for it all to be over with. Turning on the TV in my room was something they never allowed, so I didn't even bother. And that was OK anyway 'cause it only got sixteen channels. What kind of a rip off is that, for all it costs to stay there? Eventually I told myself to just completely stop thinking. Turning off my mind was such a hard thing to do sometimes. All along I wished I had some sort of knob or handle where I could put it in neutral while I didn't happen to be doing anything else.

No dreams came to me afterwards that night. Only minutes after waking up, I saw my mom sitting in the chair in my room, across from my bed, sound asleep. I wondered how long she had been waiting there so peacefully without her satiny, beige-colored goose down duvet cover from home. And when did she even come in? I hadn't even heard her. She had never done anything like this before.

Somehow one of my nurses, Beatrice, knew I woke up. She opened the door to my room enough to whisper, "Good morning." Even though she said it so quietly, it was still loud enough to wake Mom up. "I'm so sorry, Mrs. Manly. Did I wake you?" the nurse asked.

"Oh, my. No. I'm glad you did. How are you doing, dear?"

"I'm good, Mom," I told her back.

"I'll just be a minute. I have some medicine for Miguel, and I need to monitor his blood pressure and take his pulse," the nurse told Mom.

For a while longer the nurse, Mom, and me talked chit-chat stuff, then Beatrice left Mom and I alone. Mom was being so extra positive. I couldn't sense at all that she was afraid of anything that was going on, or going to happen next. "I feel certain that everything will go so smoothly for you, Miguel," Mom told me.

"Oh, good. I'm glad you're not worrying."

"There's no reason. We've both been down this path so many times. So far, so good. Am I right?"

"Yeah, that's true. Been there, done that, like Jorge used to tell us."

"You're so right. I recall him saying that. How's everything going with your father, hon? You're happy there?"

"Sure. He's going to be here, you know. Eleven O'clock, or right around there."

"I know. He and I talked last night."

"You did? How'd that go?"

"Great. He's so happy that you're getting to spend time together. Your father loves you so much, Miguel."

"I love him too, Mom. But...I miss you too."

Just as I said that, Mom turned her face to the side into the shine of the neon light inside my room, so I wouldn't be able to see all of it. I could tell she was getting a little emotional. "My life's changing, Miguel," Mom began to tell me. "More than likely I'll be moving back up to the Bay Area soon," she continued.

"Are you for real, Mom?"

"Oh, I think so. And I miss you too, hon."

"Is Hunt moving up here with you?"

"No, he's not. We're separating. He'll stay in Los Angeles. I want to be able to see you more often, so I'm looking for an apartment in the city now."

"Seriously?"

"Yes, and your father knows all about it."

"Wow, it's hard to believe you guys are talking about stuff like this now. This is so different."

"I want to help financially, too, if I can. I know he's struggling, so I want to give him a hand, as soon as I can..."

"As soon as you move up here?"

"No. It's a little more complicated than that I'm afraid. Since I married Hunt, all our accounts are in both our names. But everything will work out. You'll see."

"Mom, you know what? I never told you this before, I never trusted him from the beginning."

"You know what? Neither did I."

Hearing Mom say that made me speechless. She didn't even hesitate to tell me that. It seemed like it was just total, complete, unrehearsed honesty coming outside of her mouth.

"Good for you, Mom. You know, for knowing this."

"I guess I needed to learn that I deserved so much better. What a schemer he is."

"A schemer. That's a bad person, I guess."

"An opportunist, a manipulator. Someone not to be trusted. I, along with you, deserve better than that in life...especially when it affects my family. Enough about him."

"I'm proud of you, Mom. Aunt Shirley would be, too. You should tell her what's going on in your life."

"I'll do that, dear. So, tell me, what do want to do when you're well? Travel? See some shows? Go shopping? In a few weeks it'll be a three-day weekend. How about doing something then?"

Out of nowhere the coolest idea came straight into my head, like it was transplanted there by some surgeon. And it was way different from anything Mom and I had ever done before. "Mom, could we go to New York?"

"Absolutely, of course. If that's what you want. We'll definitely go there."

"To see the U.S. Open."

"The U.S. Open? The tennis tournament? Since when did you become a fan of tennis?"

"I like to watch it now on TV. My friend Samantha likes tennis. She wants to become a professional tennis player when she grows up. Can we please take her along with us, Mom? Please."

"Well, I haven't even met her parents yet. They may not even allow her to go."

"I'll ask them. I already met Samantha's mom, and she's kind of learning now how important it is for Samantha to overcome her fears."

"So, we'd be going to New York, to this tennis tournament so Samantha will learn to be unafraid. That's why you want to take this trip?"

"And because I want to go with you. It'll be good for all of us. Remember how cool Samantha is? Now she's sort of like a pretend sister for me. So, you can treat her like she's your daughter if you want."

After Mom said, "Well, we'll see," I knew that it was in the bag. New York had always been so much fun every time Mom and I'd ever gone there. Just like in San Francisco, people never really stared too much at me in New York City. New York's kind of like an east coast version of an anything goes kind of city. Everyone there's already seen it all.

Just a little bit before the last-minute time came when I couldn't have anymore visitors, Khadijah showed up in my room and she brought Samantha with her. It was so good to look at them both. Khadijah had seen me so many times before in a hospital bed, but Samantha never had. She didn't seem to care though. Samantha was so happy to be with me, and so was I. Immediately after seeing me, Samantha came right over and gave me a big hug. Then Khadijah came next and did the same. "Here we go again," Khadijah said.

"Yeah, I know what you're talkin'," I said back.

"We all miss you at school, Miguel. Everyone there sends their best wishes," Samantha said.

"Everyone? Yeah, right."

"Well, you know what I mean."

"Hey, guess what? My mom was here this morning and—" I began telling Samantha.

"She's still here. We just ran into her in the waiting area," Khadijah said.

"You're kidding. She must have been here all day then. Wow, I had no idea."

"She said she's not going to leave you here alone."

"Really? That's so cool. She's still here 'cause she's such a worrier. That's what it is."

"No, it's not that at all, Miguel. She adores you. I didn't get the sense she was worried about anything. She looked so different to me just now. She didn't have that frightened look on her face she usually has."

"Did she tell you guys about my plan?"

"No, nothing about a plan."

"When Mom first got here, her and I were trying to think of things to do when I get out. And you know what? I asked her if we could all go to the U.S. Open. Her, Samantha, and me."

Samantha's face was like a 7.1 Richter-Scale earthquake had just happened. "Me? Go with you both? To the U.S. Open?" she asked.

"Yeah. I'm sure she's going to go for it. As Marshall would say, '*it's kickin'*.'"

"Wow. Serena, Venus, Kim Clijsters, Maria, Lindsay Davenport…and Justine Henin-Hardenne will be there. And, we'd get to see them in person. Only, Miguel, I can't go though. It's impossible."

"No. We already figured it out. It would be on Labor Day weekend. We wouldn't miss any school at all."

"I think it sounds exciting. You should think about it, Sam. All those great restaurants, that's what I like about Manhattan most. All that delicious food."

"Yeah, that's right. It's the perfect place to chow down. Doesn't that sound good to you, Samantha? A couple of hearty meals will be good for you. You could use some meat on those bones if you're going to be kickin' some major tennis a—, I mean, butt."

"You do seem to be like you've lost some weight, Samantha. Have you?"

"I'm just nervous a lot. I don't eat very much when I get like this," Samantha told us.

Thinking about all of Samantha's fears, and adding the food-thing to that, made me wonder if something like anorexia or bulimia was going on with her now. Except, soon after their visit, I was going to have surgery. Having to worry about what was happening with Samantha would only have made my whole scenario a lot worse. Instead of becoming afraid though, it just made me way more determined to get well soon after my surgery, so we could all go to New York, hit the town, party hard, and eat like pigs big time.

CHAPTER SIXTEEN

"How come everyone's from Ireland? What's up with that?"
I'd asked Jorge in my dream.

"You got me. I guess that's who built this place. Maybe they're good workers," he'd told me, while we were still in Virginia City walking around the same old cemetery we'd been to before. This time the sun was only warm, not hot, but the dried-up sagebrushes were still tumbling on the ground in front of our feet. And the far off noises of the desert surrounded Jorge and I in a not-too-obvious way.

"Hey, they mixed the Irish people in with the Italian people. That seems kind of weird if they only wanted it to go by country."

"They're both Catholic, that's why. They organized it by religion. Jewish people are over there on that hill. The Chinese railroad workers are buried over there with people that have the same religion as them in China."

"And, these other groups. I never heard of these religions. Maybe they've just gotten to be extinct by now, these religions."

"They're all divided into groups. All buried in their own little subdivided sections. They're not religions though. The Masons, the Oddfellows, Knights of Pythias, Improved Order of Redmen, Wilson & Brown. I guess everybody was convinced they had to belong to a group back then. And after the people died they were forced to stay in them, even after they're dead."

"That sure is lame. Aunt Shirley said that that's the main problem with the world, people think they need to belong to different groups to feel like they fit in. 'We're already in a group, damn it. Having different religions, any religion, is the worst,' she always said."

"Isn't Aunt Shirley also the one who said there's probably something good in *all* religions?"

"Yeah, that's true. I like being my own man though. A rebel. You know what I mean?"

"You've got that right, dude. You're definitely someone who marches to the beat of a different drummer."

"No, I'm not. I never did learn how to play those. I took up the maracas instead."

"He's got to be in here somewhere. We can't stop 'til we find him," Jorge had told me as we moved onto the next nearby cemetery in Genoa, Nevada's first settlement.

"What's his name again?" I'd asked.

"Snowshoe Thompson. He was a hero."

"I'll look over there," I said, while pointing over to an area we hadn't visited yet. As I walked closer to this new section, instead of finding Snowshoe Thompson, I found something else I couldn't take my eyes off of, a tombstone that read:

> *Shed not for him the bitter tear,*
> *Nor give the heart to vain regrets,*
> *'Tis but the casket that lie here,*
> *The gem that filled it sparkles yet.*

It was a poem that must have been written by this guy's wife because it said, *My Husband* at the end of it. The man who died there was John H. Davis. But how did this wife from way back then know about souls and heaven? And that a casket's just a casket, but her husband lives on? Maybe Jorge had the answer. I asked him, "Hey, Jorge. When did people first know that souls go to heaven after the person dies?"

"Forever," he shouted back.

"I thought it was sort of a new thing to know that."

"No way. Catch a clue, dude."

Walking around the cemetery in Genoa was kind of the same as hiking through the one in Virginia City, because there have been people buried in both since the 1860's. At this one in Genoa though, no one else was around. Alive tourists, I mean. A lot of the headstones were from the olden times. But they didn't have all the metal fences with gates around all the graves like the one we were at before. The Genoa cemetery was like a mix of the old and new times, it had a lot more fresher graves in it. In this cemetery, death didn't seem so distant.

As Jorge and I walked up to one end of the cemetery, out of nowhere a deer appeared there staring right at us, right there inside the cemetery, frightened. It was like the deer hadn't seen a real live person in years. How long had it been since someone else was in this place? Were Jorge and I the only ones in a real long time to visit these people who died? "What if nobody visits me after I'm dead?" I asked Jorge.

The minute I spoke out loud the deer hopped straight up in the air and ran fast away. I felt so guilty for having disturbed it. It had become a much hotter day, and the deer had probably just been cooling off in the shade.

"You'll always be remembered, Miguel," Jorge'd told me.

"So it's true what it says on all these tombstones, *Gone but not forgotten*?"

"Of course."

While glancing at all the different headstones, I began realizing that some of the sayings from back then, were too hard for me to understand completely. Again, I kept seeing a saying I had seen in Virginia City from before, '*Blessed are the dead who die in the Lord.*'

"What does *die in the Lord* mean again?" I asked Jorge.

"I'm not sure. Back then it probably meant a person who's religious. Today, it would probably mean someone who accepts death as being something God meant to create, just as much as He created life, birth."

"No kidding?"

"Yeah, people don't get afraid when a baby's being born, they celebrate. Why shouldn't they feel the same when someone dies?"

"I wish I could think the way God does sometimes." Then an urgent thought popped into my head immediately after saying that. "Jorge, how come when you and I get together these days it's always in cemeteries?"

"I think cemeteries are awesome. You don't?"

"Yeah, I do. But—"

"Well then, maybe it's for some reason."

"You mean...some sort of lesson? That's it, isn't it? I knew it. Am I supposed to learn something about dying? Death?"

"You're asking *me*? How the heck should I know? I'm not God."

I wondered what He'd think of cemeteries. Just like a human person, I bet God would think some were cool while other ones were too gaudy. Get it?

Standing up like a sore thumb, one of the graves Jorge and I walked by must have been for an 1870's drag queen 'cause the tombstone had totally glittery rhinestone-things glued on all over. And, it had a man's name on it. "Fancy schmansy," Jorge and I both said out loud at the same time.

Just like in the cemetery in Virginia City, this one in Genoa was divided, too. There was a section for Masons, and another for the

Oddfellows. I thought for sure that this old-time drag queen must have definitely been considered an odd fellow for back then. Criss-crossing through the plain, fancy, and in-between graves in whatever section they were in, was what Jorge and I spent the next few hours doing. The tombstones that had the most to say on them were definitely the ones that caught the majority of our attention. Some, the way they were written, were like they were straight out of *Dr. Quinn, Medicine Woman,* or one of those Western miniseries on the Hallmark channel.

ELIZA A. TODD
Died
November 9, 1876,
Aged
38 years.
Dear is the spot where Christians sleep
And sweet the strains that Angels pour,
O! why should we in anguish weep,
They are not lost but gone before.

"That's a cool one, isn't it?" I told Jorge.

"Yeah, I like it a lot."

"It's just, once in a while, I don't really get these old poems though. What does this one mean exactly?"

"In an old-fashioned way it's saying, *'Been there, done that'.*"

"Sleep?"

"*Die,* you dork."

"So, *that's* what it means."

"Death has been going on since the beginning of time. Nothing new about it."

"What's up with the *Christian* part?"

"This woman, Eliza A. Todd, and her family, must have been Christians."

"What if you're some other religion? Do those people die and get born again and again and again?"

"*Everybody* does."

"Everybody? No kidding? Hey, I've been meaning to ask you, what religion are you now that you live in heaven? The same one you had before? Catholic?"

"I don't have one. No one in heaven does."

"For real?"

"Totally. Religions are man-made. Most religious people think it's the only way to truly believe in God, through some man-made religion. In heaven, everyone's the same. I mean, everyone's different, but we're all the same."

"On earth it's still pretty much like it was when you lived here. Different people still get treated way differently, *not* the same. There's still lots of wars and riots. And there's still tons of people around who hate tons of other people...just 'cause they're different."

"Another lesson."

"I guess that's a big one, isn't it?"

"Huge."

In the Genoa cemetery, Jorge and I didn't play our version of *Survivor* like we had in Virginia City, where we had to find the absolute oldest buried person. We didn't need to, because right off the bat we'd already found a tombstone that said, "FIRST MAN BURIED IN CEMETERY, Louis Scossa 1840-1866, Malvagia Switzerland."

Jorge and I must have walked in a full circle, because there we were again, right in front of the cemetery's first man. I wondered who the first lady was. Right acrosst from Mr. Scossa, in a special place, were three flags waving in the warm breeze; a U.S., a Nevada, and another I thought was the Swiss flag. "Hey, what's up with that? Did Nevada used to be part of Switzerland?" I asked Jorge.

"Miguel, you've got a long way to go, dude."

"Hey, Jorge! Look!" I yelled to him, while pointing at a small, green-painted sign. It read, "Snowshoe Thompson's grave →."

"Let's hit it, bro."

I'd forgotten that that's what we'd been looking for in the first place. Finally, there we were, both standing in front of the grave of Snowshoe Thompson, with a painting of some man wearing skis on top of it.

"This man was a true hero, Miguel."

"Just 'cause he invented snowshoes?"

"*He didn't invent snowshoes.* For twenty straight winters, up the Sierra Nevada mountains, through blizzards and freezing temperatures, Snowshoe Thompson delivered the mail. Up here all the way from Placerville, California. It took him three days to do it, entirely on foot, snowshoes."

"Get out."

"I'm serious. The government had put an ad in the Sacramento newspaper, looking for someone to bring the mail all the way up to this remote area. He'd even been warned that others had tried to do this by horse. That was a total flop. They became too ill, and had to abandon their horses that ended up freezing to death. Snowshoe chose to deliver the mail anyway."

"Why did he decide to do it?"

"He wanted to. Maybe deep down he realized that that was his purpose in life. He was helping others, he brought mail to those isolated people who needed it. And, he never took any pay for doing it."

"He could have easily died from all that snow though, doing a job like that. Duh."

"Snowshoe was never afraid of dying. That's exactly what gave him the strength to do it in the first place."

After Jorge said that my dream with him was over, and I woke up. How strange, I thought.

Knowing that Aunt Shirley was going to come to the hospital the very next morning to be with me, I wanted to tell her all about my dream with Jorge. Although the hospital people had told me a million times not to log on when I should be sleeping, I couldn't wait any longer. The reason I couldn't wait anymore was because for so many times, on so many occasions, lots of the very same things Aunt Shirley had told me in life were the same exact things Jorge was telling me from heaven, almost word for word. How could Aunt Shirley know all this?

Without waiting too much longer, I booted up the laptop in my room, logged onto AOL, and activated my Point & Speak so I could write and send e-mail without having to type it all in because of my lack of fingers.

After hearing Lisa Kudrow, you know, Phoebe from *Friends* say, "You've Got Mail," I began dictating my e-mail super quietly, so no one would come in and catch me.

Yo Aunt Shirley,
What's up? How's it going in Berkeley? I hope I'm still awake when you come over tomorrow morning. Guess what? Mom was just here, and we've had some excellent talks together. You probably know this already, but did you know she's dumping that loser guy, Hunt. Cool.
Khadijah came over too, and she brought Samantha with her. I really want to go to the U.S. Open in New York with her and Mom. And, I hate to be the one to tell you this, my instinct says that Samantha

probably has anorexia, or bulimia, or something like that 'cause she's getting way too skinny. Does all that food-eating stuff start from fear, by the way?

You know what else? A few minutes ago I had the coolest dream about Jorge. Just as usual, it's like somehow he's still alive when he's in my dreams. Check it out though, there's something that's soooo weird. Every time Jorge talks to me in my dreams, he tells me really smart stuff that he never used to know when he lived on earth. And, to top it off, it's usually always stuff you had already told me, but you've never *really* been up to heaven. Have you? Well, I guess you just got near it when you had your coma. I guess that's kind of close. Close, but no cigar.

You know what I keep remembering all the time now? What you told me about what you learned from being in your coma, "The minute people lose their fear of death, that's when they begin living." Does that mean I haven't even been living yet? See now, I always thought I had been. I thought for sure I was doing a hella of a good job. When I see you tomorrow, can you please tell me. This is what I want to know more than anything.

It's going to be heavy drama when you come over 'cause you, Mom, Dad, and Khadijah are all going to be here for my surgery at the same time, a total first. Hey, what if this is my final go 'round? Everyone all together to say their last goodbye? Like the way they do in the movies? Uh, oh. I don't want to get you pissed. I know how you hate pessimistic talk, so I'll just get over it for the moment.

Anyway, I just wanted to touch base. And, please give me an answer to my question when you get here, OK? How in the world do you know all this? You've definitely got to tell me what's up. Are you really an alien from heaven or something? Just kidding.

Lots of love,
Miguel

Only the second after I sent my e-mail to Aunt Shirley, I heard a loud knock at the door. It frightened me so much. I could tell that I was about to get busted for using my computer when I wasn't supposed to. Then I realized the sound had come from my AOL, the knock that comes on right when you get an IM. The message was from Samantha.

PleaseDon'tSaySam: Aren't you supposed to be sleeping now?

bandagedboy:	How did you know I was online?
PleaseDon'tSaySam:	I put you on my Buddy List.
bandagedboy:	You're the black cat?
PleaseDon'tSaySam:	Yes, that's the icon I picked out.
bandaged boy:	Cool. I like it.
PleaseDon'tSaySam:	There's something I forgot to tell you.
bandaged boy:	What?
PleaseDon'tSaySam:	Keep thinking about me tomorrow.
bandagedboy:	What do you mean?
PleaseDon'tSaySam:	I'm counting on you to get well soon.
bandagedboy:	I'll try, Samantha.
PleaseDon'tSaySam:	No, you've got to. Don't ever give up, Miguel. Never.
bandagedboy:	I won't.
PleaseDon'tSaySam:	Only, that day when you didn't care. Remember that?
bandagedboy:	Yeah.
PleaseDon'tSaySam:	That made me so sad. It made me hurt like nothing before.
bandagedboy:	I'm sorry.
PleaseDon'tSaySam:	Please keep doing what you've always done. Please keep doing what you've always told me to do. Please keep believing, Miguel. You're my best friend.

CHAPTER SEVENTEEN

When I woke up from the operation, I wasn't surprised really. I expected to. That usual *I-don't-care-anymore* attitude I normally get before or after surgery, never got off the ground. Someone else was relying on me to get better quick. I didn't want to let her down. I knew she needed my help, and I'm pretty sure I wanted to hang around not just for myself but for Samantha, my new best buddy.

Just to be sitting on the couch with Dad, on a freezing windy night, was like a total grand prize for me. I was safe, recovering fully weeks after my time in the hospital, doing one of my favorite things, watching Nick-at-Nite with my dad. "Wow, this one's way different. It's way more serious than all the others," I told Dad as we watched an unusual episode of *All in the Family*.

"Archie's still talking in stereotypes. That'll never change," Dad said.

"About Jewish people, you mean."

"At least he didn't call this guy a Heeb, like he normally would have."

"I know. Archie even said, '*Oy*'."

The particular show we were watching was about an older man who had become Archie's business partner. He'd invented a remote-controlled doorbell ringer, except they found out that it ended up being way defective, 'cause it rang everybody's front door in the neighborhood at the same time. It was a complete dud. The old Jewish man seemed like he had experienced failure so many times before. Maybe this was the last shot he'd ever get at succeeding, at least that's the way I saw it.

As Dad and I watched the TV, neither one of us were laughing anymore. The man who had such high hopes, and early on became so excited about having discovered a winning invention, lied down in pain on Archie and Edith's couch. Maybe this last failure was just too much for him. Then, he closed his eyes and he must have had a heart attack or something, because he never got back up. As the show finished, the man ended up dying right

there at the *All in the Family* house on 704 Houser Street. It was all so sad.
"How come they made a show like this one?" I asked.
"A message, I assume. A very strong one."
"A message. About dying, probably."
"Or, a message about living with hope. Never giving up."
"Being optimistic, right?"
"Oh, I think so. That's how I like to see it. It's all in the way you look at life. You get to interpret the message in your own, unique way."
"Like the way poems are."
"That's a perfect example. Almost every poem can be interpreted in a variety of ways. What's your take on this show? How would you interpret it?"

After thinking about that one for a second, I said, "I think that way too many disappointments in a person's life makes them have to die. There's just too many over the limit. It all ends up being way too much."

"I'm so glad you inspired me to keep going, to somehow find a way to persevere. I believe there's always a way to make anything happen, if you want it badly enough. You're the reason I'm free, Miguel."

When Dad said the word *free* I thought of one of my favorite movies Dad and I used to watch together, *Sybil*. That's exactly the way it ended, when her psychiatrist, Dr. Wilbur, said something like, "I don't know if she's happy, but I know for sure she's free." That was the best part of the movie, when Sybil got to completely change at the end, and totally learn from the terrible past she'd had. Her life got to start all over again, and she didn't have to have all those extra personalities anymore. She got to be just herself, and that was good enough.

Sometimes, without understanding why too good, I seemed to feel like a boy-Sybil, a boy who really had lots of way different boys inside just one, me. Was I free? The way Sybil ended up being? I never told another person this, but happiness was something I never really ever felt, even halfway. All my life it seemed like there was always sadness inside me, a kind of sadness or permanent pain all over I'd never seen in anyone else, except for Samantha. Without ever talking about it, I could tell that that's why we had become such close friends.

Samantha had told me that she always felt like she never fit in, anywhere. For sure that's always the way I felt, too. I liked the way I finally got to meet someone else like this. I never had this feeling with Jorge, he trusted way more people than I ever did. That's why he'd made more friends than me, kid friends. In my life way too many kids had been mean to me, so

I decided that I just wouldn't have any anymore. It was that simple. Samantha told me the same about her. "Being alone is what suits me best," was what she'd tell me.

"Did you have many friends when you were my age, Dad?"

"I think so. Well, not all that many."

"You probably had some that were real close friends though, right?"

"I think I was closest to my family. They were my whole world when I was your age, my best supporters. That's the way it is in El Salvador, family's everything."

I'm so glad Dad came back to be my family again. Into the night, he and I watched *Coach*, *The Addams Family*, and *Andy Griffith*. And then we watched a scary movie together he never let me see before 'cause it had too many swear words in it. It was *Misery*, about a woman who traps a writer man inside her mountain house, all because she says that she's his Number One fan. "I like it when she oinks like a pig. I hope she'll do that again," I told Dad.

"She's a little creepy, in my opinion."

Dad and I watched the movie 'til it was over, and when we saw the end credits come on, it said thanks to the people of Genoa, Nevada. "Oh, my God," I said to Dad.

"What?"

"Genoa. That's the place I had a dream about. And Jorge was in it."

"Genoa? I thought your dreams took place in Playa del Carmen."

"No, not lately. Jorge and I are always in cemeteries now. Remember, Aunt Shirley took me to that one I told you about last time? In Virginia City? This other one is close to there."

"A cemetery in *Genoa*? Where in the world is that?"

"It's right over the mountain from Lake Tahoe. Except I never knew *Misery* was filmed there. That makes it all even better, more real."

"That's showbiz. In the movie they say Colorado, when all along it's really Lake Tahoe."

"No, Genoa. They're way different even though they're real close by. Genoa and Virginia City are like desert ghost towns, and there's still real people, alive ones, who live there."

"Well, what a coincidence that is. Finding this out just before you leave tomorrow. By the way, you're all packed, aren't you? I'm taking you over to Shirley's very early in the morning at around seven."

"Yeah, I'm all packed."

"And now, it's bedtime for you, pal. And I just know she's going to run you ragged as usual, so you'll need all the sleep you can get."

I couldn't wait to go to Crystal Bay with Aunt Shirley again. And getting to spend such a perfect night with Dad was the best way to start the weekend off. My homework was done, and I was ready to hit the road the very next day.

As soon as we arrived at the cabin this time, the weather was getting to be so dramatic outside. Flashflood warnings were predicted, and tons of rain was drenching everything in sight, bringing down piles of dead pine needles from the trees along with it. Aunt Shirley had been so excited about driving to Lake Tahoe again, except she talked me out of going to the cemetery in Virginia City one more time. "We need to go somewhere we haven't been yet," Aunt Shirley said. Getting out of her car in the pouring rain made us have to dry off for a while before we began doing anything fun. So we spent some extra time inside the cabin with not too much to do except look out at the huge flashes of lightning, and listen to the massive thunder that came right after.

I wasn't really scared. It just made me wonder about nature a whole lot more. "Why's there thunder and lightning anyway?" I asked Aunt Shirley.

"It's a reminder. A big, in-your-face reminder."

"A reminder to be careful around powerful, electrical stuff like that?"

"A reminder that God's out there, around us all the time."

"'Cause He's the one who makes thunder and lightning in the first place."

"Right. Not to scare us, just a reminder that He's truly there, here, period. He's saying, 'Hey, just because you can't see Me or hear Me, here I am. And, don't you forget it."

"That must be what happens when He makes an earthquake shake stuff up or makes a volcano explode."

"You got it, mister. The very same."

"I bet there's still lots of people who probably don't know that that's really God who's making all that happen."

"They think *they're* all that. They think they've got it goin' on more than He does. Boy, do they have lessons to learn."

Aunt Shirley's reasons made so much sense to me when I looked out the window. The sight of Lake Tahoe sitting there below the dark cloudy sky was like something man could never have come up with. It was all too mysterious, too one-of-a-kind. The lightning that was happening right over the lake was like God was saying, "Hey, y'all. Look at what I made! Notice it. It's a big freekin' deal. Places like this don't grow on trees."

"*I* really appreciate this, Aunt Shirley. Being at this cool, old cabin up here with you."

"Me too, doll. Something to be grateful for. Isn't it?"

As soon as we both showed some mutual gratitude, a peek of sunlight came out and shined right onto us both from the sky. It felt warm. It made me feel healed. Not just on the skin on my face, but on my insides too. It made me feel blessed because I knew that the light I was feeling was made by God.

As quickly as it all had begun, the rain turned into a drizzle and was over. The clouds had vanished. And when Aunt Shirley opened the doors to the deck, the air smelled fresh, as if everything dirty and bad had been washed away. Somehow, the way all this had happened, I not only felt a little bit closer to Aunt Shirley than I ever had before, I felt closer to understanding a little bit more of what God's all about.

Because the weather could have changed back at any moment, Aunt Shirley and I decided to stay kind of close to Crystal Bay where the cabin was. We ended up going to have lunch at the Cal-Neva Hotel off of Highway 28, right there in town. Aunt Shirley told me Frank Sinatra used to own it a long time ago in the 60's. Half of the hotel is in California and the other half's in Nevada. It's divided smack down the middle, just like the lake itself.

As we sat down to eat lunch, the view of everything was like nothing I had seen before. It was like the view from the cabin except way more huge. "Do you know who Mark Twain is, doll?" Aunt Shirley asked me.

"Yeah, he's the *Huckleberry Finn* guy."

"That's right. He wrote it. And, you know, when he first laid eyes on Lake Tahoe he said, 'I thought it must surely be the fairest picture the whole world affords'."

"I think I'd agree with him. Isn't he the guy with the with that massively way big moustache? The guy with that Albert Einstein kind of hair?"

"Yes, he was. You're right. Mark Twain, even though he was such a successful writer, was also one of the most *hated* men in America."

"How come?"

"He didn't believe America should protect other foreign lands, nor acquire or control them. He was an interesting guy. Extremely, extremely witty."

"He probably wasn't afraid either. To have the guts to say bold stuff like that."

As usual Aunt Shirley liked that in a weird kind of way she was once again teaching me more about someone brave, someone who wasn't afraid, and the rewards they got from being that way. In front of window at the hotel restaurant facing Lake Tahoe, we sat and watched a few of the remaining clouds come and pass by. It was all awesome, and while we were there together I figured I had to ask Aunt Shirley one more question about why we're here. I had to ask her which one was more important, wanting to stay alive or being unafraid of dying. "Hey, A.S. I'm still confused about something."

"About what, M.?"

"You told me that life begins when people lose their fear of going to heaven, but what about people like me? All those things you taught me about how I can stay well, my *To Do* list, saying positive words out loud, and believing? Which one is more important?"

"*Which one*? They're equal. They're the same, you goon."

"How can that be? I don't get it then."

"As long as anyone wants to be alive, they should do all they can to make sure they get in everything they want. Have a good one, that's the way to do it. A big chunk of having a full life *is* not being afraid, to not think about what may or may not happen next, or when, or how, or why. Just do it! Do it all!"

The more I thought about that, the more I realized that they both do kind of go together. They were equally important, just like Aunt Shirley said. What a great thing to begin to understand more. I wish I had asked her a while ago about that one, 'cause it had been on my mind for a whole bunch of weeks, except I always forgot to ask.

After Aunt Shirley and I went back to the cabin on the hill, I asked if I could use Lefty's computer there to check my e-mail. Somehow Aunt Shirley even had his user id and password memorized. I didn't ask how she knew that, but whatever. As soon as I logged onto AOL Anywhere, I could see that there was an e-mail from Samantha.

Immediately I opened it and began reading.

Dear Miguel,
I know you're at the lake right now with your aunt; I just felt like writing to you. Have a good time, if you happen to get this while you're still up there. Knowing you, you're checking your e-mail even though you should be enjoying your holiday with your aunt right now.

On TV last night there was the greatest special on TeenNick about the Justin/Christina tour. It was like being there all over again. Going to that concert was something I will remember for the rest of my life. Thank you for persuading me to go. You are my superhero, Miguel.

I wish you were her now though. My mother took me to my doctor yesterday and today I have to go to the hospital to have x-rays taken. I'm not sure what's going on, and if you were here now you'd tell me not to be scared of anything. So, I'll just imagine that you'll be right here beside me when I go.

I can't wait to see you when you get back. Until then, have a great time.

Love, Samantha

P.S. Here are a few more things I added to my list:

51. Ride the Big Dipper at the Santa Cruz Boardwalk

52. Taste champagne

53. Hit out on every groundstroke; backhands AND forehands

54. Sign up for all frequent flyer programs

55. Don't be afraid to prepare for the worst

CHAPTER EIGHTEEN

"Did you add anything else to your To Do list today?" I asked
Samantha outside, in between Science and Math, on a crisp late-winter
morning.

"I sure did. It doesn't necessarily have to do with fear though," she told
me back, and continued on by saying to my surprise, "I'm running short on
those."

"No, anything. Anything at all you want to do in life. Short on what?
What did you put down?"

"I want to—"

"No, you have to say 'I will...' Just saying that you *want* to do
something doesn't end up *making* it happen. If you say 'I will' means
somehow you actually already believe it's going to happen. Or at least that's
what Aunt Shirley's always telling me."

"Yes, I remember her saying that. She said it's so important to phrase
statements in this manner. I *will* read the fifth *Harry Potter* book as soon as I
have time. And the sixth as soon as it comes out."

"Excellent."

"Have you read *Book 5* yet?"

"No. You probably know this by now, but I'm not really into reading. I
kind of hate it. That's just me."

"I wouldn't know what I'd do if I couldn't read my books. What have
you put on your *To Do* list lately?"

"I actually jotted down something for the both of us. I found a tennis
tournament, a big one that's in Florida every year. And, since Serena and
Venus had to withdraw from the U.S. Open, we'll go to this one instead."

"The Nasdaq 100. I know all about it. I've heard it's an awesome
tournament."

"Yeah, that's what it's called. You'll really love everything about it, for
sure."

"They call it the *fifth* major. All the top men and women will be there.

But…"

"What? I know you're not afraid of going, 'cause you were way psyched about the Open last fall. It'll be great. Mom will take us both."

"No, I don't think I'd be too afraid of going, I just don't know how I'll be feeling by then."

"Well, neither do I. I *never* do."

"I get so tired these days, and it's nearly impossible to predict when these high fevers are coming on." Then, Samantha paused for a second or two, seemed to realize something or other, and said, "That's true, isn't it? That's how you've lived your whole life. Not knowing what's going to come next."

"Yep. Now Aunt Shirley tells me to just *go for it!*"

Since the doctors never did figure out what's wrong with Samantha, I thought it couldn't hurt for her to keep remembering all the things she wanted to do in life. Except, something deep down told me that she and I wouldn't be able to go to that tennis tournament in Florida after all. I didn't tell Samantha this though, so I thought of something else to say to her.

What I kept remembering all the time, ever since Aunt Shirley told it to me, was how much of a good thing it was to thank God for all the good stuff in your life. On a Friday afternoon, Samantha and I walked over to Marina Green, a place where tons of people always did lots of different kinds of sports in this huge field there. There were always massive amounts of people playing soccer there, softball players, Frisbee throwers, roller bladders, runners, and walkers.

After we got to the Green, Samantha and I found a bench to sit on, almost right on top of the bay where the shoreline meets the bike path, and I told Samantha what was on my mind. Normally, anyone else would have thought I was nuts, but I knew Samantha would never think so. She always got the unique way my mind works right from the beginning, and I was thankful for that.

The first thing that came out of her mouth though, I had a hard time believing. Looking out at the bay, with the waves crashing small, quickly onto the rocks, Samantha said, "This is so amazing, Miguel. I've never been here before."

"Where?" I asked.

"It's incredible. I've never been this close to the ocean, never."

"Are you being serious?" I asked. I kind of knew she was telling the truth or else she definitely would've known that what we were sitting in front of was the bay, *not* the ocean. Duh. I corrected her anyway. "The ocean's over there, on the other side of the bridge," I said.

"Oh, that's right. Anyway, I love where we are right now, the water, the bay, the marina, wherever it is."

"I love it out here, too. Being able to hear the waves splashing so close to me is my favorite part. Listen."

For a few moments, like a parade of sounds, we heard the foghorn, the waves splashing, some sailboat honking at another coming too close, and a little girl on a bench far away, crying out "Mommy, Mommy" over and over again.

"I love it all. Alcatraz, right in front. Angel Island. What an experience."

"It's definitely the best. When I lived on Nob Hill with my mom, I used to thank God for letting me live here. I learned to do that from Aunt Shirley."

"You already know my family's not so religious, Miguel. I wasn't ever taught to do that."

"Aren't you grateful for all the goodness you have? Grateful for who you are? The way you're turning out?"

"Grateful? Yes, I guess so. I'm not that grateful for what's been happening to me lately though. I'm still not feeling right. Even though those x-rays and tests came up with nothing, something's going on with me."

"Maybe yes, maybe no. Aren't there still lots you're grateful for? I'd definitely think so. I think one of the best things for you to do is to think about what you're grateful for, and say so."

"Is that why you brought that pad of paper with you?"

"Maybe."

"You want me to write something down, don't you? Something I'm grateful for, I'd imagine," Samantha told me.

"Yeah, it's perfect for you. A thank you fan letter to Serena or Venus, or someone else. You pick."

"What? Are you crazy, Miguel?...I could never do that. I wouldn't have any idea what to say to either one."

"So, aren't you thankful that you get to watch them on TV whenever they play a match?"

"Well, of course I am. I think they're the greatest."

"Pick one, and tell her that."

"I guess I could. I don't really see the point though. I also don't know how appropriate it would be."

"How are they going to know unless you tell them," I said to Samantha, while handing her the paper along with my favorite red-gel ink pen I took out of my shirt pocket.

"Now?"

"Yes, now. And, read it out loud to me as you write it. Whatever you say out loud makes it all twice as meaningful."

Several moments passed by as Samantha hesitated and told me about five or six times that I was being silly. Then she just looked down at the page, staring at it long and hard, before she began. But in a flash Samantha got right on it, and seemed to know exactly what to say. Out loud, at the same time as she was writing it, she spoke her letter to me.

"Dear Venus,

Even though you don't know me, I hope you don't mind me writing this letter to you. You probably get many letters like this, but now that I think about it, I do want you to know how much I enjoy watching you play. What I like about you most is the way you take risks. And up to the very end of any match you play, you seem to believe fully in what you are doing. That's what makes you a champion. When your matches get tight you don't retreat, you take even more chances. You're probably the only player who competes with this much confidence.

My friend Miguel and I were even going to go all the way to New York to watch you and Serena at the Open. When you both had to withdraw though, we didn't bother. Instead, we're planning on going to the Nasdaq 100 to see you there.

I wish I could think of something new and different to tell you that no one else ever has; I'm sure you've heard it all by now. What I do want to say though is that you give me strength, Venus. Even without knowing you, I can still recognize that you like your privacy, and even though you seem like you enjoy having fun, I can tell you like peace and quiet too. This is exactly the way I am. It makes me glad to watch you; you go out there knowing you're a winner the moment you step onto the court. Then again, you probably like being by yourself right after your match has ended.

It seems like you never doubt, you never look scared of anything. My friend Miguel always tells me that anyone who's unafraid is always the ultimate champion. You will always be one to me, Venus. And, something else I'd like you to know, more than anything I can say, is that I'm grateful to be able to watch you and the incredible talent you display. Thank you for allowing me to learn to believe in myself from you, just as I've also learned through being able to witness the strength and courage you possess off the tennis court as well.

Your two-handed backhand is fantastic and your serves out-wide are awesome, although what's inside your head is what I appreciate most. You've always believed in yourself. You're a true winner, Venus. And you always knew you would be. I guess victories do come from having confidence. Without it, perhaps none of us would ever attain any of our goals.

Good luck with all the tournaments you enter, and good luck with all you do in life. It's not only a pleasure, a privilege, and a joy to watch you play tennis, you and your accomplishments are ingredients that have enriched my life forever.

Thank you, Venus.
Sincerely,
Samantha Austin"

"Perfect," I told Samantha.

"That was kind of fun. I liked doing that. It was a good writing exercise."

"It was no exercise. Whether Venus Williams ever reads it or not, you told her *thanks*, and that was the whole point. You showed that you were grateful. If you think so or not, saying it out loud, and writing it all down in the first place makes it known that you don't take anything for granted."

"Makes it known? To God?"

"Just makes it known. Aunt Shirley's the one who told me, 'Why should God help you in the future if you never appreciate what He's done for you now or in the past?'"

"That's interesting. Well, either way, I liked writing Venus that letter, even though we're never really going to send it."

"Sure we are."

"How? I don't know her address, and I doubt if you do."

"Aunt Shirley will know. She says that anything's possible. She'll find the right place to send it."

When I headed home I not only wanted to call Aunt Shirley to see if she'd know where to send the letter, I also couldn't wait to tell her what I'd taught Samantha about showing gratitude. As it turned out, I never got the chance to phone Aunt Shirley though. When I got home Khadijah was there waiting for me, waiting to take me to the clinic in San Bruno so I could see

Dr. Rosenzweig. I had totally forgotten that I was supposed to go there that afternoon at four.

Having to rush to get there made me more nervous than I'd usually be. Better late than never, I figured. By the time Khadijah and I walked inside the Care Center, the new, blond-haired receptionist girl with braces seemed more frantic than we were because Khadijah and I were so late. "Dr. Rosenzweig is beside himself. I wasn't quite sure what to tell him," the receptionist told us.

"I am so sorry. I tried calling from the car, but—"

"I'd better take Miguel inside an examining room now."

Another nurse lady, someone I had also never seen before, with tightly-permed gray hair and the same frantic look as the receptionist, quickly took me into the faraway examining room, a place I had been in a few times already. "Is Dr. Rosenzweig really mad?" I asked her.

She didn't answer. She just looked down to the floor, away from me, and said, "The doctor will be with you shortly."

What I couldn't understand was that they still weren't letting Khadijah in the room with me, she still had to wait in the front. So, that meant I had to face Dr. Rosenzweig all by myself. A million things went through my mind. I decided that I felt sorry enough for being late, and whatever he had to say to me was whatever he had to say. I guess this is what I deserved.

"Young man, you've squandered I don't know how many of my hard-earned dollars. I have nothing to tell you. Except that you'll undoubtedly be late for your own funeral," Dr. Rosenzweig said as he flung open the door to the examining room.

"Gosh, I'm so, so sorry, sir. I just forgot that I had an appointment today," I said in the same panicky voice as everyone else who's scared of the doctor.

"Well, you've just wasted not only my time but everyone else's in our office. You most likely only think of yourself."

"No, sir."

"No, *Doctor*. Do you know what Squamious Cell Carcinoma is, young man?"

"Yes. I do, Doctor."

"So you understand how likely it is that it will affect you someday?"

"Well, I know what it does. My other doctors told me all about it."

"Then you realize all these psychic gimmicks you discuss are a waste of time? All this metaphysical hocus pocus won't prolong your life by a single moment. All they're doing is stealing your father's money."

"What money? Dad doesn't—"

"I certainly don't have the time to be arguing with you. Suffice it to say, and although unfortunate, at some point SCC will most likely get the better of you, probably by the time you're twenty."

Why was he trying to make me so afraid? Then, something almost slipped out of my mouth right after he spoke, except I was able to prevent it from happening. Stating facts was not what he was doing, Dr. Rosenzweig was telling me this for some other reason. Every time I ever saw him all I could see was his anger, his big red anger. I never knew why he was angry. It wasn't hard to figure out though that it wasn't me at all that he was really angry at.

"Negative people don't like positive people," my aunt had always told me. "Don't waste your time trying to make them treat you well, the way you deserve to be treated, because they never will. They're too busy being angry at the world, they enjoy being this way. Treating you poorly somehow makes them feel better," Aunt Shirley had said.

After remembering that, I just did what I was supposed to in the examining room. I let the doctor do what he had to. Most of me just pretended I wasn't even there. Somehow I regretted that I'd never told Dad or Khadijah the truth about what this man was really like.

CHAPTER NINETEEN

Waking up to find an e-mail from Mom on my computer was totally unexpected. But what surprised me even more was what she had to tell me.

Dear Miguel,
To say that you have influenced me in a variety of positive ways would be a complete understatement. All along I thought I was helping you by being protective and cautious, where now I realize that I was keeping you from living fully. How lucky that fate stepped in to correct my horrible error in judgment. I am proud that you now live without fear, unafraid of what comes in front of you in life. And, I am so grateful that I was able to learn from the miraculous example you set.
Seeing you in the hospital recently; the way you live life, the way you respond to others, and the way you interact with your dear friend Samantha, was my wake-up call. Because of you; learning from what you've been able to do in your life, has prompted me to examine my own. All those limitations I've imposed upon myself, and most of all, the fears that have prevented me from moving forward. I've now been going to counseling on a regular basis for the past two months. This has opened up my eyes immeasurably. When I speak about you in these sessions, I speak of you as my hero, my mentor and teacher.
Thank you, my dear Miguel, for helping me recognize all I was missing from life as a result of the paralyzing fears I've lived with these years.
There's so much more I want to tell you. I'm hoping you will have the chance to come and visit me here next weekend just as we discussed. I will pick you up any time you'd like to arrive.
Until then, my dear son, thank you.   All my love,
                                                                        Mom

Hearing that from Mom made it so clear to me, all over again, that making people understand about fear, about how dangerous it is, was somehow definitely connected to the reason I was still alive. Of course I was going to visit Mom in Los Angeles, it was something I was really looking forward to. Getting the chance to see my *new-and-improved* mom was exciting to me. And being able to see her there without that loser guy around was going to make the whole trip sort of fun.

When Dad and I talked about my trip down to L.A. he had no problem with it at all. He just wanted me to make sure all my homework was finished before I left. Part of me felt guilty for going there when I still didn't know for sure what was going on with Samantha, but then nobody did. Whatever was going on with her remained a mystery. Plus, I'd only be gone for the weekend. So I know I wouldn't have even been gone so long at all. I figured by writing her an e-mail from L.A., we'd still be staying in touch.

Dad helped me pack all my medical supplies, although I knew that Mom, even in L.A., still had lots with her anyway. I couldn't wait to go. When I told Aunt Shirley about leaving, she was also excited for me that I was about to see Mom again. Aunt Shirley's feelings about L.A. hadn't changed though, she still called it the "armpit of the world."

For some reason, only minutes before walking out the door, there ended up being a whole ton of things Dad wanted me to tell Mom. At first he began saying them one by one. Then there got to be so many that he began writing them all down on a list. When the stuff Dad was telling me started to get kind of personal, I just asked, "Why don't you just tell all this to Mom yourself?"

"Oh. I figured that since you'll be seeing her, you might want to mention a few of these things," Dad told me.

"I don't mind, Dad."

"You *are* coming back on Sunday, aren't you?"

"Yeah. Of course."

"Oh, you're right, Miguel. I'll give your mother a call soon, and we'll have a chat. You go finish getting ready."

Some of the questions Dad was asking made me think that he may have been wondering about the whole custody-thing again, since that had happened so many times before. Because I knew he wouldn't mind, I thought I'd ask Mom all about that anyway. Having to move all over again, and be with a different parent one more time, was totally more than I could handle for a long while.

On the northbound side of 280 I saw a place that had made me think of

Don't Be Afraid of Heaven

Dad when he was still in jail. "A long time ago, Dad. That's where I saw a boy and his father waiting there on the side of the road, for someone to help them with their old Toyota pickup that had broken down. I remember telling Mom about that when we were driving over to the airport to pick Aunt Shirley up when she first moved here from Boston."

"Why did you mention that?"

"Seeing them made me think of you. I had no idea when I, *if* I'd, ever get to see you again. I missed you so much."

Dad almost didn't know what to say after I told him that. Instead he just looked away out of his driver's-side window, so I wouldn't be able to study any part of his face at all. That was the worst part about Dad's having been in jail, all the guilt he must have felt by just being there. Except, if things hadn't gone completely the way they did, he never would have gotten out of jail, out of El Salvador, and come back to San Francisco again to be with me.

"I don't ever want to lose you again, Miguel."

"You won't, Dad. Everything's going so good. I'm not going anywhere."

"But, after your visit, if you'd really rather be living with your mother, I'll just have to accept that...and do my best to understand that that's what you truly want."

"That's totally not going to happen. I live with you now, and that's the way it goes. Period. End of story."

Dad managed to put on a whole lot calmer look onto the outside of his face, and within a short time we had gotten to the airport on a day when many screaming anti-war protestors were there. I guess that a lot of his anxiety about my visit with Mom had kind of vanished, or just gotten a whole lot smaller. Or maybe he's just gotten a whole lot better at pretending. It also made him extra comfortable after I'd promised I was going to e-mail him, just like I'd promised Samantha.

Getting a real close by parking space made us both real happy. That's kind of like winning the lottery, because close by parking spaces at the airport are so totally hard to come by. As Dad turned left into it, a man in the car right behind us even seemed a little bit mad 'cause we got the space instead of him. Dad didn't cut in front of him or anything. But maybe the man thought he did. Just two seconds later though I could see that the guy had luckily found another space near where Dad had parked. And as he got out of his car while Dad and I were walking away from ours, I recognized that the man was Mr. Ramirez, the principal from my old school. "Mr. Ramirez, what's up?" I asked him, noticing that he had less hair. Not shorter hair, just less. It also looked like he had lost a little weight too.

"Miguelito. So it was *you* in that car? I had no idea," he told me.

Without having to introduce the two of them, Dad came up to Mr. Ramirez, sticking his hand out to shake Mr. Ramirez's. "Hi, I'm Miguel's father, Joaquin," Dad said.

"Oh, gee. I'm so sorry for honking at you back there. I apologize. It's been a tough few weeks for me. I'm Larry."

"Yes, Miguel has told me all about you. He's wished many times that you were the principal of his new school."

"Marina Middle School is excellent. You made a great choice."

"So, Mr. Ramirez, you going somewhere today?"

"I'm headed for the Midwest, Miguel. On a trip I wish I didn't have to take. I'd rather just stay home."

"Why are you going then? To visit mean relatives?"

"Miguel, Mr. Ramirez doesn't need to tell us why he's going on his trip. It's none of our business."

I could tell that Mr. Ramirez was reluctant to answer my question, but he did anyway. "Two funerals. Two of my friends died only a few days apart. So I'm going to two of them back to back."

"What a bummer."

"Wow, that's too bad," Dad told Mr. Ramirez.

"I hate to use it as an excuse. That's what's making me so upset. It seems like I always have a funeral to go to these days. Oh, well. Enough about that. Moving on. So, where are you two headed?"

"Miguel's going to visit his mother in L.A."

"Yeah, that's right. You definitely remember Mom, don't you?" I asked.

"I certainly do. We had more than a few…interesting discussions. She must like it there."

"She's moving back to the city though. L.A. kind of bites."

"I remember when *you* were going to move down there, to be with your mom and her husband."

"It wasn't meant to be. But, living with Dad was."

Then Mr. Ramirez began to snicker before he said, "I'd forgotten the way you talk, Miguel. Oh, and I was so sorry to hear that your aunt had been in an accident. Is she all right now?"

"Yeah, she's OK. She ended up being inside a coma. And, you know what?" I asked, while somehow feeling I should repeat what Aunt Shirley had said after coming out of it. "She actually said she didn't mind being in it, because it taught her something huge."

"That woman's forever learning," Dad reminded Mr. Ramirez.

"Seriously, Dad. She said if she hadn't ever been in her coma she wouldn't have known that going to heaven wasn't a bad thing. She said it's the *best* place to go. So when you've got to be at your funerals, don't be sad, be happy for them. According to Aunt Shirley, both your friends are the lucky ones to have even had the chance to go there."

"Maybe you're right, Miguel. That's a unique outlook all right. You're fortunate to have your aunt around again. The way she views life *and* death. You're even more fortunate that she's OK now."

Since both of our planes weren't going to take off for a while, Mr. Ramirez, me, and Dad all decided to hang out at Quizno's Classic Subs, a decent kind of fast-food place at the airport. It seemed like all three of us had so many things we wanted to talk about, except I had no idea how serious it would all get. Maybe it was good that I was there, or maybe not. If I hadn't been there, Dad and Mr. Ramirez wouldn't have met, and never would have had any kind of conversation in the first place. When they started talking about all the friends they had known who died from AIDS, it turned out that they knew some of the very same people, friends, co-workers, and neighbors.

Dad confessed that that was one of the main reasons why he mostly stayed away from having a relationship with anyone. And, Mr. Ramirez maybe seemed a little like the same way Dad did by agreeing with him. Looking at the two of them, and listening to what they were saying, made me realize how totally hard it must be to be a gay person. What I liked most about Mr. Ramirez meeting Dad was that they said they'd stay in touch. It was perfect because Dad didn't have too many friends in America anymore, and as Mr. Ramirez had said, most of his friends had died. It's great that the two of them got to know each other. It's good for people not be too alone in the world.

Being on the plane all by myself made me feel like I was totally on display for all the passengers and crew to stare at. I guess having had someone else with me before always erased how aware I was that people constantly looked at me. Even the flight-attendant lady appeared uncomfortable every time she happened to look over in my direction. She smiled at me. But it was a smile her face made out of nervousness though, it wasn't from her heart. That's OK though. If there's one thing I completely learned from Aunt Shirley, it was to grow a thick skin over being stared at.

In my head I just imagined that stares were shy people's way of greeting someone they didn't know too well. Thinking of them that way usually made the whole thing way easier to deal with.

Since I really didn't have anyone to talk to on the plane, it made me so much more excited about all the things I was going to say to Mom. Did she already know that Aunt Shirley and Lefty had become a hot and heavy couple? Did she still want to go someplace to travel to with me? Did she know that Samantha had gotten a little too tired to be able to go anywhere with us? I wondered what I was going to pick to tell Mom first.

As usual, my United flight ended up taking a short time since Los Angeles is really sort of close to San Francisco. Waiting their turn to drive up to the gate took the plane forever. I'm not the type of kid to pee my pants, but some other person may have if they'd been as excited as I was. Getting off the plane and walking to the inside of the airport was more confusing than I thought it would be though. I couldn't find Mom there waiting for me. Then, after about a few minutes, from behind, someone tapped me on the shoulder. When I looked back, it wasn't my mom at all. Or was it? "Oh, my God. Mom, I didn't even know it was you," I told her.

"And, I don't know how I could have missed you," Mom said.

"You look so different again, did you forget to put all your makeup on this morning?"

"It's the new me, the natural look. *You* look great by the way. How was your flight?"

"It was OK," I said, as it became Mom's turn to stare. She just looked so totally different with her new short dark hair and plain-style clothes that probably came from JC Penney.

"And, how's everything going? Are you still enjoying your new school?"

"Everything's cool, Mom. Well, everything except that Samantha's not getting better. That part's not too good. Dad's OK. And, you know what? At the airport parking we saw Mr. Ramirez. He was going somewhere in Texas, I think."

"I remember him. He's a smart man. That sure was lucky."

"Yeah, we all hung out for a while there together. He'd never met Dad before."

"Maybe they'll become friends. That would be nice. Don't you think?"

"Yeah, I guess so. You seem so different, Mom."

"I do? I've been working at it. *No fear* and *the past is the past*. That's my new mantra."

"Good job, Mom," I said without knowing what mantra meant, as we walked over to the United baggage belt area where the suitcases fall out.

Something way more peaceful and relaxed was going on with Mom. She stayed like this the whole time going to where Mom's car was, even as we headed north on the Pacific Coast Highway to where she lived in Malibu. Anything she had to say about Dad was always something positive. She even seemed happy that I had finally gotten to have some time to spend with him, instead of just the little visits I had had with him in the past. "Has your father met anyone? You know, to go out with?" Mom asked me.

"No, he works too much. He's still got three jobs."

"I think it would be nice for him to settle down with someone. Maybe have a life together, a partner to travel with."

"You *want* him to do that?" I asked.

"Sure. Why not?"

"'Cause you used to say that he ruined our lives."

"That's the past...time to move on. Life's too short. That's how I see it all now."

"Life *is* too short. You're right, Mom. So, is the *moving on* part for everything that ever happened before?"

"Absolutely. What's done is done. Time to move forward."

"What about when you had that bad fight with Aunt Shirley? Remember when you talked about her baby that was killed?"

Mom looked like I had just ripped all my blistery skin off my body after I'd said that. She was dead silent for the rest of the time driving to her home. When I thought about what I had mentioned, I never knew it was going to have such a huge effect on her. I didn't mean to make Mom feel bad. I was just asking her a question, something that had to do with what happened in the past that never really got finished yet.

Dear Sam, I mean, Samantha (Just kidding!),
What's up? Malibu's kind of cool. So far I haven't seen too many movie stars.
Well, except for Joyce De Witt from *Three's Company*. She has longer hair now. We saw her when she was buying chocolate soy milk at Von's yesterday.
Maybe you should drink some. They say that soy makes little anti-oxi dents on the inside of your body, so it'll get way more healthy.
Anyway, I got to go. Mom's yelling at me so we can leave for the La Brea Tar Pits now. That's where dinosaur fossils come out of. Cool,

yeah?
Take care of yourself. Write back soon, OK?
Love,
M.

While rushing to logoff right after sending Samantha's e-mail, I immediately received a strange and confusing message from MAILER-DAEMON, whoever he is. It said, "Delivery failed: returning message; recipient unknown." What the...?

Although Mom was still yelling at me from the other room to get going, I had to call Samantha on my cell real quick to see what's up.

"They're coming to get me," Samantha cried out.

"Who? What are you talking about?" I asked amongst the panic.

"I don't know who. I'm so scared, Miguel. It's happening all over again."

CHAPTER TWENTY

Nearly a week had passed since Samantha's last panic attack, but I was still concerned about her all the time. Somehow I even began getting bad stomach aches every time I thought about her, just like the way I used to when I was around Mom's fears all the time when we lived on Nob Hill.

Standing on the street just before she left our apartment to go home, I asked Samantha, "Did you ever go to that online-pharmacy website I told you about? The one that shows which prescriptions interact bad with each other?"

"No, I haven't had time," Samantha answered.

"What about all your doctors? What if they're telling you conflicting advice? How do you know which one's right?"

"I guess I'll rely on my instinct."

"Are you sure you're ready to go back to school? There's only a few weeks left, and right now is more stressful than ever."

"Yes, Miguel. I *want* to go back."

My breaths began coming faster and faster, then I said, "But you might get a panic attack while you're in class. The nurse at school really isn't that great. What if—"

"Miguel, stop being such a worrier."

"How come we have to go this late at night?" I asked Jorge, as we by mistake got off one stop too soon at the West Oakland BART Station.

"I really want to surprise Aunt Shirley," Jorge said, while we continued talking about heading over to Aunt Shirley's house in Berkeley.

"Dude, this place scares me. Lots of bad stuff happens here, crack deals, robberies, car-jackings. Haven't there been something like eighty-five murders here in Oakland so far this year?"

"Wow, no kidding. Hey, I really got to go to the bathroom. Especially now that we've got to go all the way back to 12th Street Station to transfer to

Berkeley. We're going to have to wait around here all night."

"I want to go back home, Jorge."

"No way. We'll get there. This is something we *need* to do."

"What? Are you kidding me? Then this is some kind of lesson? That's what it is. You're trying to scare me, and I need to get over it. Right?"

"I never said anything about any lesson. We just have to go to Berkeley now. We've got to."

What we were doing made absolutely no sense to me. *Why* was it so important for Jorge and I to get over to Aunt Shirley's at around three in the morning? Normally, I never would have even been awake then. What's up with all this?

While leaving me all by myself in the outdoor station with only half its lights working, and waiting for the train to take us to Berkeley, a really strange, loud-yelling lady came walking up to me. I didn't know for sure if she was going to go past me, or stop to say something, but that's what she did. The lady stopped to talk directly to me. "Too late, too late. Too late for somethin' different," she screamed out right in my direction.

I totally didn't know what to say, so I didn't say anything. Her hair had more than just hair in it, like orange lint or something. Her face was dirty with a few scabs on it, although I shouldn't talk. And she was wearing clothes full of stains and smudges. "You too young, you don't know. Too late, too late for us all," she told me.

The woman kept looking at me, expecting me to answer her in some way. All I kept thinking was *how could Jorge have left me alone* with this strange woman? I still hadn't answered the lady.

"Too late, too late for us."

I shook my head like I was kind of agreeing with her, 'cause I didn't know what else to do. Then I almost felt obliged to repeat what she was saying, so she'd leave me alone. "Too late," I said in a way quieter voice right back to her.

"We all gonna die. Too late, too late to do anything 'bout it now. *Tooooooooooo* late," she told me.

What was she talking about? Was she just nuts? What was making her say, *too late* over and over again? When I was able to take a closer look at something other than her face I could see that she was wearing about six crosses with Jesus on them as necklaces hanging down her front. Each one was a different color and shape, but I could definitely tell they were all crucifixes. Again, when she looked into my eyes I shook my head to agree with whatever she was trying to tell me.

"The Lord gives, then He take away. Too late for nothin' else, too late for us all."

Too much of me was left wondering not only what that lady was trying to tell me, but how she got to be that way. By the time she had walked to the other end of the platform, I could see her look back at me as she ended up finding a faraway bench to sit on. It felt like she wanted me to help her, or at least make me understand her in some way. How could I have helped when I never knew anything about what the problem was? What exactly was it that it was too late for?

Above my head, the sign for the 12th Street/Oakland train began flashing, and within a few seconds I could see it moving down the tracks to me. Where was Jorge? If he didn't get back soon, we'd have to wait about another half hour or so for the next one to come. I didn't know what to do. I didn't know where to look for him. The train had now approached the platform where I was standing, but no one else was there to get on, just me. The lint-haired lady stayed on the bench yelling something to herself, and she continued staring only at me. I didn't think she was mad. She just looked at me, and I still felt sorry for her. I wondered what her life was like, and how totally different it must be from mine.

"Get on!" I heard from the distance.

I turned my head and could see Jorge running up the escalator towards the train. "Go!" he shouted out to me.

As I stepped aboard the train I could hear Jorge's loud footsteps pounding the pavement right behind me. Before you knew it we were both inside the train, and the woman on the bench was still looking through the window at me, while talking constantly at the very same time. Inside of me I felt such a sad feeling. So much of me wanted to understand her, except I had no idea how I could go about doing that.

At a fast speed the train left the station, and all I could feel was that I had let that lady down in such a huge way, because I couldn't figure anything out about her message to me. Maybe Jorge would know, I thought. "Jorge, the whole time you were gone there was a lady that came up to me. And she kept saying a bunch of stuff, except I didn't know what any of it meant. I think maybe she wanted me to help her."

"What was she saying?" he asked.

"Stuff about it's too late, too late for us all. What do you think she meant? Too late for what?"

"I have no idea."

"And she seemed like she was kind of poor, and maybe kind of crazy. I wanted to help her."

"Help her with what?"

"Help her with whatever she was trying to tell me about. Maybe if I could have understood her, she would have calmed down a little bit."

"Did she ever ask you to help her?"

"No, not really."

"Bro, if she never asked you for help, and you could never figure out what she was trying to tell you, what makes you think she wanted any help in the first place?"

"I don't know. But maybe I could have."

"Don't you think God made her that way for a reason? Why would you have anything to do with her purpose in life if she never asked for your help?"

"Maybe I really could have helped her though."

"Dude, you've got *your own* purpose. You've got your own life. It's not your place to tell other people what their purpose is, what their lessons are. You've got enough goin' on."

"I know that already."

"And, *you* ain't God."

"Duh, I know. Why did you say *that*?"

"If you're going to be telling everybody what their lessons are, then how the hell are they going to develop the strength they need to want to learn them themselves?"

"That's like what Aunt Shirley said about psychic people. She said that when you tell someone what their lessons are beforehand, then there's nothing about them that's going to make them *want* to change, and learn those lessons on their own. They just kick back and *expect*."

"If you know what they are beforehand, or someone tells you what they're going to be...there *won't be* any lessons. It's like they're automatically cancelled, or they come up a *whole* lot later, when you're not expecting them."

"I thought that was part of my own purpose. To help other people, to help them get over fear."

"Yeah. It probably is. To help people who *want* your help. People who don't want to change *won't*. People who feel there's nothing wrong with their lives will never change. It's unlikely they'll ever learn lessons either. That's their thing, not yours, not anyone else's. That's between them and God."

"I guess that's an important thing to know, or else you wouldn't be going on and on about all this."

"All I'm saying is that the life *you* live should be as full as it can be while you're still..."

Before Jorge could finish his sentence my dream ended, the nap on my Laz-E-Boy was over. It didn't take much to guess what Jorge's last word was going to be. Did he know something I didn't? Spending any time thinking about it anymore didn't happen because Aunt Shirley had arrived at my front door. "Open up, doll," she yelled out.

"Hey, A.S. What's up?" I said, while letting her into our apartment.

"No time to come in. It's already too late, too late for us to chat. That damn BART train took forever."

"That's OK, we'll make it on time."

"Another bomb threat. That really pisses me off."

"I thought those happen all the time."

"This time someone was mad because the trains always run late, way too late. Time's an illusion anyway and nobody gets it. Or maybe I still need to be a bit more patient myself."

Knowing that we still had plenty of time to get to the sandcastle-building contest at Aquatic Park, Aunt Shirley decided to take a moment to calm down a little as we got onto the jammed-full *J-Church* streetcar. And I guess it was seeing all those people who seemed to be mostly in couples on the streetcar that made Aunt Shirley start talking about relationships. "Elefterios and I are getting pretty cozy," she told me. "How would you feel if we decided to get married someday?"

"No way. Are you for real?"

"Well, maybe. You never know."

Part of me was real happy. The other part reminded me that this was what Aunt Shirley's destiny was waiting for, what seemed to be her very last lesson on earth, trusting someone. Rather than guessing any more about it, I thought I'd ask her, "What if you don't have anything after left to learn? I mean, I'm happy for you, for you both. But then, what's left?"

Aunt Shirley thought about that one for a moment, then said, "It makes me appreciate life all the more, every second that goes by. All the time I get to spend with you, that's what it's all about."

"So, you really trust Lefty?"

"Completely."

"Hey, that's so cool. Does this mean you'll be done soon?"

"Done? Gee, doll. Only God knows that for sure. If I spent any time thinking about what's left, what's ahead, I wouldn't be living my life now. Learning *that one* was a lesson in itself, let me tell you."

"How many times can a person be born, go to heaven, and be born again and again? I mean, what's the maximum? I forgot."

"You're too much, doll. I truly have no idea, I don't think there is a maximum number. People learn lessons when they're ready, when they want to. When they've learned all they want to, all that God has in store for them, they get to *stay* in heaven, I guess. I don't really know. I doubt if anyone does."

"Why don't you think up more things you'd want to learn. That would be a good idea, don't you think?"

"Maybe so. Who knows? Maybe, if this is the last time I'm here, and when it comes my time to go to heaven, maybe I'll like it so much I'll want to stay there."

"You mean if it's that nice, you won't *want* to come back?"

"I just don't know yet. Maybe there'll be a day when I can look back where I've been, and I'll say to myself, 'Been there, done that'."

"OK, then maybe I'll do that too."

"In the meantime, what's on your agenda this go 'round?"

"Um. Well, when you want to help a person, but they never wanted your help in the first place, is that kind of like a waste of time? That's what Jorge said to me when I dreamt about him last night."

"A waste of time? I think it's good that you want to help. *You* come first though. Focus on yourself, and people will learn from your example. By helping yourself, others will be helped."

"Oh, I like that one. That makes sense to me. That's just like the Boy Scouts or the Army or whichever one says, 'Be the best *you* can be'."

The way Aunt Shirley explained it made me understand even more of what Jorge was trying to teach me. For a real long time I thought the way I could thank God for all the good stuff He's done for me was to help other people, especially people who have fears. But Aunt Shirley and Jorge were right, God didn't put me on earth to be doing everyone else's bizness. After all, I can't be learning other people's lessons for them. They have to do that part on their own.

It's hard to imagine, but by the time Aunt Shirley and I got to the sandcastle-building contest we both decided that we'd rather do something else. "I want to be *doing* something not just watch," she said. I had heard her say this before. So we walked instead, to the end of Aquatic Park Pier, Ghirardelli Square, The Cannery, and all the way to Fisherman's Wharf.

Aunt Shirley seemed to always feel that she had to be *doing* something, and that watching someone else do something, didn't have much to do with her own purpose in life. Aunt Shirley told me that that's what I did sometimes. Once she called me "the kid who's always peeking through the fence of life, like some speck-tater."

I never knew for sure what a speck-tater was. I had the feeling it was somebody who wasn't doing their own thing. "I'm going to swim to Alcatraz someday, maybe that's what I'll train for," Aunt Shirley said out of nowhere. "One more goal to put on my list. That's all I need."

"But you *always* make your goals happen. It seems like you never let them stay undone."

"I figure if I'm going to take the time to write them down, I'd better end up doing them all, at least most of them."

"What if a person dies before they've done all the things they want to? Does that make them feel like a loser?"

"I wouldn't think so. Nobody's a loser. Anyone who makes it through life is a winner. Look at you. Anyone who sees you, doll, sees your strength. They know in a glance that you're exceptional, you're a winner, a champ. They may not know what E.B. is, but they've got to know that living with it ain't so easy."

"That's what you meant by learning from my example."

"You got it, pal. They're in awe. Instead of staring at you, they're acknowledging you and all your courage, lucky to be in the company of a first-class, Number 1 hero. Someone to emulate."

"Really?"

"Exacta-mundo, doll. Bark up your own tree. Toot your own horn. You're doin' it. You've got it goin' on. Keep helping *yourself*...and watch what happens."

CHAPTER TWENTY-ONE

Helping Mom move into her new, small and average in-between apartment on Vallejo Street ended up being a lot of fun, mainly because she made it that way. The in-between part was that it wasn't on Russian Hill and it wasn't really on Telegraph Hill either, it was in-between them both. Mom had planned out a few really cool contests for Samantha and I beforehand as we began to do the unpacking. Mom even promised that she'd give an extra special prize to the first one who could find the box with her Sarah McLachlan CDs in it. I could tell Samantha was having a totally good time. To her, it wasn't a chore at all. And it was giving us both a chance to hang out with my *newest-version* mom.

"Here you go, hon," Mom told Samantha, as she handed her the prize for finding the box with her favorite coffee in it, Peet's. The prize was the fifth *Harry Potter* book, that she had ordered from Amazon, a book Samantha really, really wanted to read.

"What do you want us to find next, Mom?"

"How about a little lunch first? You two certainly must be hungry by now. You've definitely earned it."

Neither one of us knew too much about this new neighborhood Mom had moved into. It was way less upscale than our old apartment on Nob Hill. Seeing that Mom didn't care as much about impressing people actually made me impressed. Her new apartment didn't really have a view of anything except for the neighbors across the street, and that seemed to be OK with her.

"Now, what would the two of you like?" Mom asked from the kitchen.

"You're going to *make* us something?" I asked.

"Sure. Why not? Unless you'd like to go out. What would you like to do, Samantha?"

"Either one is fine with me, I'm starved."

It was so good to hear that Samantha had an appetite again. She'd even put on some weight. She still didn't seem to be quite the same though.

"Miguel? What's your pleasure?"

"Go out. Show us what North Beach is all about."

"Done."

As we walked through the lawn-covered, rectangular-shaped park at Washington Square, I asked Mom about a really cool-looking, huge church there. "Can we go into that church, Mom? Or do we have to be another religion to do that?"

"No, anyone can enter, I'd imagine. I'd actually like to see it myself."

All three of us walked up the steps of this beautiful, old church that was more like a European cathedral to me. It's called Saints Peter & Paul. And even though it sounds like two separate churches, it's really just one. You know, like Sonny *and* Cher. Get it?

Mom was never really a religious person, except walking in seemed to make her kind of quiet, maybe respectful that the church was a holy place. "Can we sit in one of these benches for a while, just to look at all this stuff?"

"Of course we can, hon," Mom said in a whisper.

All the stained glass was awesome, with all those baby Jesus and Virgin Mary scenes on them. I didn't really know what they meant, but they were still cool. On the wooden benches with no graffiti carved in yet, we all three sat for a few minutes until Mom asked me and Samantha to stay there for a while so she could go do something. Really silently, Mom walked up to the front of the church to where a bunch of candles were burning. She looked so serious, like she was returning a way-overdue library book. She grabbed a long match and lit a fresh candle as I could see her whisper something when she looked up at the cross of Jesus. Then, when she was done, she put some money in the donation box.

When she walked back to us, I could see her wipe both her eyes with one of the aloe Kleenexes she'd pulled out of her purse. "Are you OK, Mom?" I asked.

"Yes, Miguel. I am. I was remembering someone who left much too soon. That's who I lit the candle for."

"Who was it you were thinking of, Mom?"

She paused for a while before deciding to tell me, "Shirley's little girl."

As we walked up what seemed like hundreds of the Filbert Steps to the top of Telegraph Hill, Samantha and I had to stop to catch our breath halfway up. At least that gave us the chance to admire all the pretty vines, ferns, gardens, and trees along the way. Mom had gone back to her apartment to make a phone call, and she said that Samantha and I could explore the neighborhood if we wanted to by ourselves. Something about the confused and curious way she looked made me feel for sure that Samantha was going to end up asking me about Aunt Shirley's baby girl. She stayed polite enough in front on Mom though to know not to have asked about it then.

When we reached the top, Samantha and I both had the same victorious-like feeling inside of us. Like we were on top of the world. From the kind of circular deck we were standing on, it was like a virtual tour of the bay, except this one was for real. All the way from the ocean and the Golden Gate Bridge on our left to the bay, the Bay Bridge, and the East Bay on our right. All the rest was smack in the middle, directly in front of us. Alcatraz, Marin County, Angel Island, Pier 39, Fisherman's Wharf, and lots of other touristy stuff I had been to before with Aunt Shirley, was in-between.

Coit Tower was cool looking, and I could tell that it was built a long time ago. "How old do you think this thing is?" I asked Samantha.

"I'm not sure. Maybe close to a century old, I don't know."

"I think they made it for some sort of dedication to somebody."

"A fireman, a fireman who died during the '06 earthquake. Would you mind if we sat down for a while? That walk up here made me tired."

"Sure. No problem. It's a good thing Mom gave me her cell phone. That way she can pick us up."

"Your mom's so nice."

"Yeah, she's hell'a cool. She never used to be able to drive by herself though. We used to always just have to take limos and cabs everywhere. She used to be too afraid to drive, too afraid of everything."

"I remember she'd said that. Your mother said she's changed a lot."

"A whole lot. Mom said the thing that helped her the most was talking to people who were just like her, afraid."

"Just like you and I do."

"That's exactly the way it works, it's a two-way street. Aunt Shirley told me that helping other people get over what you've gotten over actually ends up helping yourself, too. It heals *you*."

"When you teach me about fear versus faith, do you feel you're healing yourself? Making yourself better?"

"I think so. Especially 'cause you said you wanted help to get over your fears. If you didn't ask, then it would be a waste of time for us both. At least that's what Jorge told me."

"Your brother?"

"Yeah. I mean, he told me that when I had a dream about him. You can only help people who want to be helped. There's actually a ton of people out there who need help, but they don't think they do. So, they won't ever change until they want to. Get it?"

"Yes, that makes sense. Then, your mother must have wanted to change."

"I guess so. Maybe it was after having to live in L.A. that made her want to change."

"Why L.A.? What's wrong with it?"

"Oh my God. Don't ever ask Aunt Shirley that question. She'll go on for hours telling you exactly why L.A. sucks so much. She calls it a city without soul."

In a real hesitant way, Samantha finally got to the question I thought she would have asked me long before. "Your aunt had a baby that died?"

"Well, that's a real long story, Samantha. And, that was from a real long time ago."

"Is she still sad about that?"

"Deep down, I think she's spent her whole life being sad about that. Even though she's a real optimistical person, I'm pretty sure there's a real sad part to her that she never lets anyone ever see. Not even me."

"I get sad sometimes, too. My doctor refers to it as depression."

"What is it that makes you sad the most?"

"Sometimes I think my life will go by, and I won't ever be really happy."

"I know what you mean. Check it out though, guess what I figured out? *Nobody's* ever really happy. That's not what life's all about. That's a made-up thing, for sure."

Just as I told Samantha that, Mom's cell phone started ringing. When I looked at its display, all it showed was *Private Number*. "Hello, Mom?" I answered.

Before speaking right away, Aunt Shirley said, "Miguel? Is that you? What's up, mister?"

"Hey, A.S. I've got Mom's cell phone 'cause she's picking us up pretty soon. Me and Samantha."

"Oh. That's smart, doll. Your mother just called me, and left a message. I don't have her new number at home though."

"Uh, oh. I don't know it either."

"She said she needed to talk to me. About something important. Do you have any idea what's up?"

Since maybe I only had a clue why Mom had called Aunt Shirley, I figured that I wouldn't be lying, so I said, "Gosh, I don't know."

"She sounded a little upset. Not mad, upset."

"Well, how about if I tell Mom to call you back when I call her to pick us up? Oh, but wait, I have a question for you. Actually I'll ask it, and you tell Samantha the answer. OK? She's right here."

"Sure. Shoot."

"Is life all about getting to be happy?"

Aunt Shirley began to laugh as I soon as I handed the phone over to Samantha. With both our ears pressed to the listening part, I heard Aunt Shirley say, "Sam? Are you there, sweetie?"

"Yes. Hi, Aunt, I mean, Shirley. It's me."

"Hey, doll. How's it going? I know what that loon is getting at. Lessons, lessons, lessons. In my opinion, that's the first, second, and third reason why we're here. All you can do with happiness is, take it whenever, and wherever, you can find it. Why?"

"Miguel was just telling me that being happy shouldn't necessarily be the main goal in life."

"I'd have to agree with that one, doll. To me, true happiness is something you only see in the movies. Especially the old ones."

"Told you so," I yelled out.

After Samantha was done talking to Aunt Shirley, we just sat a little longer on one of the cement benches that looked out to everywhere. Samantha got to reserve up her energy by staying in one place, and out loud we began listing in a row a bunch of lessons we thought we've learned in life. The biggies all kind of had to do with learning to get over all kinds of fear. Samantha's even the one who taught me not to be afraid of getting better grades. "You're smart, Miguel. What's wrong with getting *A's*?" she had asked me. So, I figured what the hell. Maybe I'd go for it.

When Mom came to pick us up, I'd told her that Aunt Shirley called on her cell number. That's when Mom realized that she had forgotten to give Aunt Shirley her new home one. I can tell that they hadn't talked in a while. Then out of nowhere, Samantha asked Mom, "Mrs. Estes, do—"

"Sharon. Please call me Sharon."

"Do you think that learning lessons is what life's all about?"

"Learning lessons. What a very sophisticated question that one is. You must've been speaking to my sister."

"Yes, I did. Just for a little while."

"Well, I'm ashamed to say that it took me forever. But having learned from experience, I'd have to say 'yes.' That *is* what life seems to be all about."

After just a little bit more, Samantha asked Mom to take her back to her house 'cause she was starting to get a headache. She'd been having more and more of those lately, and the medicine the doctor had been giving her wasn't working too good anymore. We dropped Samantha off in Pacific Heights, and I made sure to thank her for making my day so much fun.

Since Mom's new apartment had this comfortable futon in it, and since it was already unpacked, and since I had actually gotten kind of tired, too, I asked ahead of time if I could take a nap on it. When we got back to Mom's apartment I went right to sleep. It seemed like I was meant to.

Immediately Jorge was in my dreams. As usual we were in a real familiar place, and he had something he wanted to tell me.

"Lifetimes on earth are very short," Jorge said.

"Especially back then. All these kids that are buried here. They hardly had a chance to do *anything* in life."

"Not just back then, now. Forever. Life's *always* been short."

"But some people get to be like ninety or even a hundred. They used to have pictures of people over a hundred on the *Today* show nearly every day. Seriously."

"That's nothing. Since the world began, one hundred years, or even two hundred's like nothing. Hardly anything at all."

"Yeah, right. Like anybody's ever going to live to be two hundred."

"Let's keep looking. This time, for the *youngest*. Let's see who the youngest person who's buried here is."

I couldn't understand why Jorge chose for us to do that next, but what the hell. Spending time with him was always something that made me happy, even though we were once again inside the Virginia City cemetery in northern Nevada. Together we hiked up and down the different deserted hills there. And again I thought about the *buried-in-certain-groups* thing. "Do babies have to be Masons, or Odd Fellows, or Knights of Pythias too?" I asked.

"I'm not sure. Let's see," Jorge answered.

He and I walked around more and more, to all the different parts we had never gotten to before. There were babies buried almost everywhere. This was something that never made sense to me, even though I noticed this before, the very first time Jorge and I had been to this cemetery. Why would God make a baby born if it never gets to be at least a teenager? Maybe I should have been more grateful, when I turned fourteen, to have even made it that far.

"Holy sh—, Jorge, this one was only two-days old. What's up with that? That's not very long at all."

"No kidding? Two days."

"I don't get why they had a headstone and a grave for a baby that was hardly *ever* alive."

"Out of respect, I guess. Although this baby was only alive for a couple of days, it was still alive. Life's short. Getting the chance to live at all is still a privilege, an opportunity to learn at least something."

"What can a two-day old baby learn? It probably didn't even get to learn English yet."

"I don't know. I guess the baby wasn't ready to learn lessons. Maybe it had second thoughts about being born. Maybe the baby dying so soon was, in actuality, a lesson for the parents."

"Hey, you know what? Since you know all this stuff, do you know what's going on with my friend Samantha? She's not doing very well, and the doctors haven't figured any of it out. Do you know anything?"

"I'm not a doctor. I do know one thing though, no one may ever know. Maybe that's the way it's supposed to be."

"*Someday* they'll know, right?"

"Maybe, maybe not. Most of what life's all about, no one will ever know. Life's short. Learn what you can, and make the most of your life while you've got one."

Of all the times Jorge had been in my dreams, I'd always been too scared to wonder about a certain question. This time, I had the courage to ask, "Jorge, how old am I going to get to be? How long will I end up living?"

Without saying "goodbye," and before answering my question, Jorge was gone. I woke up somehow knowing that something big was happening nearby. "I've waited all my life for you to forgive me, Shirley," I heard.

"It was all meant to happen exactly the way it did. Of course I forgive you. Cecilia wasn't here that long, maybe she wasn't supposed to be. I'll never forget her. She brought so much meaning to my life, to yours."

"I wish we had this talk a long time ago."

"You didn't learn courage until now. Cecilia helped you learn it, she put something inside your head, and it stayed there until it was ready to come out. You never did anything wrong, how can I possibly hold you responsible."

"I don't know what to say."

On the futon in the living room I pretended to go back to sleep, thinking they'd come walking in at any moment. I never did say "hi" or "bye" to Aunt Shirley, I just stayed pretending...thinking about her little baby Cecilia. A girl who was only alive for a little while, a girl whose short life left lessons so many years after. Cecilia's life mattered a whole bunch, no matter how old she ended up being.

CHAPTER TWENTY-TWO

As we sat together on the #80 Golden Gate Transit bus, headed towards the Golden Gate Bridge, Samantha said, "I'm beginning to feel exhausted, Miguel. I don't think a long walk's going to be possible today. I'm sorry. Can we get off at the next stop?"

"Sure," I told her.

Seeing that Samantha had no energy was not news to me. Maybe the best thing to do was to just relax, I thought. When I walked up to the bus driver and asked him to stop at the very next one, he said OK, and let us off right in the middle of the Presidio.

I don't know what it was that made me want to go to a certain place there so badly. Without thinking too much about it, I asked Samantha, "How about if we head up there? We could sit under one of those big Eucalyptus trees, and do nothing but chill."

"That's a *cemetery*, Miguel."

"Yeah, I know. Check it out though, Jorge and I do it all the time. Well, you know, in my dreams."

"Do what?"

"Hang out in cemeteries. It'll be cool. I want to see what the view's like from up there."

It wasn't that the hill we were walking on was the steepest, but we still took our time getting up it after Samantha finally agreed to go to this cemetery with me. We ended up sitting under some other kind of huge tree with lots of big hanging branches, and the view from there was like one of the best I'd ever seen. There was no fog at all, so the view we saw seemed like it kept going on forever. Everything about being up there seemed to be so magical. "Wait 'til I tell my parents about this. They'll never believe that you and I actually spent time in a cemetery," Samantha said.

"I think it's the best. All these people buried here. It makes me wonder what they were like, what kind of lives they had."

"And, these people were all in the military at one time."

"Or they were family of military people."

"My father's very fond of the military. He and my mother argue about that sometimes."

"Aunt Shirley is way against any kind of violence. She says the people who are in it, the military, are pretty brave though. But, she can't believe wars still exist. And even though she's one herself, Aunt Shirley says Americans are the worst. She says that too many Americans see war like a football game, one team versus another. Like some huge competition."

"But there's no prize after any war, just corpses. That's what my mother tells my father anyway."

"Samantha, do you ever think about what it's like when a person dies?"

"No, not really. I try not to. It scares me too much. Even being here is scary to me."

"I used to be that way too, until I started having dreams with Jorge in those cemeteries. Now it just makes me curious. I still get afraid when I think about me dying."

"I do too, Miguel. So can we please talk about something else?"

Sometimes I could never figure out what made me so obsessed with dying, especially when I'd never really even been like that before.

Samantha and I began to compare and contrast the lives of the Olsen twins, and as we did, Samantha seemed to relax a whole lot more. And then, for some reason, she wasn't so eager to leave. There was something especially calming about this place that we'd both noticed. Was this the same type of feeling dead people in cemeteries experienced after they had died? Or were we both just imagining this?

Watching the massive cargo ships pass under the bridge in the distance, coming into the bay, while others were going out to sea, made me ask Samantha, "Do you think you've gone to all the places you wanted to go to in life?"

"Yes, sometimes I do. I've traveled a lot with my family. I seem to like being here now, right here in San Francisco."

"Once in a while I wonder if I've been everywhere I ever wanted to go, or if I've done most everything I've ever wanted to do."

"You're life's pretty eventful, Miguel."

"It seems like I've learned a whole lot about life, why we're here, and stuff like that. Except, having more fun without having to learn lessons is what I'd like to do more of in my life."

"What you've already tackled is the toughest part though. Didn't your Aunt Shirley tell you that everyone *chooses* or *doesn't choose* to learn their lessons? It's your choice, and you decided to go for it. I think that's the best."

"I always keep thinking that something better's going to come along. Like a whole chunk of time is going to come to me where I don't have to learn *anything*, it'll just be so easy."

"I'd like to have that for myself someday."

"I'm not so sure that time will ever happen though. Sometimes I feel that I know more than most kids my age should have to know, and I've had to think about tons of stuff that only grownups should be thinking about."

"Maybe you're really older than fourteen. That's the way I feel all the time, Miguel. I've always had the feeling like, in some ways, I'm an older person living inside a thirteen-year olds' body. I've never felt like a normal kid. I've never actually felt like a kid at all, ever."

As soon as Samantha said that, I looked over at her, and for the first time I witnessed exactly what she had always been feeling. For the first time I knew I was seeing someone who was much, much older than the person I had known all the time before. It wasn't like Samantha was all of the sudden a stranger to me, it's like we were both somehow older than our age. This is the same way I had always felt about Jorge when he was still alive. What did this mean? And why was I just starting to see Samantha this way?

Whatever the reason was, I was glad to discover one more way the two of us had something unique in common. Samantha was starting to feel like a sister to me. Maybe she was even some kind of replacement for Jorge who had left me, sort of like a sibling exchange. I enjoyed this feeling a lot. Samantha and I had never had any fights the way Jorge and I always used to. It's strange, and meant to be at the same time, that I had had Khadijah as my nurse, then Mom's husband let her go. And then after Dad got custody of me again, he rehired Khadijah. Without her, I probably never ever would have gotten to know Samantha. The way God makes everything happen is something that will amaze me for the rest of my life, I thought.

I could tell Samantha was getting even more tired, and out of nowhere, she told me she needed to take a nap 'cause her blood sugar energy level was so low. It made me feel real strange to see her put her head down on the grassy knoll full of graves, close her eyes, and fall asleep right there in front of me, while we're both still in the Presidio cemetery overlooking the bay. I saw this as the perfect time for me to do something I hadn't done in a very, very long time. I decided to ask God for some answers.

Taking a walk through the tombstones was the proper thing to do while I let Samantha sleep peacefully. Knowing that she wouldn't be able to hear me, I quietly began out loud.

"Dear God,

How's it going? What I learned today is that I'm really grateful to have Samantha as my best friend. I don't think I need to ask You this, but I'm supposed to know her for some reason, right? Never mind, duh. That's like a no-brainer. I think she's sort of like the sister I never had from the beginning, a pretend *from-birth* kind of sister. Anyway, thanks for making us know each other now. Samantha even likes talking to homeless people, just like I do.

I kind of need to know something now though. When is she going to get better? I don't know what to think about that one. I had a weird feeling inside. And, as You probably kind of already know, I still feel guilty about Miguelito. You know, that I didn't do enough, that I didn't do my best to help him. I kind of feel responsible for all that. Aunt Shirley keeps telling me that we're only responsible for ourselves in life. Is that true by the way?

Everything else in life is OK. My health has been pretty good. I'm still not so sure what's up with this new doctor I've got. I don't have to spend that much time with him, so maybe that's all right. I know I'm only supposed to tell the truth, except I haven't told anyone about how mean Dr. Rosenzweig is. Maybe he just happens to be having totally bad days on the days when I have to see him.

But God, You know what? I think I need to know something else, too. What is it Samantha's supposed to learn from me? Or is there something I'm supposed to learn from her? Or did You plan it to be a two-way street? I kind of have the feeling this is supposed to be something I need to know sooner than later, one more really important lesson. Am I right?

Samantha's still sleeping right now. Can You believe it? She decided to take a nap right here in this cemetery. I guess when a person's that tired, they got to find a place to sleep wherever they can. Even though Samantha said this place scares her, it seems like a peaceful and beautiful place to both of us. Is this sort of what heaven's like? Can You please tell me? Or am I supposed to keep guessing? Or just be surprised when it's my turn to get there?

I don't really need to know that part. I was just wondering, so never mind. All I want to say again is thanks. And, if there's something more I should be doing, please let me know what it is, and be specific if

You can, 'cause I'm mostly bad at having to read Your mind.
Take care, God. I'll talk to You soon.
Love,
Miguel"

I had no idea what kind of answers God was going to give me. When I walked back over to where Samantha had fallen asleep, she was gone. I hadn't even realized that I had walked that far away from her. It frightened me a lot. Where did she go? "Samantha, Sam," I started yelling out. I began running all around the area where we had been hanging out all alone. How could this have happened? I wasn't gone very long at all.

Worrying about what could have happened to Samantha was making me more and more sick as each second passed that I didn't know where she was. "Samantha, where are you?" I cried out.

In the distance, it seemed like I was maybe able to see her or someone who happened to look like her. The girl I could see was standing in front of some grave. "Samantha, is that you?" I yelled out.

The girl turned around and looked over at me. She didn't say a word. She was staring right at me, but didn't seem to recognize me. I began running towards her, and that seemed to have scared her too much. It *was* Samantha. What was she doing? Why was she in this spot? "Samantha, it's me, Miguel. Don't be frightened."

Then she seemed to realize it was me. But I still had no idea what was going on. Why was Samantha acting this way? "Miguel, I was so confused. I'm frightened. Where were you?"

"You fell asleep. I just stepped away for a few minutes."

In a real foggy-like way, Samantha pointed to the headstone she had been standing in front of and asked me, "Who's this?"

"I don't know."

"I remember now. I did sleep for a while, didn't I?"

"Yes, duh. You fell totally asleep. That's what scared me so much. You were gone, you walked away after I left you alone while you were asleep."

"I had a dream. That's what it was. It was so strange. I was, I mean, it's me, but it was someone else. I was a different person. A woman, a white woman...from France."

"Get out."

"Yes, Miguel. A white woman, and I was...with my husband."

"Your *husband*? It's your imagination. I have really weird dreams too, sometimes."

"No, that's just it. Even though I was asleep, it was too real. Something about this was true. I loved this man, he was my husband…no, he was going to be my husband, however he had to go to a war before we were able to be married."

"What? What war?" Was she joking about all this?

With a total serious look on her face, Samantha said, "World War II. He was sent to Europe. That's where he was killed."

"I get it now. You probably had this dream 'cause that's what we're studying in history class. We have a test on World War II next week."

"No," Samantha said. "This was real. This happened."

"Samantha, get serious. There's no way."

"I can't talk about this anymore…it's scaring me too much. Let's go, Miguel."

"OK, sure."

"Being here gives me the creeps. I want to go home."

I totally agreed with Samantha. Getting out of the cemetery was exactly what we needed to do next. Immediately before we stepped away though, something made me look down at the headstone Samantha had been standing in front of all that time. I didn't know what made me need to pay attention to it in the first place. It seemed to be glued to the inside my head the whole time as we walked down the hill to catch the bus back towards the Marina, back near our school.

Since Samantha lived so close to school, she decided she felt well enough to walk back to Jackson Street where she lived. "Are you sure you're feeling OK, Samantha?" I asked her.

"Yes, Miguel. I feel fine now. If you want to study later on, over the phone with me, call, OK?"

"Yeah, that'll be cool. I totally don't get anything we're doing now in Math anyway."

Samantha and I said "goodbye." And as I saw her walking up Fillmore Street, all I could think about was the time we'd just spent among the graves in the Presidio cemetery on the hill. What a nutty thing to have been hanging out there, when there were way more fun things we could have been doing together.

It was nearly six o'clock and Dad still hadn't gotten home. Khadijah had made my Spaghetti-O's dinner for me ahead of time, so I just heated it up all by myself. But somehow, something kept telling me to check my e-mail. Dad had always told me that I wasn't allowed to logon until all my homework was finished, except this was just something I felt I had to do. So, I figured I'd take a chance.

When I signed on, all I could see was a bunch of junk. 24 e-mails had come in. 22 of them had *Viagra* spelled a ton of wrong ways in the subject line. AOL says they've got good SPAM filters, but they totally don't. An e-mail from Marhsall was there. I ended up reading his first. It ended up being way too boring though. Marshall always talks about himself the whole time anyway.

Since Dad hadn't gotten home yet, I typed in *Jerome P. Gustafson, PVT* into the Google search box, and in only two seconds I found a link I ended up going to immediately.

It was an archived, online obituary for this guy with an old, black-and-white photograph on the very top of the page. As I read about this man, the name I'd gotten from the headstone at the cemetery, it said that he had been killed in Italy during World War II. The photo caption read,

> *Private J.P. Gustafson alongside his fiancée, Yvette Desliens, three weeks before their intended nuptials.*

CHAPTER TWENTY-THREE

"*'That these dead shall have not died in vain,' is the way in* which President Lincoln stated it in his Gettysburg Address," Mrs. Morales, my history teacher, told me in our private, after-class conversation.

"So, that's why it's called San Francisco National Cemetery," I said to her.

"Yes, his address actually led to the National Cemeteries Act being passed by Congress in 1863."

"It's all for war-people?" I asked.

"For veterans and members of their families," Mrs. Morales said.

"Were there veterans from a bunch of wars buried there?"

"Yes, Miguel. Wars spanning three centuries."

"That includes World War II, doesn't it?"

"Yes, Miguel. It does."

"Even people who were really killed somewhere not in America? Like maybe in Italy?"

"Yes, the bodies were transported here to San Francisco for a proper military burial."

After talking with my teacher, I became more and more curious, even though I should have been spending time studying harder for this horrible, rotten Math test I still had to take. On our lunch break I went over to the Marina library to log onto AOL Anywhere, so I could look up one more thing. The obituary I'd looked at at home said "funeral services pending." So, I thought I'd do another search to find out more about this man whose name I had remembered from the cemetery.

I had little time to find what I was looking for, although I ended up not needing much. Right off the bat I found something about this man, Private Gustafson. Something that talked about him being buried in the National Cemetery in San Francisco, the same one Samantha and I were at in the Presidio. This confirmed that the name I had seen on the headstone was the exact same one I had found information about on the Internet.

Clint Adams

Samantha fever was too high for her to come to school, so she and I never got to talk about the stuff I'd discovered. Something inside my gut told me I was absolutely right. What Samantha had was no ordinary dream. Maybe parts, or all, of what she was telling me was totally the truth.

Since I now had a couple of minutes before having to be in my next class, I decided to check my e-mail from the library computer. There was only one in my Inbox, and it was from Samantha.

Dear Miguel,

I hope you did well on the Math test today. Mr. Porter said I can take it tomorrow after school if I'm well enough to go in then. You'd be so proud of me today. I began doing something I've been wanting to do forever. I was all caught up with my studies, so I decided to read *Harry Potter and the Order of the Phoenix*, Book Five, the one your mom had given me. I love it. Are you sure you don't want to read it when I'm done? I know you don't like to read. I have the feeling you'd really enjoy this book.

Are you glad I'm progressing with all those new activities I wrote down on my *To Do* list? By the way, has studying ever been on any of your *To Do* lists? I really wish I was able to have gone to school today, because so much of me is feeling so incredibly good about myself, about my life. So much of me feels like a new person, Miguel. I feel stronger, even though I'm so listless these days.

Now I'm doing what you've always done. Now I thank God every day for helping me to become such a strong person, a person who's so close to living without any fear at all. My whole life seems revitalized, like a brand new me. What I thank God for most is that I met you and became your friend. I know that in my entire life I will never meet anyone who loves people as much as you. Nor will I ever meet anyone who's as positive and optimistic about life as you.

Unfortunately though, what you warned me about, happens to be coming true. Friends and even some cousins of mine have become jealous of me simply because of my new strength, because I now choose to live my life without fear. It's a shame, but thanks to you I understand it all. If you hadn't explained it to me prior, I would have thought that I had done something wrong. Or would have felt obliged to feel guilty over having done something I never did in the first place. I know you know what I mean. These people have chosen to treat me poorly, with disrespect. Now I know I deserve better. I deserve to know only people who treat me the same way I treat them. I can't do anything about the fact that I am changing and they have chosen not to. Having you in my life makes up for all of them put together.

Thank you for not being scared of my power, my power to be me, my power to change, my power to move on, and my power to be unafraid of anything.

Thank you for helping me become so strong, Miguel. It makes me feel so happy and proud that you are my one, true, best friend.

All my love, Samantha

In the time I was reading Samantha's e-mail more had come in. None of them were readable because I began crying so hard. Never before had I felt so many feelings all at once, feelings that took over my entire, blemished body.

"Are you all right, son?" a stranger asked, while running up to me.

It took me a while to get the words out, but eventually I was able to say, "I'm fine. Do...you...know where the bathroom is?"

The concerned man pointed halfway down the library hallway to the right of the reference desk, before he also asked, "Are you sure?"

I nodded *yes* and ran as fast as I could to get to the bathroom. As soon as I got in, I locked the door and stood in front of the mirror. Samantha's e-mail was still so very fresh in my head. Of course all my thoughts were about her. When I looked at my blistery face staring back at me at that moment, all I could be was proud of myself, proud of whatever part I'd played in Samantha's massive transformation. I felt so lucky to have had anything to do with the positive changes she's experienced. It was like the most perfect feeling I could have ever imagined, just like a day without blisters.

There was one thing Samantha got kind of wrong though. She should have been thanking herself as well. After all, Samantha's the one who wanted to change, she's the one who sought out help, and she's definitely the one who made it happen. Realizing that Samantha's the one who made all this happen also made me believe and accept that she had just, in a period of only a few months, learned *the* lesson of her lifetime, to be afraid of nothing.

By the time I returned to school, I could hear the bell ringing. It was almost time for my last class of the day. But something about me felt like such an outsider, an outsider with some serious questions. Part of me was beginning to understand why I had always felt so different from all the other kids. I had always thought in an obvious way it was 'cause I had E.B. and everything that goes with that. I was totally wrong.

Over and over, I thought, why was I in school learning about things that didn't even come close to the importance of all the lessons that come directly from life? From the life God has given us? Without having heard it come out of Samantha's mouth, I still would have thought I was nuts for having felt so old on my insides. I had always felt like I knew things that most other kids would never know about 'til all the way when they'd become old people.

This is the exact same way I had always felt about Aunt Shirley, too. Like even though she was barely thirty, and acted like a kid most of the time, she was still the oldest person I had ever known. Somehow to me, on the inside, it seemed like Aunt Shirley was the oldest person alive on earth.

And now, Samantha had also learned that she was a really, old person too on the inside. Being proud of Samantha, and being proud of myself, were seeming to come from the very same, one feeling. Never ever, at all before, had I experienced someone *getting it* so completely. It was like all those lessons about fear I had learned from Aunt Shirley were all rolled into one...and Samantha *got it*. Samantha learned it. Samantha passed the test with flying colors. She'd fulfilled her purpose in life.

While sitting in my last class of the day I observed my teacher, Ms. Chatterjee, very carefully. What feeling did she get inside the minute she realized that her students finally understood the biggest lesson she had to teach? Like on the very last day of the school year? Whatever feeling it was I imagined, it still couldn't have felt sadder than what I was feeling about Samantha. I couldn't think of anymore she needed to learn from me.

Although everyone else on my school bus was busy talking about a bunch of stuff, I stayed by myself and said nothing...until Marshall Glickman jumped up on right before it was ready to leave. "Yo, Miguel. Sup?" he said, while almost landing on top of me as he hopped into the seat.

"Hey, Marshall," I answered back.

"What's up with F.A.A.T., homey? I heard it won't exist no more, ever since you got busted."

"I didn't get busted. Mr. Lau just felt that since some parents didn't seem to like it too much, we shouldn't have it anymore."

"Bummer, dude. It was a cool idea. You know what? I never told you this, I really joined it so I could hookup with more chicks."

"Oh, I see."

"That fear-thing your aunt kept telling us about was a major bore, a massive yawn. Whatever."

"Some people don't think that, Marshall. I definitely don't. Samantha doesn't."

"What's up with her anyway? Is she really dyin'?"

After being completely unable to believe what Marshall'd just said, I asked, "Who told you that?"

"Everybody. I heard it from a bunch of people. The word's out. Total bummer."

"Samantha's *not* dying, Marshall."

"Dude, I—"

"And whoever told you that is a moron, a total dumb ass."

Marshall and I had virtually nothing more to say to each other after that. He got off in Noe Valley, way before I did, so I had time to let my anger pass by. It never did though. Samantha may have been tired with fevers, and everybody knew something was wrong with her, but why did all these dumb ass students think Samantha was dying? I hate them. They're so mean. I hate them all.

Everyone I had to look at on my way home after where the bus dropped me off made me mad. Everything before had been going so perfectly. I was feeling so absolutely great about me, my life, and about Samantha. All it took was one jerk to screw it all up. Why does God do this? Just when things were going in the most excellent direction, He made this happen. Even by the time I opened the door to my apartment, I couldn't tell who I was more mad at, Marshall or God. I had been mad for so many years that God gave me E.B., and every day I did my very best to understand that He did this for some reason, some reason that I knew I'd probably never be able to identify for sure, for the rest of my life.

Before I was able to get my apartment door open, Dad was right there on the other side opening it for me. He was so startled to see my face the way it was. My face must have looked just like his when he was in prison for that whole time. Mine didn't end up changing for at least one or two more hours.

After another hour or so after that, I came out of my room and Dad asked me, "How are you doing?"

"Better. It's definitely not true though. I was mainly mad 'cause it had been such a perfect day, with a bunch of perfect things happening."

"Oh, I can certainly understand, Miguel. Especially since it all has to do with Samantha."

"Not just her, Dad. Everything was like all perfect for me too."

"Wow, a double whammy. Every time I've ever experienced perfection of any kind, I've always had some sort of letdown immediately after. It's almost a natural occurrence."

"Seriously? So I should have known that that perfect feeling wasn't going to last forever."

"Perhaps so. What I learned was to never again think of anything as being *perfect*. On the other hand, the most perfect moment I've had in recent years was being able to see you again, after being gone for so long."

Talking to Dad made everything seem a little bit better. My huge, raging anger was mostly gone, and I was back to my normal mood. Still nowhere near that perfect feeling I had felt from before. Maybe that's just the way it goes. If normal was what I felt most of the time, I guess I should have been grateful for just that. What my normal mood was, after I thought about it for a bit, wasn't too shabby after all.

Something Dad had said also stuck with me, too. When he had said that the time he spent with me was perfect, I also not only felt that same way about him, I felt that way about Samantha too. And one more person, Jorge. Sometimes I spent a lot of time wondering what my life would have been like if he hadn't died. I know that thinking like that is way out of line 'cause that's what God *made* happen. I wonder anyway. Although Jorge came to me so often in my dreams, and in them we always seemed to be in cemeteries together, I still couldn't ever force myself to do something I'd been avoiding forever.

"This feels like we're going to my doctor's," I told Aunt Shirley.

"I know. Colma's right next to San Bruno. But no doctor today, doll. Are you positive you're up for this?"

"Yep, I'm sure."

As we got closer to the cemetery where Jorge was buried, I was still a little nervous. Even the weather around us was unsure, as it began raining hard from a clear blue sky.

"Are you sure you're sure?" Aunt Shirley asked me.

"Um, yeah. I definitely want to go see him."

Everything about Colma and Daly City was so plain to me. It all looked the same, nothing special about it at all. Plain, average, dull, generic, and uninteresting. All the way up to where the road took us to go to the cemetery, lined with cookie-cutter houses that have rock-garden front yards, nothing had changed. All basic and blah. Blah-blah-blah.

"What are you thinking, doll?" Aunt Shirley asked me.

"This is just kind of weird for me. It's like I wanted to forget about this place after…"

"Think about it though, doll. When you're with Jorge in your dreams, you both seem to find cemeteries so interesting."

"That's just it. They were interesting because Jorge was *with* me. That's what made them all interesting and fun. I got to be with Jorge again."

Something inside my stomach felt like it was going to explode. I guess Aunt Shirley could tell that I was feeling something way weird and queasy, so she asked, "Tell me the absolute truth, doll. You really want to do this? Or skip it?"

"Aunt Shirley, it's just that I like to remember Jorge the way he is in my dreams. Maybe it'll spoil it if we go inside here, and see that it's really him that's buried in the ground. Will it end up canceling out my cool dreams altogether?"

"Gee, Miguel. I don't know."

"If I see that grave, it means he's really gone." Then it took only one more second to ask Aunt Shirley, "Would it be OK if we go back home? Like right now?"

"You got it, hon. I'll hang a u-eee right here, pronto."

CHAPTER TWENTY-FOUR

"Guess what I do now whenever they stick needles in me," Samantha said.

I shrugged my shoulders up, showing my astonishment at Samantha's creativity. I couldn't even imagine how she'd ever be able to cope with this one.

"I pretend they're vaccines. I believe that the fever-reducers, pain relievers, minerals, and vitamins they're giving me are going annihilate whatever I've got. I think of Jonas Salk, Baruch Blumberg, and John F. Enders."

"*Hel-lo*. I'm not Dr. Phil, here. Who the hell are they?"

"Oh, I'm sorry. I forgot. These men invented vaccines for polio, hepatitis, and the measles, respectively."

Even being sick in the hospital, Samantha was still at least ten times smarter than me. Oh well. It made me glad to see that she was using her mind to its fullest potentiality.

"Recalling them, and believing deep down that these shots are helping me, made me unafraid of them. I'm no longer scared of needles."

"Wow. You go, Samantha."

"By the way, can you cross that off my list, please. It's over there in the middle drawer."

As I reached way over to the get Samantha's *To Do* list, something fell out of my jacket pocket, hitting the floor with a loud clunk.

"What's that, Miguel?"

"Holy Sh— I almost forgot. I'm supposed to give you this. It's my watch that doesn't tell time. Aunt Shirley had given it to me when I was in the hospital once."

"Doesn't tell time? Well, I'll have to thank her for it...although I don't have a clue."

"No, Jorge said I was supposed to give it to you. You know, from my dreams. And he said that too, that you wouldn't know what it means. He said you'll know later. Anyway, it's totally special to me, so I want you to have it."

Because Dad had to work his new nighttime job at U.C.S.F., he wasn't able to join us. Mr. and Mrs. Austin were coming over to pick me up, so just the three of us could have dinner together. Samantha was still in her room at the hospital. And since she was asleep a lot of the time, the doctor suggested that her parents leave for a while to get refreshed.

Samantha's mom and dad told me they had something they wanted to tell me. I had no idea what that was, and they were two people I had never really known too well, so it was a good chance to see if they knew anything more about Samantha than I did. Going to whichever restaurant didn't seem to matter too much, 'cause it was mostly Samantha that stayed on my mind. I was still excited that they were taking me to the Carnelian Room. It's on the 52nd floor of the Bank of America building in the financial district.

I had to get kind of dressed up extra fancy. So Khadijah, when she was over in the afternoon, picked out something real nice for me to wear, my black cotton slacks that go with my black cotton jacket. Sometimes it's kind of hard to look classy with all these bandages I have to wear all the time. But that's the way it goes. If this place has a dress code, I was sure hoping it included gauze strips and surgical wrappings.

Just like clockwork, right at five-forty-five on the dot, Samantha's parents were buzzing me from downstairs, just like they said they would. I figured they didn't care too much about getting to see Dad's and my apartment, because compared to their huge mansion-ish-sized house in Pacific Heights, mine probably didn't seem so special. So, I ended up walking downstairs and meeting them there, outside our building.

The minute I saw them both there, waiting for me to come down to them, they looked way different from when I had seen them before. They were *totally* dressed up, real proper-like and fancy. Without thinking too much beforehand, I asked, "Are you guys going to the Opera afterwards or something?"

"Oh my. No, Miguel. We always try to look our best," Samantha's mom said, with tons of diamonds hanging out everywhere. Hearing her answer made me immediately remember what Mom was like when we lived on Nob Hill, when everything always had to do with the way things had to look on the outside. Seeing Samantha's parents up close and personal made me feel even more grateful that Mom had changed, and became more down-to-earth. Maybe that's what a lot of money forces a person to do. They feel that they have to look and act a certain way, just 'cause they feel like that's what they're supposed to do *because* they've got money.

Something about me had to realize that that's just how some people are. And like Aunt Shirley taught me, I shouldn't judge nobody. I mean, anybody. "Is this OK? The way I look?" I asked the mom.

"You look marvelous, dear. Doesn't he, Geoffrey?"

"Ready for the Opera, in my opinion. Tonight, only dinner I'm afraid," the dad answered.

"Cool."

"Our car's parked a few blocks away. Would you like Geoffrey to get it, and pick us up? Or shall we walk there?"

"Let's walk. I like walking."

For a split-second, out of nowhere, I stopped to remember that when a white person and a black person have a baby together, the baby's probably going to be considered black to outside people. I don't know what made me think of that, except it was hard for me not to look at these two people, and not know that they're the people who made Samantha. It also made me remember from way back that this was another thing Samantha and I had in common, mixed types of parents. I wished she could have had dinner with us. But I knew she'd probably be out of the hospital soon, after the doctors were done with all their observations or whatever it's called.

When we got to their car, I couldn't figure out why they had the one they did. "Wow. Is this yours?" I asked.

"Yes, my wife doesn't care for it. I love it," the dad said.

"I mean, you *own* it? It doesn't belong to the army or marines? It looks like the kind of car they drive around in wars, like a military kind of car."

"I couldn't agree with you more, Miguel," the mom said.

"It's a Hummer. They're very *in* right now," the white dad told me.

After a second passed I asked, "In what?"

"In style," he answered.

"Oh."

I had never been to the Carnelian Room before, and I couldn't wait to go inside. I made sure to remind the mom that there were only certain things I could eat, and she said it should be no problem. As we began driving up 16ᵗʰ Street towards the financial district, I happened to ask them both, "What kind of food do they have there?"

"New American cuisine," the dad answered.

"Oh, they're my favorite."

What I noticed as we drove along the streets, especially through my neighborhood, the Mission district, was all the people staring at these parent's shiny-painted war car. The dad seemed to like it though. Ever since the day I was born, people have stared at me, and I've always hated that. It was strange that buying a certain car that got stared at a lot was something anyone would actually enjoy. See, 'cause remember I'm really big on privacy, and minding your own business.

The looks from the people on the street never stopped. All the way through Potrero Hill, China Basin, up the Embarcadero, and into the financial district, right where Montgomery, Jackson, and Columbus all come together. I wanted to yell at all these people and say, *"Haven't you ever seen an army car before?"*

What a total coincidence it was that the dad ended up finding a rare parking space right in front of my favorite restaurant, Clown Alley, that's painted up like a circus on the outside. They probably got the idea from Jack-in-the-Box to have clown pictures plastered all over the inside walls, except Clown Alley's still mostly unique and original. They've got really good burgers and stuff there. "I always wanted to take Samantha here," I told the parents.

"Really? This place?" the mom asked.

"Oh, for sure. I told her all about it. She really wants to come here. The next time we go to Chinatown or North Beach, we're definitely coming here to eat."

"Well. Good for you, dear."

It seemed like they never imagined that Samantha would ever want to do such a thing. Maybe they didn't know her the way I did. Maybe they never got to know the real Samantha inside the outside one. And worst of all, maybe they didn't even know how much she'd changed. If they didn't, I had to make sure they knew this, because it was such a totally huge accomplishment.

As we walked through the financial district with all its really tall buildings, I began wondering about the earthquakes that happened in the Bay Area. Just like Aunt Shirley *always* kept telling me, "It's only the smartest people who ask all the questions. That's what makes them smart." So I asked the parents, "How come they still build these buildings, if they know earthquakes happen here all the time?"

"They've all been constructed to code. Or retrofitted, son," the dad said.

"So they weren't scared?"

"Of earthquakes?"

"Yeah, they weren't afraid of all the damage that could end up happening?"

"I guess not."

"Samantha's told us all about your life, dear. She said that learning to be unafraid...saved your life," the mom said.

"Well, I guess that's kind of the way it is."

"And you learned to be this way because of your aunt."

"Oh, definitely. My aunt taught me a whole bunch of positive things. You'd really like her, she's way cool."

"So we've heard," the dad said.

Into the Bank of America building elevator all three of us walked. I got to be the one to press 52 with my knuckle before anyone else could. "This is the tallest building in San Francisco," a bald man-tourist inside the elevator bragged to other tourists he was with.

With a lot of confidence, I politely corrected him and said, "It has the most floors. The actual highest one is the TransAmerica Pyramid."

"Oh, is that so?" the tourist said with a ton of surprise.

"Yes, sir. So it's kind of a tie."

The tourist didn't say anything else all the way up to the restaurant, so nobody else did either. Maybe I shouldn't have said that. It's just better to get it completely straight, if you're going to bother saying anything at all. When we all got out of the elevator, and the tourists walked way ahead of us, Samantha's mom said to me, "You certainly are sure of yourself, Miguel. I wish our daughter could be more like that."

"Oh, she *is*. Samantha's so strong now. She's not afraid of anything. I'm totally proud of her."

"And, so am I. Although, she still has those dreadful phobias to contend with. They're not helping the situation at all," the mom said.

"No, you're wrong. She *used* to have them. Maybe they're still there, but they're *waaaay* smaller now."

Just when the mom was going to say something next, the really polite waiter guy with a turban took us to our table right at the window. Smack in front of us was the tip of the Pyramid, and the entire bay behind that for us to see. As we sat down, the mom had more she wanted to say. "Miguel, as you're well aware, our daughter's not doing well. And the doctors we've seen don't seem to be making any head..."

Since the mom couldn't finish her sentence 'cause she seemed to be getting a little lost for words, I helped her out. "She'll get better. You'll see. Samantha can do anything now. She can make anything happen. I'm totally sure."

"You're very optimistic, son. What exactly is it you *do* to stay this way?" the dad asked.

"Well, it would take all night to tell you all about E.B. It's really bad. I have to be wrapped up all the time. And I have to take special baths, and, anyway, there's tons of stuff I need to do. But, there's tons of things left I still *want* to do in life, and I *believe* that I'm going to be here to do them. I believe that totally. I have faith that I'll be here to do everything that I've written down on my *To Do* list."

"Samantha mentioned this to us before. It's your faith that sustains you."

"Faith in myself. That's why God put us here, to believe in ourselves, and all the things we can do. If you ever doubt, you're a goner."

"To you, faith is the opposite of fear, isn't it?" the mom asked.

"Definitely. *Faith* or *belief* is the total opposite of fear. Faith and belief *make* things happen. Fear prevents anything from happening."

"What kinds of fear, dear?"

"All fear. Aunt Shirley says people aren't born with it, they learn to be afraid of change, afraid of leaving a bad husband, afraid of leaving a mean wife, afraid of taking a vacation, afraid of spending money, afraid of changing jobs, afraid of failure, afraid of success, all that kind of stuff. She says *most* people are this way, and God didn't make us alive to be like this. He made us be born so we could do whatever we wanted. So we could fulfill our purposes."

"How wise you are for your young age," the dad said.

"Most certainly. I told you, Geoff, it's more than an optimistic attitude that Miguel has. It's the power of belief. Is that what you'd call it?"

"Yeah, that's exactly what it is. Belief-in-yourself. It's the strongest thing there could ever be."

"As well as your belief in your God?" the dad asked.

"Yeah, that too. I totally believe in God, except that's the main part where people screw, I mean, mess up. There's tons of people out there who pray, but that's *all* they do. They're still totally afraid of *making* any kind of change happen *themselves*. God doesn't do nothin' for people who just, you know, sit on their ass. Pardon my French."

Just as I said that part, our waiter came over, and asked us what we'd like to order. I realized that I'd been mouthing off ever since we sat down, and I hadn't really had a chance to see what I could eat. All the time I have to be extra careful of what I eat 'cause of my digestion. Normally I could have picked out at least a few things on any menu, but not this time. Samantha's mom asked me what I'd like to have, and I honestly had to tell her that there was almost nothing I'd be able to eat there. On some other night I could have, just not this one. "Oh, my heavens," she said.

The dad looked kind of embarrassed that they went to all this planning, and I couldn't even eat there. I felt really bad. Then, it completely surprised me when the dad immediately said, "You know, I've had such a craving for a Clown Alley burger lately. Maybe we should give it a go."

"Are you for real? You eat at Clown Alley?" I asked.

"Well, no. Not really. Nevertheless, there's a first time for everything."

"It doesn't have a view, you know."

"Absolutely. We've eaten here much too often anyway. Why don't all three of us be unafraid of change, together…and hightail it over to Clown Alley," the dad insisted.

The mom didn't seem to mind, except I could also tell that she'd never been to Clown Alley either. As it turned out, the dad ended up paying the waiter some money, even though we never actually ate anything, which was a way-courteous thing to do. And, right after that, we were once again inside the express elevator going down. This time with no tourists in it. As we crossed Kearny Street, we arrived at the corner of Columbus and Jackson. "Well, I'm looking forward to this adventure. How about you two?" the mom said.

"I'm way excited, Ma'am. I love it here."

"So am I. Maybe we can even order one for Samantha to go. They're microwavable, aren't they?" the dad said.

"She'd like that. Or maybe we can all even bring her back here after she gets out," I said.

"Marvelous," the mom said.

In all our fancy opera clothes we ordered our totally casual dinner. At first they were surprised that I didn't order a burger. They never knew that I couldn't ever eat those. So, I ordered my regular Tuna Delite hold the onions, since it looked just like a cheeseburger anyway.

Just as a homeless lady snuck in, the mom brought up the topic we were talking about before, fear versus belief. "…Miguel, that's what we really wanted to speak to you about. Is there any way you can you help Samantha through any of the methods you've been able to use yourself?" she said.

"Samantha's already learned *everything*. You'd be amazed. She's totally changed, she's fearless now."

"Perhaps that's so. In spite of that, something's still not right."

"It's all up to Samantha though. It all has to do with how many more things she wants to do in life, how much she wants to make them happen."

"And that's what it is? It's her desire that will make herself well?" the dad asked.

"I can't say that. It doesn't really make a person well, it makes them *want*. And when you want something bad enough, and believe, it's definitely going to happen."

"So, that's what keeps you healthy and well."

"I guess so. But there's also a part of me that knows I could die at any time. Maybe even tomorrow."

CHAPTER TWENTY-FIVE

After a couple of months had passed, I began sleeping less and less at night. So much was on my mind. This is something I realized that had always been dangerous for me in the past, too. Not getting the sleep I needed usually always made me real sick every time. Going to the hospital was definitely something I was not in the mood for, especially since Samantha was forced to be in there every day now. Her parents also seemed to be spending about 99% of their time worrying, mainly because after doing a million tests, the doctors never really could find out exactly what was going on. For the few seconds when they didn't happen to be worrying, the mom and dad just seemed like they were totally in shock.

Every chance I got to see Samantha though I felt happy, and I could tell she felt the same. Whenever I visited her my spirits moved way up into the clouds. By the time I got back home though, or whenever I was in school, my spirits came back down to earth again. After a really nice visit with Samantha, I went back home and became so tired that I actually fell right to sleep. Right away I had a dream, and as usual Jorge was in it. In the beginning, it was a little confusing to me, for the *me* inside my dream. A whole lot of me felt like I couldn't really tell if it was actually a dream or not.

"I'm so glad you guys brought me here," Samantha said.

"I'd been here once already. That was with Aunt Shirley. This is so totally cool, isn't it?" I said.

"But, it's not really like heaven. You're a little wrong about that, dude," Jorge said.

"Oh, I think it is. Heaven can be whatever you want it to be. In my opinion, Big Sur is very much like heaven," Samantha said.

"How would you know?" I asked her.

"Because I've been there so many times before."

"To heaven? You have?"

"Many, many times. So have you, Miguel. Don't you remember what it's like?" Samantha asked me.

"I've never been there before. Aunt Shirley and I just kind of guessed that it was something like Big Sur."

"Did you know your aunt's probably been to heaven more times than anyone?"

"Oh, yeah. That's the truth. *Everyone* in heaven knows Aunt Shirley," Jorge said.

"Get out. You never told me she's been up there before."

"Sure I did, fool. You don't remember me telling you that this was her last time? Her last time on earth? She's learned *everything* by now," Jorge answered.

"So, that's for sure then?" I asked, just to be positive.

"Nothing's for sure, dude. And, if anything was, I'm certainly not the one to tell you."

"Hey, Samantha. What about me? Will I be going to heaven soon? What do *you* think?" I asked.

"You mean *back* to heaven. I don't have a clue. But, you should try hard to remember how perfect it was."

"Nothing's perfect, Samantha. Dad and I agreed that there isn't really anything that's perfect."

"Heaven *is* perfect," Samantha said.

"Without a doubt, dude. Dad was right though. Nothing *on earth* is perfect. There's a lot about life that really sucks. They're all lessons. And lessons definitely got it goin' on. They're the main event, junior," Jorge said.

Once again, what Jorge was telling me were the very same words I'd heard a million times already from Aunt Shirley. And it was so strange that Jorge and I were again in a location I'd been before with Aunt Shirley, Big Sur. Being in this miracle spot made me remember the restaurant we had gone to there, Nepenthe, the place that seemed to look out onto the rest of the world. So vividly I was beginning to remember that special lunch she and I had together, the one when we looked out to see the whales jumping up and down in the sea. "Hey, are you guys hungry?" I asked Samantha and Jorge.

"I sure am," Samantha said.

"Duh. When am I not hungry?"

"Aunt Shirley took me to this totally cool restaurant before. It's just up the highway, right off this cliff-kind of thing."

"The Post Ranch Inn?" Samantha asked.

"No, Nepenthe."

"From the *Odyssey*. Nepenthe's mentioned in it. A drug used to remedy grief. It also means something that makes you forgetful of sorrow, it eases pain. Nepenthe makes you feel better. Maybe that's why your aunt took you there."

"She never told me any of that stuff though."

"Aunt Shirley's good at knowing what to teach you, and knowing when to let you learn on your own."

"Discovery leads to lessons learned, Miguel," Samantha said.

"Well then, sis. Just call me Vasco de Gama."

"Yo, Vasco. What's your claim to fame?" Jorge asked.

"He's some dude who discovered some place. I remembered his name from history class. I forgot the place he founded though."

When all three of us got over to Nepenthe we walked up all the steps, through a mixture of heavenly gardens, to where the restaurant is. As we kept walking up and up, Samantha still had enough extra energy to tell us all the names of every plant with flowers hanging off them, from both sides of the steps. "Freesias and hibiscus on our left, and on our right are tiger lilies and gardenias."

"Hey, how come you're not huffing and puffing like most times when we're walking?" I asked Samantha.

"Just like we said before, *perfect*."

"Perfect? What does—"

"Oh my God, check out the line to get in. We better get over there fast!" Jorge said.

The three of us ran as fast as we could to get into this huge line, just so we could get a table somewhere, and eat. "Indoors, front deck, or back deck?" The hippie-ish worker-lady at the high-topped desk asked us.

Without giving it any thought beforehand, I said, "Front deck."

"It'll be about thirty to forty-five minutes," the lady told us.

"That'll take forever," I said to Jorge.

"Dude, that's nothing. You got something else going on?"

When I agreed to wait, Jorge and Samantha took me over to where this huge fire pit was, something I'd never seen the last time. I guess the restaurant people used it to keep the customers warm during the times when it got too foggy or cold. For us, there was no fog around though. Sitting near massive flame sure made me feel a lot warmer though. "Miguel, thanks for bringing us here. I just love it," Samantha said.

"Me too. When Aunt Shirley brought me here we were both thinking about you a lot, Jorge. And, I thought maybe for a second you even turned yourself into a baby whale so you could kind of like say 'hi' to us both. That's what we saw that day from here, whales. Isn't that corny?"

"That was nice that you were thinking of me then."

"So, that really wasn't you?"

"No, I don't think I was ever a whale. That probably just happens in the movies, you know, the animated ones."

"Yeah, I was a lot younger way back then when I was thirteen."

"Miguel, you're only fourteen now."

"I know, but I've matured a lot in the past year. I'm a whole lot smarter."

Jorge rolled his eyes, thinking that I wouldn't see him do that, but I did. Even though he moved to heaven, I guess he'd always stay my older brother, someone who can get away with rolling their eyes like that right in front of me. "What else did you and Aunt Shirley do when you were here?" Jorge asked.

"Tons of special stuff."

"Did you go down to Hearst Castle?" Samantha asked.

"No, we didn't have time to go all the way down there. Aunt Shirley had to be back in the East Bay for some meeting that night, even though she totally didn't want to have to go. She said she'd never set foot in Piedmont again, unless she absolutely had to."

"What's wrong with Piedmont? I've been there, it's lovely." Samantha said.

"You *have*?"

"Sure, the homes there are gorgeous. And those views of the bay are incredible."

"Samantha, you're black. Didn't you know?" I asked.

"Yes, Miguel. I know I'm black."

"No!!! I mean, didn't you know how Piedmont got started? You know, how it was founded? No offense, Aunt Shirley told me that Piedmont was started just to keep black people out of it. Even though it's right in Oakland, the Piedmont people wanted to make it separate, just for white people."

"That was a long time ago, dude," Jorge said.

"Aunt Shirley said that some of the people who live there even today still think that way…keeping all the different kinds of people separated. Aunt Shirley said it makes her sick in her stomach to go anywhere near it."

"Heaven's not like that. Everyone's all together. No one is judged. No one is treated differently from anyone else," Samantha said.

"You say that like you know. Aunt Shirley told me that too, that no one is judged up there. She said that God doesn't judge people when they get into heaven. You think that's true?"

"Only people judge. God doesn't. That's fiction," Samantha told me.

Looking down into the fiery flames right in front of us, made me think of something else Aunt Shirley had told me. "What about hell? You know, some people believe that if you're a bad person you'll burn in hell."

"That's a load of crap. People on earth'll believe anything," Jorge said.

"It's all those religions that have been around for too long. They've corrupted just about everyone."

"The Catholic people believe in purgatory. How about that one? Is there really a place like that?"

"Having to think about all the rules and regulations that go with all those different religions gives me a headache," Jorge said.

"You can get headaches in heaven?" I asked.

"I'm making a point, you dope. *There is* no purgatory. Never has been, never will be."

"Well then, what about Mormon people? They say you have to accept Jesus Christ before you can get in."

"No, no, no. I can't imagine where they came up with all this. What were they thinking?"

"You don't have to accept nothin' or nobody. When you're done on earth, heaven is the only place you go right after that. It's a done deal. No two ways about it. Get it?"

"For real?" I asked.

"Yes, it's all so simple. It's like these religions seem to help the people who need to rely on them. Religions can also distort the truth though, and get people pretty confused at the same time."

"You said it, Sam. They've totally messed with people's heads. All those do's and don'ts. And you've got to do such-and-such in order to get into heaven. That's what's got a lot of people freaked. No one should have ever been afraid of heaven in the first place."

"I'm not afraid of heaven," I said.

"I think you are," Jorge said.

"I think you may be, too. Or else you would have probably remembered what it was like all the times you were there before," Samantha said.

"Or maybe because you still have so much more to do. You know, on earth. Helping people once in a while to get over fear is your thing, dude. So do it."

"I'm doing it. I helped you a whole bunch, Samantha. You don't have fear anymore at all."

"I know. You did a perfect job. I'm so grateful to you, Miguel. That's what actually gave me the strength to leave."

"Leave? For where?"

"Heaven. It's my home now."

"Yeah, Samantha lives in heaven with me now."

"It's the perfect place to be."

Something about me couldn't respond to what either of them had just said because I was too confused. And they could tell that I wasn't getting it. Then I had to remind her by saying, "You're in Big Sur now, Samantha. With me and Jorge."

"I'm only here visiting. Just like Jorge is. Just like Jorge has always done. We both are in heaven now."

"No, you're not. You're not in heaven. Not yet."

"You should be so happy for me, Miguel. Nothing about you should be afraid about me being in heaven now. You should be celebrating. Please be happy for me, Miguel. I learned my lessons, and now I'm free. Going to heaven is my ultimate reward."

"It really is, dude. Someday you'll understand."

"No I won't. No, no...

No, no! You can't be gone!" I yelled out, while waking up from my dream.

For almost the next whole hour I was in shock. Why had I had such a dream? Why was there something about it that seemed so real to me?

In the night everything had become all so quiet. No sirens. No foghorns. No homeless people yelling at each other. No trolley cars. Nothing. In the silence I needed to communicate what I'd just experienced. It was way too late to be calling anyone, and Dad was sound asleep. So I decided to write an e-mail to Samantha. Ever since she got put in the hospital for good, I've sent her e-mails every day. She always loved it whenever she got one from me. In the darkness of my room, I turned on my desk lamp, booted up my computer, logged onto AOL, activated my Point & Speak, and I began.

Dear Samantha,
Sup? Remember how Marshall used to say that all the time? He's still sort of weird, always driving everybody nuts at school. You're

definitely not missing much there. It's the same old, same old.

I'm still coming to see you on Friday. Is there anything special you want me to bring? Just let me know, OK? Khadijah's, I mean, your Aunt Khadijah's going to bring me there, so you'll get to see her too. You already know this, but she's graduating from Cal next week. That's all she's been talking about lately. I'm way excited for her. Are you doing OK? I know you'll get better real soon and be back home. And we'll have tons of stuff we can do together. I hope your *To Do* list is full, especially since it's summer vacation soon, we'll have plenty of time to get everything done that we want.

You know what though? I just had the totally weirdest dream. That's why I'm writing to you now, 'cause I just had it. As usual Jorge was in it, but you were in it, too. And the whole time you kept repeating that you were in   You kept saying you were in   Big Sur. You said that you'd never been there before. We had a great lunch. And, we got to see the awesome view from the Nepenthe restaurant there. It was a really good time.

I better get back to sleep now. Take care. And, I'll see you on Friday. Lots of love,

Miguel

CHAPTER TWENTY-SIX

When Khadijah handed me the greeting card with a pretty picture of clouds in a blue sky on it, I asked, "What's this for?"

"Samantha asked me to give it to you. She said it was stuck to the back of another card she'd received from one of your teachers, unused, still blank inside. Samantha told me it was meant to be, no accident."

I laughed a little as I said, "It's funny to hear Samantha talking that way."

As I took the card into my room, I looked out my window while still holding the card from Samantha in my hand. Outside, up above, was the exact same scene that appeared on the front of the card, a few white, billowy clouds in a sunny blue sky. Then, I opened up the envelope, and began reading.

Dear Miguel,
　　　Please forgive me. I'm sorry I've become so ill. I'm sorry I can't be there for you now. Always remember how strong you are. Don't be afraid to keep telling the truth. Your Dad's right. Stand up for yourself whenever you can.
　　　You're such a nice person. This also makes you a target.
　　　This is all I can think to tell you now.
　　　Always know that I'll forever be with you in spirit.
　　　Love,
　　　Samantha

When I had finished reading, I placed the card on my window ledge and with my eyes I compared the two skies with clouds. Was it the sky and clouds after all? Or was it heaven?

There was nothing about me that was glad to be there at my doctor's office again. Even though Khadijah was with me, I was still not in a good mood. I was mad. Mad at a whole bunch of things. Mostly I was mad about my E.B. "It'll just be a few more minutes, Miguel," a brand new nurse I'd never seen before told me.

Normally I would have smiled or said "thank you" after what she'd just said, but I didn't care. I totally didn't want to be there. And I especially didn't want to have to see Dr. Rosenzweig or listen to anything he had to tell me. He's a bad person and I hated him.

"Maybe we can go see Samantha tomorrow, or the next day, Miguel," Khadijah told me.

"Yeah, whatever."

"So, you're having one of those days, huh?"

"Yep. A real pisser."

"In some way, you've got to try to remember that these people are here to help you. Or, if you want to stay angry, that's OK too."

"Good. Then that's what I'll do."

"Miguel, we're ready for you now," the nurse said, while opening the waiting room door.

As I've done a million times before, I stepped into the room in the very far back of the clinic, and sat on the table. The nurse carefully unwrapped all my old bandages right before the doctor was about to come in. She said a few things to me, although I wasn't really listening. When she got done with all the regular procedure stuff, she said, "The doctor will be in to see you in just a few minutes."

I nodded my head, and I still didn't say anything. Instead I waited, and waited, and waited. As I waited, I got madder, and madder. Finally, after having to wait inside that room for almost a lifetime, the doctor came in and said, "How are you doing today, young man?"

"My name's Miguel. Not young man."

"Well, excuse me, *Meeg-iall*," the doctor said, then shook his head sideways.

I just stayed sitting there, completely mad. Not saying another word.

"This doesn't look good at all," he told me, and then he continued to say, "I'm afraid this one's rather severe. Are you sure that nurse of yours is preparing those ointments correctly? Precisely as I instructed?"

"Yes. Khadijah's a good nurse. She knows exactly what she's doing."

"...*Doctor*."

"She knows what she's doing, *doctor*." Then he just glared at me in a real stinging way. "Do you have anything positive to say, *doctor*? Or are you just going to stay as rotten as usual?"

At first Dr. Rosenzweig gasped at what I'd just told him, then he responded by saying, "I beg your pardon."

"*You* are a rotten person. Aunt Shirley and Jorge told me that I wasn't supposed to tell anyone else what they're lessons were, but you're probably totally mad at everyone in the whole world for something that happened to you from way before. Or for something that someone had done to you. Or you're unhappy at the way your life turned out. And that's why you're so rotten to everyone you meet, especially to positive people like me."

"Young man…you're entirely out of line."

"It's Miguel! *M-I-G-U-E-L!*"

From the opposite side of the examining room door, I could hear knocking, and then a woman's voice asked, "Dr. Rosenzweig, would you like any assistance?"

His voice was shaking a little when he answered, "No, Denise. Everything's under control."

Everything wasn't under control though. Immediately I became mad at myself for not telling the truth a *long* time ago, about the way this guy really was. I wasted so much time going to him, someone who did so much more harm than good. Dr. Rosenzweig may have gotten to be a smart doctor, while in reality, he had learned nothing at all. What happened in his life to make him want to take it all out on everyone he meets? How come he never chose to learn from his past? Whatever the answers were, I didn't care. Taking the time and energy to expect this guy to wake up and smell the coffee was something I had no interest in doing.

"I'm done, Dr. Rosenzweig."

"No, you're not. Now, Mee-kell, I don't blame you for being mad. It's not easy living with E.B."

"That's not what I'm mad about. I'm mad that I hadn't told the truth a long time ago."

"The truth about what?"

"The truth about deserving someone *better* than you, someone who treats me well, someone who doesn't make me scared on purpose just to get more money from Dad's insurance. The doctor stuff you know all about is a great, except you're like the killer poison that cancels out all the medicines you give me."

"Miguel, I'm a doctor. I know what I'm doing."

"The only reason I stayed going to you is 'cause I didn't want to hurt Dad's feelings, because you're all he could afford. I never told him the truth, I never told anyone the truth about you, what you're really like."

"Why don't we begin this examination again? We'll pretend none of this ever took place."

"No, no. I'm sorry I had to get so mad, but that's exactly what tons of people do when lessons come to them. They pretend they *never* happened. They learn nothing. No offense to you, but I'd rather die than have to see you again. I learned my lesson. I learned I deserve someone so much better."

"Miguel, I—"

"Thank you very much, Dr. Rosenzweig, for all the medical stuff you were able to do for me. I'm leaving now. I hope you get a chance to learn from what just happened...it was a big lesson for you too." As I said that, I got off the examining table, redressed all the bandages myself even after the doctor offered to help me, put my clothes on, and walked out the door. At the very same time I went through the doorway, all the fire that had been inside my belly was extinguished. This was something I probably should have done a long time ago, even though it's never too late to stand up for yourself. As usual, this was another fantastic lesson God had given me, and I passed with all tons of flying colors.

When I walked out past the nurses, and the other workers in the reception area, they didn't seem at all surprised that I was leaving. They must have heard what had happened, and I could tell from the looks on their faces that they felt either happy or proud of me. I said "goodbye" to them all, and they all said the same back. I also mentioned to them that I wasn't coming back. So they all wished me the best, and I wished them the best, too.

Although I thought I had learned to conquer all my fears, I was still learning about some new ones that were left. Fear was the thing that prevented me from telling the truth about this doctor. Fear was what kept me going to him, thinking that this doctor was all I deserved. The next step meant having to tell Dad what I had just done. Before him though, I knew I'd also have to tell Khadijah. As she saw me coming towards her in the waiting room, she had a totally dazed and confused look on her face.

"Is there anything you'd like to tell me?" she asked.

"I'm done," I told Khadijah as I led her by her left arm out of the clinic and into the outside hallway. Walking back to her car was when it began to make sense to her.

"I had a feeling there was something about this place you didn't like. So, you're certain about all this?"

"Positive. I feel like a winner...all because I had the courage to tell the truth."

"You learned that from your dad. I remember you telling me what he'd always say about speaking the truth. 'Only truthful things...' What's the rest?"

"'Only the truth's worth telling.' Anything other than that just causes problems."

"That's a good one. Well, good for you. Everything'll work out, Miguel."

"I know. Did you happen to call the hospital on your cell phone while I was inside?"

"No. Not yet."

"Why don't you do that now? Maybe we can go see Samantha."

Khadijah agreed. Except right before she called, she noticed my bandages. She could see that they weren't wrapped properly. In the back of the parking lot where the clinic was, Khadijah took out her medical bag, put all the ointments on that needed to get applied before my bandages, and then she re-wrapped me just the right way. Khadijah reminded me that I still needed to go to a doctor, back to Stanford more than likely. Not knowing how all that was going to get paid for didn't seem to worry me. Aunt Shirley always said that money'll always be there when you need it most, as long as you'll believe it will be. "Act like you already have it," she'd always say.

In my freshly-wrapped body, Khadijah and I headed over to Saint Mary's Hospital on Stanyan Street, where Samantha had been moved to. By the time we got there something had changed. The hospital people wouldn't say much at all. Samantha wasn't allowed to have visitors for about the next hour or so. They didn't make it seem like anything important was going on, they just needed to do something with her, alone, and then we could come back to visit a little later on. Bummer.

Since we were right next door to it, Khadijah and I decided to walk over to the Panhandle-entrance of Golden Gate Park. "Where to?" I asked her.

"You pick, Miguel," she told me.

"I haven't been here since I was with Aunt Shirley, and that was a while ago. The Hall of Flowers hasn't reopened, the de Young Museum is being totally rebuilt, and the Asian Art Museum isn't even here anymore."

"How about if we find a place to talk? Someplace rather quiet?"

"Yeah, I'd like that. My dogs are barkin' today. Let's find a place to sit down, relax, and have some down time. The Japanese Tea Garden. How about that? 'Cause it's still morning all the tourists probably won't even be there yet."

"That sounds perfect."

Walking through the tree-filled park made everything so peaceful for me on my insides. A part of me felt so much stronger. The rest of me felt so relaxed, like what just happened at the doctor's office never happened in the first place. We paid our admission and went straight back to a place with some shade, the little café where they serve tea and almond cookies. But just as the geisha-dressed, Japanese girl with two long, black pencils sticking out of her hair took us to a table overlooking the goldfish pond, we heard, "Yo, over here." It was Aunt Shirley and Lefty. I couldn't believe it. What were they doing there?

"Miguel, Khadijah. How are you?" Lefty asked us.

"What's, I mean, why are you both here?" I asked.

"Hi, you two," Khadijah said.

"We're taking a break from life. How about you guys? What's up with you two?"

I told Aunt Shirley and Lefty all that had just happened, leaving the clinic in San Bruno, going to see Samantha at Saint Mary's, and that we were going back to see her again in just a few minutes. Khadijah and I sat down with Aunt Shirley and Lefty at a bigger table looking out at the trees, the gardens, and the pond. Somehow we all ended up sitting at the exact same table where Aunt Shirley and I had sat when we were both there together from a long time before.

"It all happens exactly the way it's all supposed to happen," Aunt Shirley said.

"Did you know I'm going back to the Dermatology Department at Stanford, Miguel? I'll be your doctor again."

"What about the money?"

"I've got money. Your mother's got money. '*All God's children got...*' It's a done deal, doll. It was *all* supposed to happen this way. You learned something. This lesson wouldn't have come your way had it happened any differently. Ain't God somethin'?" Aunt Shirley said.

"I thought you liked Doctor Rosenzweig. I never would—"

"It happened just the way it was supposed to. It's a done deal. *The end*," Aunt Shirley said back.

"Would any of you like more tea?" Khadijah asked.

Rather than answering, Aunt Shirley politely waved her left hand in the air so the Japanese waitress, and everyone else, would see. She didn't just wave it in a quiet way. Aunt Shirley did it by wiggling her fingers back and forth, making it all way more dramatic than it ever needed to be. Lefty rolled his eyes back and forth, and I could tell that something else was going on that I couldn't at first figure out. "Oh, my God. Are you—"

"Yes, my proposal came two days ago."

"Are you for real?" I asked.

"I think so, doll. This is it. Soon you're going to have a new, uncle-doctor Lefty."

"Congratulations. Oh my God. To both of you," Khadijah said, as she hugged Aunt Shirley while she was still sitting down.

Seeing that Aunt Shirley was actually going to get married was like icing on the cake...for her. It was the ultimate way for her to learn the important lesson of finally being able to trust someone, by letting herself get close to another person. I was happy and sad for her at the same time though. It was especially lucky that the person she picked to trust was somebody I already knew and liked so much, someone I also trusted from way before.

For the next hour or so we all celebrated and talked about all the things that would come next. Everything was going to be kept simple though. Aunt Shirley and Lefty both agreed to make it happen that way. In the middle of hearing and talking about such good news, I began thinking about Samantha all over again. Even though I wasn't exactly worrying, I was still thinking about her just the same. I don't know how she knew, but while Khadijah and Lefty were talking about something, in a whisper Aunt Shirley leaned over and told me, "Samantha's going to be just fine."

"She is?"

"I'm positive. I also know that's something she'd like to hear from you. Go see her. I bet she's ready to take visitors now. We'll walk there with you."

This was like a double dose of totally great news. Hearing that from Aunt Shirley made me feel tons better. I didn't want to admit it to myself, but I was really scared and worried. Knowing that fear only made everything tons worse, I never admitted it to anyone, 'cause I didn't want it to be like an evil curse or whatever for Samantha.

The four of us walking through the park towards the Panhandle was like we'd always been together. The four of us from a time before 'cause it felt so natural, like a family. And soon we were all going to get to see the rest of our family, Samantha.

When we got back to Saint Mary's, Lefty had run into a doctor there in the lobby, some doctor he'd known from before. It seemed as if that doctor had told Lefty something specific about Samantha. They talked off to the side for a while. Then when they were done, Lefty looked right over at me before he began walking back to us all. His look wasn't a happy one. I didn't ask, and he didn't offer to explain.

We all went up to see Samantha. Aunt Shirley and Lefty stayed in one of the waiting rooms upstairs. Khadijah and I stepped up to the desk place and asked if it was finally a good time to get to see Samantha. "Samantha Austin. She's in stable condition right now, asleep. I'm so sorry, she can't be disturbed. Maybe tomorrow."

Khadijah and I were way disappointed. I *really* wanted to see Samantha, and thank her. But, I understood how important it was to get some sleep, too. I guess I'd just have to be more patient, and try to visit another time.

On our way out the front entrance of the hospital, Lefty and Khadijah went to the restrooms while Aunt Shirley and I stood there looking out at Stanyan Street full of stopped traffic. "You said she'll be fine. Do you still think that, Aunt Shirley?"

"Absolutely, Miguel."

CHAPTER TWENTY-SEVEN

"What if there's rotten people up there?"
  "So."
  "What if it's all a lie, and heaven's not really a good place?"
  "I doubt that, Miguel."
  "What if God doesn't really exist?"
  "There are many people who believe that already."
  "What if fear *isn't* the opposite of faith?"
  "Miguel, you're beginning to scare me."

Hearing Samantha tell me that at Aunt Shirley's house made me wake up screaming. Sweat was everywhere, and my bandages were soaked. I stayed panic-stricken until I realized it was just a dream.

Changing my own bandages took me a while. I calmed down once my skin was dry, and listening to the chirping birds outside made me feel more peaceful inside. What never went away though was my curiosity. It had filled up my entire body. I needed answers, so I said,

"Dear God,

Hi, God. It's me, Miguel Estes. How are You? Are You still making all kinds of things happen that make people wonder why? Most of the time I do my very best to understand that You've got different plans from what we all do. I guess that's what life is all about. Isn't it? Surprises? And to just accept that Your plan is more important than ours, 'cause Yours always has to do with lessons, and that's what matters most?

Oh well, enough with the questions. But now that I think about it, how about one more, since it's the main one I wanted to ask in the first place? Is my friend Samantha's going to get any better? My insides already know the answer. I guess I just wanted to ask. Over the past few months I learned a ton of stuff. I learned that heaven must be the best place to be anyway, even though the toughest part is missing the person when they're not going to be on earth anymore. I hope that doesn't sound too greedy. I mean, I want all the people I love to stay here. Except if they don't want to be here anymore, or they're done, then I guess it's kind of selfish to want that. Sorry.

What I don't tell anybody, God, is that I cry a lot. I cry all the time. That's a secret though. Don't tell anyone, OK? I figured out that life's mostly a sad thing. It's really hard and sad. Maybe it's not that way for people who don't choose to learn the lessons You gave them, but then what's the point of living if you don't learn. I guess that's the tradeoff. Personally, I've always liked it right after I learned from one of Your lessons. It's like getting extra credit without having to do anything extra. It's like I've been productive with my life, and it hasn't all gone to waste.

Maybe it's the people who've chosen not to learn lessons, are the only people who get to know what it's like to be happy. I'll be happy when I go to heaven knowing that I did my job, and I did a good one. Sometimes I wonder if I'll be done soon. You know this already, how E.B. kids don't get to be adults most of the time. Will I be one of them? Oops, I guess that's another question, and I promised there'd be no more. Sorry again, God.

I guess I should get to the point. I love Samantha a whole bunch. She's my best friend. Sometimes I feel like we are the only people in the whole world who get each other, and know what each other is all about. You know what I mean? All the kids at school always thought that Samantha and I were the weird ones 'cause we're sort of different. So, that's why both of us never had very many kid friends at all. But we had each other. And, that's why I love her so much.

Just so You know, I'll still love her just as much if You really do have to send her off to heaven. I'm even going to ask my school to carve her name into the outside cement wall there next to those other guys' names that are already on it. Or, if I'm the one who gets sent there first, please let her know that I'll always love her whether she ends up turning into a legend or not, and she'll never be alone. I'll always remember to visit her in her dreams in heaven, just like the way Jorge has always visited me in mine.

Well, that's the main thing I wanted You to know, God. I don't know what's supposed to happen next. I know I'm not supposed to. It's Your plan, and I'll stick to it.

Thanks for giving me my friend Samantha. She's definitely the most perfect present You could have given me since Jorge left. And, if this is the very last one You give me, then that's OK too.

As usual, please bless everyone I know. And, especially my friend Samantha, my best friend.

Love,

Miguel"

"Whoever said 'the Lord works in mysterious ways?' Who invented that, Aunt Shirley?"

"Gosh, I don't know. Why do you ask?"

"I just wonder if it was a person who learned a bunch of their lessons, or someone who learned just a few."

"It may have been a person who didn't even know that that's why we're here, to learn lessons. Maybe it was a person who thought that the purpose of life was to have fun, to be happy, or to love everyone."

"Wow, they sure were clueless, if that's what they were thinking."

"Do you think the Lord works in mysterious ways, doll?"

"Nope. Not anymore. The more I realize that *everything* happens for a reason, the less of a mystery it all is."

"That's how I see it, too. Sometimes I marvel at how things work out. I used to be surprised, now I marvel. It's all *so* perfect."

"What does *marvel* mean again?"

"To be in awe. I'm awed by the perfection of it all."

"So, you think that life's perfect."

"No, not life. The way life unfolds, the things that happen in life, the way it's all planned out. God's plan. God's plan is perfect."

"Jorge and Samantha, when they were in my dream, said that heaven is perfect. It's a perfect place."

"I bet it is. When I was in my coma, that's what I learned. It's not only a perfect place, it's the perfect place to be."

"Is it really better than earth?"

"No contest. Life's hard work. Some people think they're accomplishing a lot through their jobs, through promotions, or through their careers. The job of life is the only one that matters. You don't pass or fail, you don't get raises or bonuses, you learn. That's what it's all about."

When Aunt Shirley first told me all this, it was new to me, like it would take some time to sink in. Hearing it this time around made me realize that this was definitely the truth, nothing to question. Just as I experienced with

Samantha when I'd witnessed her huge change, I realized I was growing even older. Understanding what Aunt Shirley had just told me made me feel like I was becoming as old as she was.

For the next few hours, Aunt Shirley and I sat together in front of her window where I made my dreams. We looked out at all that was in front of us, all that we had seen from so many times before. There in the distance was San Francisco, a city with so much life going on, with its busy people living their busy lives. There was Oakland, a city with people doing the same things, but a city mostly known for all the murders that happen in it. There to the north, Marin County, a place where most people seemed to have more money that they know what to do with. And, Berkeley right down below, a place that's thought of mostly as different, unique, and maybe even strange.

I liked strange. That's always what seemed to suit me best. Having E.B. was strange. Having conversations with homeless people was strange. Talking to God out loud was strange. Sitting in front of a window where dreams come alive was strange. Having dreams about a dead brother who lives in heaven was strange. Realizing that heaven was a whole lot better than earth was strange. Although, knowing deep down that my best friend was going to go there soon, didn't really seem to feel that strange. More than anything else, it began feeling natural.

Being strange, and liking it, was normal for me. It made me who I turned out to be. A huge part of me didn't want to let go though. Hearing and learning about how great heaven was, was one thing. But to let someone go there and actually celebrate that was something else.

"Remember Reason Number 2, doll. We're not only here to learn lessons. There's another one," Aunt Shirley said while breaking the silence.

"I know. Helping other people when given the opportunity, Reason Number 2."

"Yes, sir. And, often times when you help someone else, you're helping yourself."

"I know. Like with fear? Getting over it?"

"Absolutely. Fear is a biggie. There are so many kinds. It's all over the place. It's like when you helped Samantha, and somehow in between, you learned to be unafraid of firing that lame-ass doctor you had."

"You're right, Aunt Shirley. And before that, I thought I had gotten rid of all my fears."

"They're like a virus that keeps mutating. You think you've conquered them all, then before you know it, there's one you've never heard of before....nipping at you heals. It's God's way of keeping us on our toes."

"That doesn't mean that there's more fears I have to deal with later on? Does it?"

"Later on? There's one big one on your plate right now."

"There is? What is it?"

"It's a combo platter, doll. The two reasons for living all rolled into one. A lesson for you *and* a chance to help someone else. It's an all-you-can-eat special."

"Oh my God. What a cornball. Well then, what is it?"

"Yeah, right. Like I'm going to tell you."

"Aunt Shirley, that's not fair."

"How on earth would you ever learn a lesson, if some schlub like me told you what it was going to be? It's that mystery-that's-not-really-a-mystery thing we just finished talking about."

Aunt Shirley wished me good luck, left the room to do work on her computer, and let me think more as I continued looking out to the bay. Way deep down I knew. I had always known what I needed to do. I needed to do it for myself. Mostly I needed to do it for Samantha. She and I both had one more fear that needed to be conquered. Deep down I knew that it was the hardest fear to get rid of, because it was one that I had lived with my whole life. Being afraid of dying was something I had to finally let go of. For me, for Samantha.

"I'm so proud of you, doll."

"So, you'll help me? You'll help me figure out what to say?"

"You're not going to need my help. You'll know exactly what to do and what to say. Plus, *You-know-who*'ll be right there with you."

"So, it's the right thing to do?"

"It's the perfect thing to do. The perfect gift. You'll set her free. I wish I could see more people act as bravely and wisely as you. It's their egos that get in the way. They think only of themselves. Wanting their loved ones to hang around when the loved ones were ready to depart yesterday. Me, me. me. They do it only for themselves. Keep thinking of Samantha first. Think of how much you'd like to see her be completely unafraid. Help her to be free, Miguel. You can do it."

"And that's the right thing to do. Tell me again, how come *I* have to do it? How come I have to be the one to tell her this?"

"Don't you think there's a reason why the two of you became best friends? Can you imagine there's anyone else better qualified than you to help Samantha when it counts most? Getting rid of fear is your forte, doll.

It's your purpose to help others get rid of theirs."

"And, by helping others, I'm helping myself."

"Bingo."

Aunt Shirley was talking about it all so plainly. Either she was a lot less emotional than I thought, or she just probably figured that letting someone go, helping someone actually get to heaven, was an incredibly happy, generous, and wonderful thing. Maybe Aunt Shirley felt that spending any time being sad over any of it was the totally wrong way to feel. Either way, the only feeling that ended up staying inside me was sadness. My best friend was going away, and she wasn't ever coming back.

A long time ago, Aunt Shirley told me that time never existed in the first place. She'd said, "The lives we all live go on as long as we want them to, as long as we have more lessons we want to learn. It doesn't matter if we learn them this time, or the next, or the next time after that. It's all one big, old, long lifetime divided into a bunch of little ones."

The day had passed and the evening was just about to. While back in front of Aunt Shirley's window, I sat in my chair where I made up my dreams. There, I began understanding more and more of the mystery of life that's not really a mystery at all. Instead of dreaming, I saw my own reality right out there, in the beautiful view I got to look at. Staring at the sunset over the ocean, in between the two towers of the gleaming Golden Gate Bridge, I thought back to a year before when I first had seen the same thing from Aunt Shirley's house when she just moved in. Can a person grow a hundred years older in only one? That's what it felt like for me. It was that exact same feeling as when I'd talked to Samantha about how we really felt like way-older people on our insides.

Right after the sun completely disappeared into the ocean, Aunt Shirley came from behind me, gave me a big hug that didn't hurt, and asked me how I was doing. "You missed it, the sunset," I told her.

"I'll catch the next one," she said.

"Yeah, I guess that's the way it goes. There's always tons of sunsets. They never run out, do they? Even when the fog comes in they still happen, it's just that we can't see them."

"Sunrises and sunsets. They've been happening forever, and they always will."

"And we've only gotten to see a few."

"You'll get to see just as many as you want to see."

"I'm going to miss Samantha a whole bunch."

"I know you will, hon. Saying goodbye is always hard," Aunt Shirley said, as she hugged me again.

"Sometimes I try not to think about her at all, because it just makes me too sad. Really sad."

"You're soooooo lucky though, Miguel. You were able to help someone change their entire life and the way they view it. Samantha's a completely new person now, fearless. Just think of the way she'll begin her life next time."

"So, there's going to be a next time for her?"

"I don't see why not. She's so very smart, and smart people always seem to want to know more. She's going to be just fine, and so will you."

Everything Aunt Shirley was telling me sounded real good, although this sad feeling stayed with me, like it was something that was never going to go away. Why did God make me have this life? Why did God make Samantha have hers? Sometimes it was all just too hard to believe that any of it was fair. What was the real reason God invented lessons in the first place? Just to give us all something important to do?

"What's on your mind, doll?" Aunt Shirley asked me.

"Lots of stuff. Stuff that I don't get," I answered.

"Join the club. My head's full of junk I'll never understand."

"Do you ever get sad, Aunt Shirley?"

She paused a few seconds, then she said, "Yes I do. I'm sad a lot."

"Seriously?"

"Most of the time there's a sadness inside me that never leaves."

"I think I saw you do it once before, but do you ever cry?"

"Miguel, I never tell anyone this, I cry all the time."

"You do? Why do *you* cry, Aunt Shirley?"

"For many reasons. Mostly because I'd rather feel sadness…than feel nothing at all. It means I've been somewhere. I've learned something. I've lived life."

CHAPTER TWENTY-EIGHT

The longer I lived, the more I realized that doing the things you had to do in life, are mostly done by shutting off your brain. You don't need to feel any of it, you just do them. This is the way I looked at what had to come next, something in my life that needed to be done. If sadness was a feeling that was going to be with me always, then this was something I somehow finally accepted. It was no longer a big deal. Been there...

Once I was able to accept so much of what my life had all been about, my positive side started to show again. For the past year, through my dreams, with the lessons I learned, from the people who influenced me, I realized that going to heaven wasn't only good, it was perfect. I finally got that going to heaven was the perfect thing, and it was the perfect place to go. I had begun to finally understand it so completely, how lucky Samantha was to be able to go there.

What a happy day she'd have, the day she'd go off to heaven. My life on earth would go on, while she had a much better life ahead of her. For a moment, I had put my sadness aside, and became truly happy for Samantha.

In a few minutes I was going to see her. My insides were telling me that it may be for the last time. On earth, all of Samantha's vital signs had become totally abnormal. There were times where she went in and out of consciousness, and it seemed real clear that she was not going to get any better, especially since she had been this way for such a long time. No matter what though, I couldn't wait to see her. I loved Samantha, she'll always be my best friend.

All at the same time, every one of my thoughts had gathered inside my head. All the things Aunt Shirley had told me from before. Everything I learned. All Jorge had told me in my dreams. They all led me to where I needed to go next, the hardest thing I was ever going to have to do in my lifetime. For a while there I wanted so badly to talk to God out loud, like I had done so many times before, except deep inside me I knew I was ready.

"*Don't be afraid*," I kept telling myself. "*I can do it*," I said out loud, softly.

"What, Miguel?" my mom asked me.

"Nothing, Mom," I told her, as we got closer to Saint Mary's.

"I know it's hard, hon. But I couldn't be more proud of you. In such a short time I've seen you grow lifetimes...right before my eyes. You're truly a remarkable young man, Miguel. No one I meet from now on will ever impress me more."

"Wow. Thanks, Mom."

"Samantha's so very lucky. Because of you she was able to abandon all those phobias and fears. What a fortunate girl. How incredibly blessed she is. Samantha's learned lessons I may *never* be able to grasp. You've done an excellent job, dear. I'm so proud of you."

Somehow I was planning to tell Mom "thanks" again, after listening to her pep talk. But all I could do was cry. I had become so totally overwhelmed by everything I was experiencing. Although I thought I could do it all on my own, I needed help. Mom comforted me the best she could, and I appreciated that. I needed something more to get me through what I was about to do though. So, I closed my eyes just for second, and again I thought of Aunt Shirley. "Put Samantha first...this is what she's been waiting for," Aunt Shirley had told me once before.

Soon after remembering what Aunt Shirley had said, Mom and I walked into the entrance of the hospital. When we went to the floor where Samantha was, we saw lots of her family there. The minute I saw them, and noticed what they were doing, I could see that everything was all wrong. It was like I had just woken up after being asleep all my life. After all I'd been told by Aunt Shirley and Jorge, after all I'd learned, and after deep down knowing what I had to do, I finally got it. I finally understood it all.

In the waiting room on the fifth floor the mom was crying, the dad was pacing back and forth, and Khadijah looked like she was in shock. All I kept thinking was that I hoped Samantha hadn't seen any of them acting like that. They all didn't get it. They weren't helping Samantha at all, they were all just making it a whole bunch worse. In my heart I knew that it was all up to me. It was up to me to show Samantha my happiness and joy for her.

The dad told me that Samantha "wasn't lucid at times." And when Khadijah called me beforehand, she felt that this was maybe the last time I'd be able to see Samantha. When Mom saw Khadijah in the waiting room, she walked right up to her on the couch and hugged her, something she had never done before. After that, Mom went over to Samantha's mom, then to the dad, and seemed to say something nice to them both. Being in that room made me know for sure that I didn't need comforting anymore. Khadijah came over and hugged me anyway. "Samantha would like to see you. You want to go in now? Are you up to it?"

"Oh, definitely. Let's go see her," I said.

Khadijah and I walked over to where the nurses were, and she asked if we could go in. One of the nurses said, "Yes. Now would be the perfect time."

As Khadijah opened the door to Samantha's room, I was right behind her. We stepped in quietly, and even though I had been in the hospital to visit Samantha many times before, I still lost my breath when I saw her this time. That only lasted about a second though. The shock of seeing what she looked like vanished, and in some way all I could feel right after that was happiness inside. I was sincerely glad to see her, and at the very same time, part of me somehow felt relieved that she may soon be leaving, happy for where she may be going.

"I've been waiting for you, Miguel," Samantha said.

"Hey, Samantha. How are you? It's great to see you."

What surprised me immediately was that although Samantha looked so tired and ill, her personality and everything about her was so completely alive, completely unaffected. Back and forth Samantha and I did small talk for a while, with Khadijah saying a few things in between. Khadijah's sadness was still so obvious, and I could tell that she needed to leave the room because of the emotions that showed on her face. "You two probably want to talk in private. So I'm going to go back to the waiting room for a while," she said, as she reached for the handle on the door.

"I love you, Auntie Khadijah," Samantha said with a ton of excitement in her voice.

Khadijah turned around with a surprised look on hers, like she had never heard Samantha say that before, and in the most truthful way she said, "I love you too, Samantha." Then Khadijah stepped out of the room.

"Hey, Miguel. Guess what? I met Jorge," Samantha said.

"Jorge who?"

"Your brother. I met him. He told me to tell you '*hi*'."

"My brother Jorge? Really?"

"Yes. I had a dream, and all three of us were together at some place near the ocean. It was so beautiful."

"Really? Except that's the dream *I* told *you* about. You never ever got to meet Jorge though. Not for real."

"Wait a minute...he looks like you except his ears stick out more, his hair is shorter than yours, he's a little taller, and he wears his Giants cap backwards."

I was so completely baffled. How could she have known this? I didn't remember ever telling Samantha what Jorge had looked like. And, I didn't remember showing her any pictures of him. "Yes, you're totally right. That's Jorge, my brother," I said.

"'*Hi*,' he says."

My mouth opened to say, "Then…please tell him '*hi*' back." Then it made me nervous talking this way.

"Don't be afraid, Miguel. It's OK. Jorge explained everything. We all never stopped talking."

"In the dream I had, we did too. But in my dream you were…"

"In heaven. I know. You were too. All three of us were in heaven. A place where everything's perfect."

"*I* was there too?"

"Yes, Miguel. All three of us were in heaven. We were all so happy. I'm so eager to go there now. But I've been waiting for you."

"I know. Wait a minute though. This is so strange. I thought that's what *I* was supposed to tell *you*. Not to be afraid."

"I'm not. Not at all. But, that's exactly what I've been waiting to tell *you*. Don't be afraid of heaven. Heaven's a place where fear doesn't exist. Fear only exists here, and it was never meant to."

"That's what Aunt Shirley says. And, you're OK with everything?"

"I'm more than OK. I can hardly wait. You've taught me so much, Miguel. I will always be grateful for all I've learned from you. There's nothing I'm afraid of anymore. Learning to be unafraid was the lesson I needed to learn most, and I did it. And, there's nothing about me that's afraid of what happens next. You look so shocked, Miguel."

"I just never expected this. It's all so easy now. I thought *I* was going to have to be the one to tell you that it's all OK, OK to…"

"Go. Don't be afraid, Miguel. Don't ever be afraid to tell anyone that it's OK to go. Not even to yourself. It's part of life. It's something I look forward to, and so should you."

"I can't believe you're saying this. You used to be so scared of everything. You're so different now."

"You're the one who helped me become like this. Be the same, afraid of nothing. You'll know more of what I'm feeling when your time gets closer. The sooner you feel this, the more of life you'll be able to live."

"Aunt Shirley had told me something like that too. I just can't believe you're saying these things. This isn't what I was expecting at all."

"That's the way it's supposed to be. What you expect is what you won't have. Expecting nothing makes life so much simpler. You probably worried over what you were planning to tell me. When you got here, you found that your worrying wasn't even necessary…it accomplished nothing. Fear isn't just a waste of time, it's bad. It causes harm. It creates a life different from the life we're meant to live."

"You're so smart, Samantha. I didn't want to say this, but I'm going to miss you soooooo much."

"Oh, we'll see each other again. Now it's time for you to do more. Now it's time for you to help others, the way you've helped me. That's what you're here for."

"Will you miss me?"

"I won't have the chance, because I'll always be around you. I'll always be a part of your life. Since I was in your life here, it means I'll be in your life forever."

"You make it sound so simple."

"That's the way it was supposed to be."

"So, you really are going to go?"

"I think so. Actually, I don't know that for sure. I am sure that I'm *definitely* not afraid…it's like almost being there, while I'm still here. Right now, I'm glad I get to spend this time with you."

I felt exactly the same. Being with Samantha was like getting to be with my best friend, my favorite student, *and* my newest teacher, all at once. The time I got to spend with her in her hospital room ended up being our best time ever. It was a time when I got to see someone who was more fulfilled than I'd ever seen anyone before. Samantha never worked for a big company, she never got to go to high school, she never got to be a professional tennis player, but she was the biggest success story I'd ever known. Samantha chose to learn from life, she learned to be unafraid. She was my hero, and I'm so grateful she was generous enough to want to teach me something before she left. I can't wait to see her again.

Just before she had gone, Samantha gave me back something that Aunt Shirley had given me from before, that I ended up handing over to Samantha, the watch that doesn't tell time. "Now I understand why Jorge wanted me to have this. Life *does* go on, time *is* a fantasy. Wear it always. I want you to remember me, Miguel." Samantha had said.

"I could never ever forget you, Samantha. You made me feel

worthwhile. You made me realize that what I do matters. I love you, Samantha. Thank you for being my best friend."

"Thank you for being mine, Miguel. I love you too."

Samantha and I said a few more things to each other before she got too tired to talk more. Each of us seemed to have said all we wanted. In the most peaceful way ever, I walked back to the waiting room to be with the others. I knew Samantha would be all right. She'd be taken care of the best way possible, and letting her go was the most perfect thing to do. It's what she wanted. It's what she had been waiting for.

Right before I got back to the waiting room though, I made a sharp right turn into the bathroom. I don't know why I did that. As I stepped in, I looked into the mirror so I could watch myself cry. "I'd rather feel sadness than feel nothing at all…it means I've lived life," Aunt Shirley had said to me.

As I wiped the tears away from my eyes, I closely noticed my hands. I examined them carefully. They made me think back to the mystery of life God created, the mystery that's not a mystery. I'd just then realized that a hand with all the fingers and one thumb sticking out is shaped exactly like our hearts, our heart muscle. God probably made them that way for a reason, some perfect reason. That's the last thing Samantha and I did before I left her room. I held her hand and she held mine. Perfect.

A few minutes before midnight, I was asleep in my bed at home. On that night I had no dreams. I was awoken by another image in my head. It was the most perfect feeling I'd ever experienced. It was a calm I had never known before, the exact opposite of feeling fear. My mind just then thought back to the time I dreamt that Jorge, Samantha, and I were together in Big Sur, talking about what heaven's like. Was I really in heaven with them both? Or was I still on earth? It no longer mattered. Without being positive, I still knew that heaven *was* the perfect place to be, just like Samantha had told me.

Exactly as it turned twelve o'clock, there was something else I felt for sure, that Samantha had gone to heaven. I knew she was OK, and although I'd never get to see her again in my life on earth, I immediately thanked God over and over again for having given me such a huge blessing. I was the luckiest boy anywhere for having Samantha as my best friend.

A couple of months after Samantha's funeral, her mom had something she wanted to give me. She told me that it's something that would have special meaning for me, and I was probably meant to have it. It was Samantha's *'Overcoming Fear' To Do* list she'd started when we first met at our F.A.A.T. meeting.

It took me a while to read through it, but I did. As I turned from one page to the next, I couldn't believe how much Samantha'd achieved in her life. She had gotten rid of more fears at fourteen than most people do in their whole lifetimes. I could see that as she got over each and every fear, she'd cross them off on her list. The last fear on her list remained uncrossed though.

On my desk I reached for a pencil, and crossed it off.

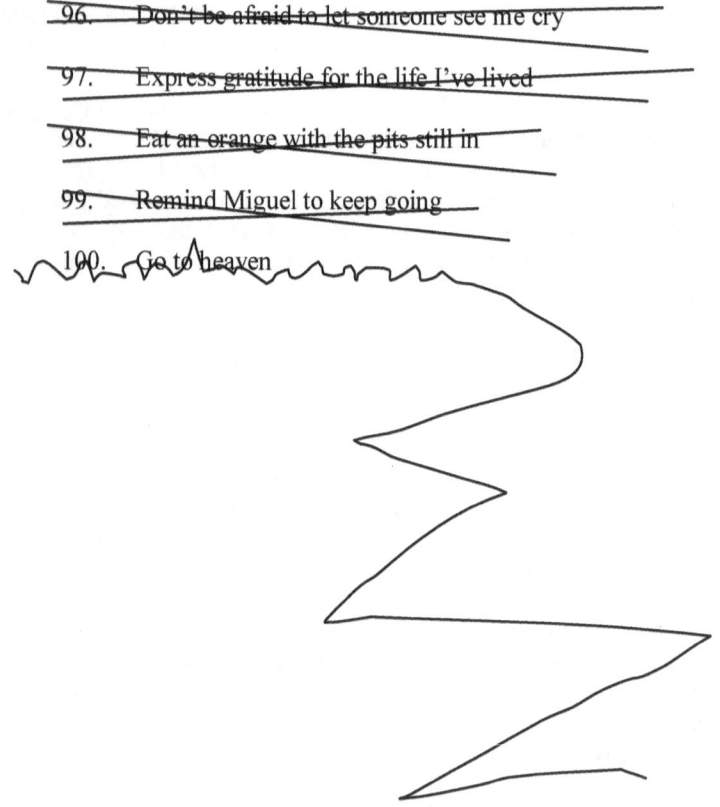

96.   Don't be afraid to let someone see me cry

97.   Express gratitude for the life I've lived

98.   Eat an orange with the pits still in

99.   Remind Miguel to keep going

100.   Go to heaven